O9-AIC-179

COLTON COWBOY JEOPARDY

Regan Black

HARLEQUIN

ROMANTIC
SUSPENSE

If you purchased this book without a cover you should be aware that this book is stolen property. It was reported as "unsold and destroyed" to the publisher, and neither the author nor the publisher has received any payment for this "stripped book."

Special thanks and acknowledgment are given to
Regan Black for her contribution to
The Coltons of Mustang Valley miniseries.

Recycling programs
for this product may
not exist in your area.

ISBN-13: 978-1-335-62649-3

Colton Cowboy Jeopardy

Copyright © 2020 by Harlequin Books S.A.

All rights reserved. No part of this book may be used or reproduced in any manner whatsoever without written permission except in the case of brief quotations embodied in critical articles and reviews.

This is a work of fiction. Names, characters, places and incidents are either the product of the author's imagination or are used fictitiously. Any resemblance to actual persons, living or dead, businesses, companies, events or locales is entirely coincidental.

This edition published by arrangement with Harlequin Books S.A.

For questions and comments about the quality of this book, please contact us at CustomerService@Harlequin.com.

Harlequin Enterprises ULC
22 Adelaide St. West, 40th Floor
Toronto, Ontario M5H 4E3, Canada
www.Harlequin.com

Printed in U.S.A.

Regan Black, a *USA TODAY* bestselling author, writes award-winning, action-packed novels featuring kick-butt heroines and the sexy heroes who fall in love with them. Raised in the Midwest and California, she and her family, along with their adopted greyhound, two arrogant cats and a quirky finch, reside in the South Carolina Lowcountry, where the rich blend of legend, romance and history fuels her imagination.

Books by Regan Black

Harlequin Romantic Suspense

The Coltons of Mustang Valley

Colton Cowboy Jeopardy

The Riley Code

A Soldier's Honor
His Soldier Under Siege

The Coltons of Roaring Springs

Colton Family Showdown

Escape Club Heroes

Safe in His Sight
A Stranger She Can Trust
Protecting Her Secret Son
Braving the Heat

The Coltons of Shadow Creek

Killer Colton Christmas
"Special Agent Cowboy"

The Coltons of Red Ridge

Colton P.I. Protector

Visit the Author Profile page at
Harlequin.com for more titles.

With special thanks to all of the authors in The Coltons of Mustang Valley world. It was an honor and delight to take this journey with you.

Chapter 1

"Pick up, pick up," she chanted under her breath while the phone continued to ring, unanswered. Today was supposed to mark the start of her new career as Mia Graves, real-estate agent. Instead of an easy-breezy morning preparing her first listing, she'd been plunged into a nightmare. They hadn't covered anything like this in her classes or on the state exam.

Her palms were slick on the steering wheel and she kept checking her rearview mirror as she drove back into Mustang Valley proper. She didn't think she was being followed. At least she didn't see any familiar vehicles back there. Yet. Her stomach cramped. This could *not* be happening.

The call went to voice mail and she used the hands-free option to end the call. Before she could redial, an incoming call came through. As she recognized the number, another surge of panic chilled her skin. She declined the call and tried the babysitter again.

At last Tamara picked up. "It's Mia," she said, unable to suppress the quake in her voice. "I'll be there in five minutes. Please have Silas ready to go."

Please let Silas still be there. Surely, Tamara wouldn't have let him go home with anyone else.

"Of course. I just put him down for a nap."

My son is safe.

"The first morning away is always the biggest hurdle," Tamara continued in her unflappable way. "Are you okay, Mia?"

"Yes. Yes, I'm fine." With Tamara's soothing voice filling the car, she reclaimed a measure of her composure. Tamara and Mia's mother Dalinda had been as close as sisters, and Mia had always called her Aunt Tammie. When she'd felt overwhelmed and uncertain about childcare options for her new baby boy, Tamara had volunteered to help.

"Just frazzled. A friend invited me to lunch and if it goes well, I might just land a new client," she improvised. "That brings the tally to two."

"How exciting!"

"Yes," Mia agreed, checking her rearview mirror once more. "My friend specifically asked me to bring the baby along."

"Well, he's better than a business card, isn't he?" Tamara chuckled. "I have his things all set for you."

"You're a dream, Aunt Tammie. Thank you."

"Don't be silly. You're more than welcome to leave that angel with me anytime. Will I get to spoil him silly tomorrow, too?"

"I'll, ah, be working from home tomorrow," she said.

Tamara knew her well enough to see right through a blatant lie. She would work from home, just as soon as she figured out where home would be for the next several days. "See you in a minute," she said, ending the call quickly.

Becoming an independent real-estate agent was supposed to be the ideal, no-brainer and no-limit career decision. She and her father had discussed several options before she'd started her classes. Establishing a base close to home would be better than the extensive travel demanded by her previous work as the manager of her ex-husband's charitable foundation. Setting her own hours gave her the most flexibility as a single mother and she'd happily daydreamed about days when her son could join her on occasional appointments.

Tears stung Mia's eyes as a foreign, desperate fear chased her to Tamara's neighborhood. Until today, she would have summed up her eight weeks of motherhood as pure joy offset by exhaustion and sharp spikes of worry. What she'd discovered today and the potential fallout reclassified those worries as trivial.

Today had been a test run for her. Her first hours apart from Silas since giving birth should have been a bit of an emotional challenge, not a harrowing ordeal. Resentment shot through her that once again her stepmother, Regina Graves, had ruined a good thing and thrown her life into turmoil.

Mia pulled into the drive and parked the car. Although her heart raced with urgency, she flipped down the visor and checked her reflection in the mirror. If anyone thought to ask Tamara about Mia's appearance and demeanor today, she wanted her aunt to report that she'd been calm and steady. Unfortunately, she was pale and a bit wild-eyed. Understandable after the vile threats Regina had made against her child, but it would cause Tamara worry and raise questions she couldn't begin to answer.

Reaching into her purse for her cosmetics bag, she applied a bit of highlighter at the corners of her eyes and a fresh layer of lip gloss. Maybe Tamara would blame the obvious signs of anxiety on her first day away from her baby boy.

She stepped out of the car and walked up the path to the front door. Tamara threw open the door, and seeing that loving, vibrant face almost brought Mia to her knees. She steeled herself. Silas needed her to be strong. Stronger than the threats aimed at him. His arrival had turned the past two months into the best two months of her life. She wouldn't relinquish that without a fight, no matter what her stepmother tried to do.

"Oh, my girl." Tamara pulled her into a hug. "The first time out is the worst."

"It is." Mia let herself rest for just a moment on that sturdy shoulder, soaking up the heartfelt support. Who knew how long it would be before she'd have anyone's support again?

Tamara beamed and released her so Mia could come inside. "At least your first client is a pleasure, right? It was so good of your father to let you list and sell his house in the country." She studied Mia closely. "Did going there today stir up memories? Your mother loved that house."

"She did," Mia agreed. "All good memories," she added because it was expected. And until an hour ago, it was true. All the memories of the country house had been wonderful, from her early childhood to weekends with girlfriends and, eventually, holiday gatherings as a married woman.

"I'd love to stay and tell you everything about this morning," she said. "But I need to be on time for that lunch meeting." She picked up the diaper bag Tamara had set in the foyer. "Thank you again."

"Everything is right there," Tamara said. "I'll go tuck him into his car seat."

"I'll come along," she murmured, gently closing the door. No sense making it easy if Regina had followed her.

Tamara smiled indulgently. "Ah, little mother. Nothing will do but to see him with your own eyes."

She nodded, her lips clamped together too tightly to speak as she followed the older woman down the hallway.

Tamara urged her to go on into the bedroom first. There in the portable crib, her tiny son slept, a vision of contentment. She watched his chest rise and fall and silently vowed to make sure he stayed safe. She stroked his soft cheek, followed the whorl of his curly dark hair as she listened to his soft breath. Lifting him gently, she snuggled him close before she buckled him into the car seat. He stretched his legs but didn't wake.

Mia wanted to take the portable crib, but doing so would raise more questions and concerns. She'd make do or buy a new one at some point. She picked up Silas and reached for the diaper bag, but Tamara insisted on carrying it to the car for her. Mia swallowed the protest. If Regina or anyone else had caught up with her, it would be better to have another witness to any trouble.

"Thank you again," Mia said at the car. After securing the seat, she closed the door and gave Tamara one more hug, praying it wouldn't be the last.

With Silas snoozing in the back seat, she had a renewed sense of calm as she drove away. From the moment the pregnancy test showed positive, her life had come into crystal clear focus. Her son was her singular priority and she wouldn't allow anyone or anything to hurt him, no matter what changes or precautions were required. She'd divorced, moved and launched herself into a new career. During her last trimester, she'd survived the helplessness and terror of the earthquake that rocked Mustang Valley. Her commitment wouldn't falter now.

Breathing easier as she left the neighborhood without another incident or threatening call, she turned her mind to logistics. Since she was currently staying at her father's house, she couldn't go home and she didn't dare call or drop in on him. Norton Graves had a mile-wide blind spot when it came to his second wife. He would never believe that Regina had threatened violence against his daughter and grandson.

Where did that leave her? She needed clothing for her and Silas, as well as cash and baby supplies. And then she needed a place to lie low while she decided what to do with the incriminating secrets she'd uncovered today.

She reached for the radio, turning on a soothing station for the baby. A few minutes later, an incoming call interrupted the music. The caller ID announced her father's name. Wary about what Regina might have told him, she used the button on the steering wheel to answer.

"Hi, sweetie," he said, sounding as jovial as ever. Maybe Regina hadn't filled his head with more lies yet. "How did it go at the house?"

"Great," she replied brightly. "Tamara said Silas was an angel." There, she hadn't lied to her dad.

"I had no doubts. How are you feeling? Your mother found it hard to leave you the first few times."

"I survived." Another truth. "It was an experience," she said. "Knowing he was with Tamara helped."

Her father chortled. "Tamara was the one who watched you for us so Dalinda and I could have a nice dinner."

"Life just keeps circling, doesn't it?" Her father rarely spoke about her mother, and never when Regina was within earshot. This was her chance to tell him what she'd seen, even if she couldn't show him the video yet, before her stepmother twisted the story against her.

"That it does." He cleared his throat. "One second. Come in. Mia? Regina's here. I'm putting you on speaker."

"Hello, Mia! How are you and the baby?"

She winced at her stepmother's overbright greeting. "Doing great, thanks." Her window of opportunity had slammed shut.

"We're both eager to hear when you'll get the listing up," her dad said.

Her father always knew how to pile on the pressure, but when it came to work, she normally thrived. He'd entrusted her with the sale of the country house— probably because Regina wanted to buy something bigger and newer—and she wouldn't let him down. "I'm not sure when the listing will go live," she said. Although she hated lying to him, it was the best of her options. "I might actually have a private buyer interested in the property."

"Already?"

"Might," she repeated. Taking a page from Regina's book, she put a sharp sparkle into her voice. "I mentioned the property to a few friends and apparently the word is out."

"That's fantastic news. For both of us. All of us," he amended quickly. "You should see the smile on my bride's face."

Bride, shark—when referring to her stepmother, the words were interchangeable in Mia's mind. "Super. I'll keep you posted," she promised. "Love you."

She ended the call and a rush of angry tears spilled down her cheeks. Would it ever be safe to see her father again?

Jarvis Colton adjusted the angle of his hat against the afternoon sunshine flooding the Rattlesnake Ridge Ranch. He'd been riding fence all day on the Triple R, a task that was often met with little enthusiasm.

Jarvis loved it. No one was more shocked by that revelation than him. He'd left a career as a management consultant—the suits, air-conditioned offices, deals over drinks and conference calls—to come out here and be a cowboy. A dark T-shirt, jeans, boots and his horse completed his new workplace uniform.

His brother and sister, Spencer and Isabella, still scolded him about this decision and he wished he could find the words to make them understand. If they ever joined him for moments like this, they might get it. As triplets, they were close, and when life had thrown them one challenge after another, Spencer and Bella were the only people he really trusted.

His siblings labeled his professional detour an emotional crisis and blamed his choice to store his belongings and walk away from a great condo and a lucrative career on bitterness and fantasy. They weren't entirely wrong. He could almost imagine that Spencer, a sergeant with the Mustang Valley Police Department, was expecting him to sabotage the ranch owned by Payne Colton, a man who had practically refused to claim any blood ties to the triplets. The next generation of Coltons—Payne's children—was closer to Jarvis and his siblings.

Jarvis couldn't deny the temptation. Payne, in addition to building the Triple R into one of the most prosperous cattle ranches in Arizona, also served as chairman of the board for Colton Oil. The family patriarch was charismatic and tough, and had ensured that his children would prosper for generations to come, while Jarvis and his siblings had been effectively cut out of the Colton family tree.

But when Jarvis traded his suits and office for barns and fields and long, hard-labor days, he'd done it with the sole intention of finding proof that the Triple R rightfully belonged to the triplets. At least the section of acreage he was crossing now.

Granted, the ranch foreman, Payne's son Asher Colton, didn't know Jarvis's motives, but he'd hired him, anyway. Jarvis had been pleasantly surprised to find his cousin was a fair boss and didn't treat him with any of Payne's dismissiveness or negligent animosity.

Working out here, Jarvis had soon discovered what his life had been missing. Cause and effect. Effort and reward. In business, his decisions didn't always yield an immediate result. While he knew the value of patience, he enjoyed the relatively quick confirmation of making decisions out here. There were short-term goals and long-range plans, but the day-to-day work made a clear and obvious impact.

And once the daily work was complete, Jarvis used his personal time to search for confirmation of the story their grandfather, Isaiah Colton, had told him when it had been just the two of them out fishing. Jarvis had never forgotten how special and important he'd felt when his granddad made him promise not to tell a soul, not even his siblings. According to Isaiah, back in the 1800s, the Triple R had been stolen from their branch of the Colton family tree, forever changing the family fortunes. Five years ago, just before he died, Isaiah had brought it up again, claiming the proof of that treachery was buried out here on the ranch.

Jarvis couldn't let the idea go. Especially not after the recent uproar within the Colton Oil side of the family. If there was any truth that Payne's oldest son, Ace, had been switched at birth, maybe Isaiah's story wasn't so far-fetched. So Jarvis gladly rode fences, not just for the protection of the cattle and preservation of the operation, but for himself, scoping out likely places to prove his grandfather had it right after all.

Based on everything he'd heard and his research into the history of Mustang Valley, he'd mentally earmarked this particular area. Now, finished with the official task of repairing any weak or broken fencing, he rode toward the place he wanted to dig. As he followed an overgrown trail, anticipation zipped through his bloodstream. Assuming Payne woke from his coma, Jarvis imagined the expression on Payne's face in court, hearing his precious land belonged to Jarvis, Spencer and Bella, and that he wasn't the wealthiest landowner in Mustang Valley anymore. How many times had Payne ignored their existence, claiming they shared a last name by accident rather than any true family connection?

If Isaiah was right, the change might shake up things in Mustang Valley more than the earthquake had a few months back. Of course, it was a long shot and a crazy notion, and it was unlikely such a scene would ever happen. But it was fun to think about. What if he actually found a deed or some other evidence his grandfather was sure had been buried out here generations ago?

Dropping out of the saddle, he gathered the reins in one hand and walked closer to where he wanted to dig today. Since setting himself on this path, he'd spent hours researching newspaper articles and photographs from four generations ago up through present day. With a landscape as picturesque as the Triple R and all the publicity surrounding Payne and his family lately, photographers were out here all the time.

He marked his position using a variation of a geocaching app on his cell phone and then started digging. Within minutes he was sweating through his shirt. Expecting anything less in Arizona this time of year would be foolish. Still, he didn't miss the cool air of a climate-controlled office. This effort, for the ranch, for his grandfather's pride, felt empowering and right, whether or not he found anything.

That was the piece no one else understood. Just looking for the truth filled him with a sense of purpose and honor. Isaiah, for all his faults, had been good to the three of them, and just about the only person in town who attempted to love them after their parents died. Due to Isaiah's well-known drinking habit, family court shuffled them off to the care of their bitter old Aunt Amelia. He owed Isaiah for trying to give them a foundation, a sense of their roots in the midst of grief and upheaval.

He pushed his hat back and wiped his brow, then cut into the earth again. A metal detector would make the job easier, but a shovel didn't need an explanation. As he used his foot for more pressure, the shovel squeaked. He thought he'd hit something. He paused, wiggling the shovel out and back in again. Silence this time. By touch, there was nothing but the hard-packed Arizona soil. He waited, listening again for the sound. When it came, he swore it sounded like a baby crying.

Raised in town, Jarvis hadn't worked the land his entire life. Over the past year he'd learned a great deal about the various wild animals and habitats in the area. Seemed early in the day for a coyote, but he supposed a mockingbird might manage that sound. He looked to his horse as the next rising cry carried on the air. The gelding merely flicked his ears, either at the high-pitched sound or a fly buzzing too close.

The sound faded and Jarvis resumed his digging. Whatever was making that sound, he couldn't waste this window of opportunity chasing it down. Unlike life in the office setting, he had to search when he had the chance. Work on a ranch could be calm one day and chaos the next. Personally, he enjoyed the unpredictability, the variety, even the long hours. As one of the hands, he might ride fence today and work on repairs around the property for the next month.

When it was clear the metal box his grandfather described wasn't in this hole, Jarvis made a note and started filling it in. With the sun sinking toward the horizon, he'd about given up on this location when he heard the sound again.

This time he was certain that wasn't a random animal. Not even mockingbirds could sustain that long, unhappy wail. If he had to guess, he'd say it was a baby, but what in the world would a baby be doing all the way out here? He tied the shovel to the pack behind his saddle and swung up onto his horse. Moving slowly, he followed the sound.

As he closed in on the sound, he couldn't reconcile the crying with the remote and rugged terrain, and yet it was the only logical conclusion. The pitiful wails drew him farther along the old trail to one of the warming huts built generations ago so cowboys could take shelter from bitter, cold weather.

"Hello?" Jarvis called out. The crying sound came again. "Everyone okay?" The last thing he wanted was to walk into trouble. He hopped out of the saddle, looping the reins around the lower branch of a tree that crowded the small rustic cabin. He was close enough now to hear someone trying to hush the baby, to no avail. "Do you need—"

"Stay back!"

He heeded the warning, stopping short as a woman stepped out of the hut. She held a sturdy stick like she was a major-league batter ready to hit a home run, using his head as the baseball. In the shadows behind her, a tiny child with big lungs wailed miserably from a carrier of some sort.

Jarvis held up his hands. "Take it easy." He used the tone he'd learned worked best with spooked horses. "How can I help?"

"You can't." She stepped forward, her grip tight on that stick. "Get out of here."

"I'm no threat." She was tall with gorgeous, light

brown skin, generous curves and defensiveness oozing from every pore, with or without the threat of violence. "I'm only here because of the crying. It's not a sound we hear out this way."

"We?" Her dark eyes went wide and her gaze skittered across the area behind him. "Who is with you?"

"No one. No one," he assured her. "Just me and my horse." He held his hands out from his sides, palms open. Something worse than the fear of being caught squatting on Colton land had her wild-eyed. "I'm a hand here at the Triple R. Did you know you were on a working ranch? I was riding by, checking fences. How did you find this place?"

She shook her head, stick still held high, the baby still protesting.

"Show me some ID," she demanded.

"Okay, sure. Should've thought of that." He reached for his back pocket with slow, deliberate motions. "Just reaching for my wallet." He held it out and inched forward.

"Stay back!" He froze. "Toss it to me."

He obeyed and the square of leather landed close to her feet. "Do you need some cash? Help yourself."

She glared at him, dark eyebrows snapping together. "I don't need your money."

Great, now he'd insulted the woman holding the weapon. What else was he supposed to think? Who would bring a baby out here if they could afford better options?

He took a visual inventory while she flipped through his wallet. Her dark hair was pulled up high in a messy knot, a testament to the heat, he figured. She wore a dress in sunset hues that hugged her lavish curves, the soft fabric flowing over her body. Her face looked familiar, but he couldn't place her. She wasn't a woman he would've forgotten if they had met before.

"How about you put the stick down and take care of the baby? Is it a boy or a girl?"

"Boy." Her gaze darted between his identification to his face a time or two. "Jarvis Colton? This says you live here in town."

"Yes."

Her brow pleated over her straight nose. "I've never heard of you."

Why would she? No one had heard of Jarvis or his siblings. They'd never run in the same social circles as their wealthier cousins.

"If you're really one of the Coltons, why are you all the way out here riding fences?"

The judgment was loud and clear as her gaze skated over him. "It's my job. If we don't keep up with the maintenance, the cattle tend to wander off." Did she need to see the dirt under his fingernails or the calluses on his palms? He struggled to keep his cool. This woman was frightened. Though the tone was similar, she wasn't his sister, lecturing him on giving up his "silly cowboy quest."

No, this woman made him feel like stepping up, the proverbial hero riding to the rescue on a white stallion to protect her from the world.

The outrageous fantasy rocked him. First, the horse with him today was Duke, an average, hardworking chestnut gelding. Plus, Jarvis wasn't built for that kind of heroism. The only family he needed or wanted were his brother and sister. He took a step closer, despite his certainty that she would knock his head off if given the chance.

"I'm no threat," he promised. "Why not get him settled down and then we can talk. I can keep watch for you."

She opened her mouth just as the baby's cry changed, going from that high-pitched squeal to a wet gulp. She immediately dropped the stick and his wallet to tend to the child.

Jarvis picked up the discarded items, pocketing his wallet and leaning her stick against the open door of the small cabin. He hovered in the doorway, to keep watch and prevent scaring her further.

Her touch calmed the baby straightaway and the maternal, soothing croons lifted faded memories to the top of his mind. It had been years since he'd thought about his mother's warm voice and gentle hands. The soup and crackers and comic books she'd brought to him when he had a cold or sore throat.

"Your son?" he asked unnecessarily.

"Yes." She angled away from him, and a moment later the only sound in the cabin was the baby's muted suckling.

Jarvis studied every inch of the cabin, keeping his gaze well away from the nursing mother. It was so intimate and strange and he was intruding, an interloper of the worst kind. Leaving wasn't an option, though it was clear she'd rather he disappear. She and her son were vulnerable out here. He couldn't walk away without doing something.

"You know my name," he said. "Will you tell me yours?"

"Mia," she said. "This is Silas. He just turned two months old."

She shot him a cool glance over her shoulder and he remembered where he'd seen her. Magazines, catalogs and the stunning swimsuit editions. The first time he'd seen her in one of those, she'd posed near a rocky outcropping with her hair loose around her shoulders and her showstopping curves showcased in a coral bikini. Water swirled around her knees and beaded on that marvelously smooth skin. His gaze skimmed over her body, filling in details he remembered. Was the tattoo on her left hip real or had it been added in postproduction for that last commercial she'd done?

Mia Graves. Local girl turned modeling superstar. Why was she out here in the middle of nowhere? Her father, Norton Graves, was a high-profile investment banker. Anyone doing business in the region had passing knowledge of the man. "You're Norton's daughter."

"I am."

Whoa. He jerked his thoughts back into line. "Do you need me to call—"

"No." The baby whimpered at her sharp tone and she twisted slowly side to side, patting him gently, murmuring apologies. "I don't need anything," she insisted. "Not from you or him, or anyone else." There was steel underscoring her words. "Some privacy here is all I need."

"You can't stay here." He should've phrased that better, but this wasn't any kind of place for a mother and infant.

"I know I'm trespassing," she said. "Please, it won't be for long. I can write a check or make a donation or something."

"But—"

"Please," she interrupted. "Do you have to report me? I'm not hurting anything. I just need another day or two to figure out my next step."

It didn't take a genius to know she was holding back. No one, not even a ranch hand, would consider this hut habitable for more than a few hours. "How long have you been here?"

"Overnight." She shifted the baby, resting him on her shoulder and patting his back. "I didn't plan this."

"Obviously. What happened?" His thoughts were whirling. Was this a custody thing? He'd noticed the headlines from his sister's reports in the *Mustang Valley Gabber* about Mia's recent divorce. If she was in trouble, why wasn't her dad helping out? According to his limited knowledge, Norton valued his family and treasured his only daughter.

She rolled her eyes. "What will it take?" she asked.

"Take?"

"To keep you quiet," she said. "I can—"

He cut her off this time. "Don't finish that sentence." If she wanted to bribe him, he didn't want to hear it. "I don't need your money, either." He didn't want to dwell on what else she might be desperate enough to offer. "What kind of trouble are you in? How did you even get here?"

"I drove," she replied. "My trouble isn't your problem. I didn't think anyone would find me out here."

"You weren't wrong."

"Just lucky you happened along?"

"Well, yeah," he replied. That was how he saw it. The hut was just that. An unfinished, bare-minimum structure that hadn't been maintained or updated in years. There was no running water or even a bed. It was a glorified firepit. "I can help you."

He was already making a mental list of what he might pull together to make her more comfortable until he could convince her to move someplace more secure.

"Thanks, but no thanks. We're fine right here, unless you plan to report me." She turned her back to him again as she continued to nurse the baby.

"I won't report you." Her skepticism didn't bother him half as much as her location. "But this isn't adequate," he insisted. "You can't take care of a newborn here." He didn't have any real experience with mothers or babies, but this couldn't possibly be the right environment. Mia Graves had been raised with the best of everything money could buy. How she'd successfully managed one night here baffled him.

He saw a grocery bag in the corner, next to a stylish tote overflowing with what appeared to be baby paraphernalia. "There are guest rooms at the ranch. I can make arrangements and you can clean up and rest."

"Wow." Her gaze was flat, annoyed. "Way to make a woman feel special."

She was a wall of stubbornness. "That's not what I meant. You look great."

One eyebrow arched in challenge.

Fine, he'd spell it out. "You don't have a bed. No real bathroom. That one chair is better used as firewood. Should I go on?"

"Please, just *go*."

He crossed his arms. He'd match her stubborn streak. "I'll let you stay, if you tell me what kind of trouble you're in."

"What you don't know can't hurt you," she said with a slow shake of her head.

Oh, she was completely wrong about that, but this was about her. Her and the baby. *Baby*, a voice shouted in his head, lest he forget that gorgeous women were for dating only. Babies came with relationships and starred in family photos on holiday cards. He wasn't cut out for *any* of that.

"What I don't know can absolutely be a threat to this ranch. It'd be good to have some advance warning if a furious husband is on the way."

"Allow me to clear that up." Her voice snapped like a whip. "Neither my *ex*-husband nor my father will be storming your ranch in pursuit of me."

Your ranch. He knew the words meant nothing to her, but they sent a pleasant sensation coursing through him. If he found the proof Isaiah told him about, it might very well become his ranch. He and Spencer and Bella would own the Triple R. Wouldn't that be a kick?

"What is that face about?" She circled a finger in the air around her own face.

"Nothing important." He wasn't about to let her shift the focus of this conversation. "Lover? Real mother of the baby? Who are you hiding from?"

Her gaze lit with fury. "Silas is *my* baby. I'm the one nursing him. Or did you miss that detail?"

He hadn't missed anything. In college, he'd been infatuated with Mia Graves, model. Everything from her sly and sultry expressions to her wide, gregarious smile captivated his imagination. Her meteoric rise had set the advertising and marketing world on fire. More than one of his professors had made them study either her career or the brands she represented.

"Okay," he allowed. "That was ridiculous. So clear it up for me. I can't protect you or the ranch without information."

It was hard for people to understand just how much territory was out here, how much ground the crew had to cover. "If you found a way to sneak in, someone else could do the same." He didn't want to think about coming back to check on her and finding a tragedy. On the flip side, he didn't want some crazed person destroying the ranch in an effort to find *her*.

"I'm here because this is the last place anyone will look for me. Can't we just leave it at that?"

"Afraid not." He couldn't allow her to stay here at all. Infatuation or sympathy aside, his responsibility was to the ranch.

"Why should I trust you to do the right thing?"

"Do you have a choice?" Her gaze dropped to the scarred plank floor and he felt like a jerk. "You don't have to tell me everything," he added quietly. "You aren't hurting anyone out here and no one needs to use this place. But you're isolated. I'd rather not come back to find someone hurt you."

"I really can't tell you anything."

"If not your dad or your ex, what other man has the resources to drive you to this?"

Her shoulders hunched and she cuddled her son closer as her bravado vanished. "Not a man," she said. "A woman. A woman with influence and access to far more resources than she deserves."

Chapter 2

Frustrated, Mia looked to the doorway and the stick she'd thought to use against Jarvis Colton, Triple R ranch hand. He hadn't tossed the stick aside or out of her reach; he'd placed it inside the open door. He looked like he'd walked straight off the set of a modern cowboy photo shoot. He might resemble a model, the type of man she used to deal with on a daily basis, but he wasn't. She had to remember he was a stranger and posed a very real danger to her plan.

Plan. What she had in mind so far barely qualified as an actionable concept. And now there was a witness to her current incompetence. She wanted to pull at her hair, this entire mess was so embarrassing. She tucked Silas back into his car seat so she wouldn't upset him if she got emotional again. And she didn't want to be at a disadvantage if Jarvis tried to force her out of the tiny cabin.

He had a powerful build and the dark T-shirt he wore revealed strong, sculpted arms. She wasn't exactly a lightweight, but he posed a clear risk, physically and logistically. When she'd started modeling, her agent had suggested she study self-defense. The skills she'd learned hadn't been tested in years and she'd prefer not to test them now.

"Mia."

The kindness in his voice nearly reduced her to tears. It wasn't fair that this chance encounter should make her feel less alone. Since escaping yesterday, Regina had sent her one threat after another. She'd sent pictures from Tamara's neighborhood as well as the courtyard in front of her ex-husband's condo. A night of worry and nightmares interrupted by her restless son hadn't helped Mia figure anything out. Unfortunately, Jarvis was right about this place. She didn't see good sleep coming anytime soon and Silas needed her at her best.

"I didn't know I was on the Triple R," she said. She caught herself working the gold band she wore on her thumb as her weary brain tried to get ahead of this stalemate with Jarvis so she could return her focus to the stalemate with Regina. "I thought I'd found an old hunting cabin."

"You basically did."

"Well, the good news is my problems shouldn't find me here."

He removed his hat and raked his fingers through his dark hair. "Let me get you to a better location," he said. "Somewhere up-to-date and safe."

He had no idea how much the idea tempted her. "There's no such thing as safe right now," she said. "My stepmother, Regina, is gunning for me." She glanced at her phone, resting at the top of Silas's diaper bag. Thank goodness the woman didn't have real guns. "This spot is only safe *because* it's run-down." Jarvis frowned. "She thinks I'm too spoiled to rough it to this degree."

"You're not."

"No," she replied, though it hadn't really been a question. "We've never gotten along. The Graves family is a walking cliché. We have the trophy wife and the bitter, resentful daughter of a wealthy father determined to overlook any unpleasantness in favor of building his business."

While she vented, he'd stepped close enough that she couldn't ignore the scent of sunshine on his skin. This place might suit her and the baby temporarily, but he took up more than his share of the space.

"What happened?"

"What didn't?" She spared him the gory details of years of bickering and snide remarks and cut straight to the current issue. "Being newly divorced by the end of my first trimester, I talked with my dad about career options. Real estate felt like the right fit, so I took the classes. When I passed my state exam, he offered to let me handle the sale of his country house once I was ready to get back to work."

"Your stepmother doesn't want to sell the place?"

"I have no idea what she wants aside from wanting me out of Dad's life." Mia was too tired for this. "The house is an asset. If Dad's selling it, he'll buy her something better." Mia pushed at her heavy hair. Why couldn't this have gone down during cooler weather instead of this presummer heat wave? She wanted to change her clothes and freshen up, but she couldn't do any of that with an audience.

"Tell me what I'm missing," Jarvis prompted.

She reached for her bottle of water and drank deeply while she debated how much to share. She wanted to believe the sincere concern in his gaze, but in her experience, voicing anything negative about Regina blew up in her face. "Yesterday I learned Regina has been using the country house for an affair. Probably not her first," she added. Her father was several years older than her stepmother, but not by so much that he couldn't claim they were happily married. It made her stomach pitch. "My marriage wasn't perfect, but we were loyal to each other," she muttered more to herself than the cowboy waiting for the rest of the story. "Long story short, I inadvertently caught her and her boyfriend in the act when I was there taking video for the online listing."

"Let me guess—you told your dad and now they're both mad at you."

"I wish it was that simple. I will tell him," she said. As soon as she figured out how. "As it stands, I can't tell anyone. Yet." She was so ashamed at how poorly she'd handled the moment. "If there was a chance to press an advantage, I missed it," she confessed.

In his car seat, Silas gurgled and kicked his feet. She'd let him down and now she was backed into a corner. "The man she was with saw me first. He thought I was there at her request."

She caught the wince on Jarvis's face, assumed her expression at the time had mirrored his. "Agreed." The *ew* factor had been off the charts. "So there I am, video rolling while my stepmother and a much younger hottie are all over each other. Naked, in case there was any doubt about their intentions."

Her son yawned, and love, protective and fierce,

surged through her. She would find a way to get past this nonsense and give him the stable life she'd planned so carefully. "I ran out of the house and headed straight for Dad's office. Then the first call came through. Regina offered me money."

"Which you don't need," Jarvis said.

The quip made her smile. "Correct, but Regina goes for the easy out first. Every single time. I stopped answering her calls, determined to reach my father before she did. Then he called. Naturally, I picked up. Before I could say a word, he asked if I'd meet him and Regina for lunch to celebrate my first day. He said it was her idea and I knew I'd been outmaneuvered."

"How so?"

She stared at him. It was such a challenge to admit that the mistakes she'd made as a heartbroken teenager were still impacting her life today. "If I told him what I saw without any proof, he'd only be disappointed and lecture me about being too old for games."

"You're serious."

The way Jarvis studied her, she felt more exposed than she had on lingerie shoots, and more regret and shame than she'd ever felt as a kid when communication had completely broken down. "I did try to break them up. After they married, I put zero effort toward a smooth transition."

"What kind of effort did your stepmother make?"

No one, not even her husband, had ever asked that. To be fair, she'd been out on her own for years before she'd met and married Roderick Hodges. From the start, her ex had more important things on his agenda than delving deep into the rocky parts of her childhood. She'd happily left the house and those years behind. Until she'd accepted her father's invitation to move back in.

"That's all water under the bridge these days. Things are civil now. Or they were. I asked for a rain check on lunch, disappointing my father in the process, but I wasn't sitting through a meal in a public place while she gloated about getting away with it."

"What changed?"

"She threatened Silas," Mia said. Just thinking about that phone call and the text messages that followed brought angry tears to her eyes.

"What?" He frowned as if he'd misunderstood.

"You heard me. She told me that if I tattled on her to Dad or the police, my baby wouldn't wake up from his nap. Her words." It was too fresh, the fear too close to the surface. She swiped at the tear that spilled down her cheek, then hugged herself because she was too distraught to hug her baby. "I wanted to call the police, but what could I say? It would be her word against mine and my father sides with her." Every time. She brushed away another tear. "So I ran," she said in a whisper.

Jarvis swore.

Silas turned toward his voice and Mia bit back a request for him to watch his language. Her son was way too new and still far too young for it to make any difference.

"Of course you ran," he said, "But here?"

"Regina has always seen me as prissy and spoiled. Entitled, because Dad and I were so close. As if that was abnormal after Mom died." Mia deliberately unclenched her jaw at the memory of those old insults spoken when her father was out of earshot. "Despite everything I've done on my own in my career, she'd never expect me to hide out alone, definitely not in anything less than a five-star hotel."

Mia would love to hide with Tamara, where her son would have the best backup. But her mother's friend would be one more pressure point Regina could use against Mia. And while a resort vacation sounded perfect, she didn't have enough cash for that and using a credit card made it too easy for Regina to track her down.

"What about a guest room down at the house?" Jarvis suggested. "The place is massive, and almost no one would know. Everyone's distracted with Payne's recovery."

She shook her head. "I've been to the main house," she said. "As Mrs. Norton Graves, Regina runs in the same circles as the Coltons. She might be there right now, pretending to comfort Genevieve. She and Selina Barnes, Payne's second wife, are friendly competitors in all things of wealth and privilege." She smiled down at her son. "You've heard him cry. If we're within earshot of anyone, we'll be discovered within a day."

"But you'd be safe." He moved closer, filling the small cabin even more. "There's a chef and housekeeping. Hotel amenities without a credit card trail. You'd be able to care for him and yourself properly."

"Properly?" She bristled. How dare this cowboy come in and question her ability to care for her son? "Out. We are not your problem." Her primary concern was whether or not he would become a problem for her. "All you have to do is forget you saw me."

"As if." He folded his arms over his chest.

Unless she went on the attack, there would be no budging him. She looked around and started to gather the items she'd brought in from her car, stuffing them into the diaper bag. Within a minute she could be out of here. But where could she stay without drawing notice?

"Mia, stop. Let's assume you are out of her reach here. Have you sent the video to your father?"

She wanted to snap at him, this stranger who thought he knew her and was so sure he had all the answers. "Please leave me alone." Contrary to Regina's belief, Mia didn't beg anyone for anything. "I don't need you to solve this. I just need you to go."

"I could take the video to the police for you."

"Infidelity and sleeping around isn't exactly a criminal offense." Mia tugged at her hair. "She has the upper hand right now," she added, her chest tight. "Just, just look." She pulled out her phone and pulled up the text messages.

Having memorized the entire string of threats and pictures, she watched Jarvis's face as he scrolled through. He stopped, eyes narrowed, and she assumed he'd found the first set of pictures.

First, at the restaurant her father had suggested for lunch, Regina was pouring red wine into two glasses, her showy wedding set obvious. The next picture was a sickeningly sweet selfie of Regina and Norton, cheek to cheek, glasses touching.

The text that followed posed a question regarding Norton's medications and alcohol consumption.

"Is there an interaction risk?" Jarvis's query confirmed her assessment of where he was in the sequence of messages.

"Upper hand," she repeated. "There is a risk, but it's low. She wouldn't put an outright death threat against him in writing."

He swore again, this time under his breath. "She certainly didn't hesitate to threaten your son via text."

"No, she didn't. Knowing her, that means she has a plan to cover her tracks if it comes up."

"So what's *your* plan? You can't hide here forever."

She didn't appreciate the challenge in his tone as he returned her phone. "Of course not." She needed space to breathe and think and come up with a way to expose the woman who had, as of today, effectively shoved her out of the life she'd known. "I'll think of something."

She would find a way once she was sure her father and son wouldn't pay the price. Her father had been her rock, her idol throughout her life. She hadn't agreed with him on everything, particularly not his latest marriage, but they'd found a way to maintain their relationship. They weren't as close as they'd once been, but close enough. For years, Regina had been undermining that relationship. Jealousy, selfishness… Her reasons didn't matter. Mia knew she was wallowing out here, but she felt entitled to the time. Silas was safe. She could manage out here for a few days while she made up her mind how far and how soon to push back.

"If you could ignore us for a couple of days, I'll be out of your hair."

He stared at her for a long moment, then his gaze dropped to her son before cruising over the cramped cabin. "I can't ignore you." He settled his hat on his head. "I'll pick up some supplies for you."

"That's not—"

His mouth flattened and a sharp head shake cut her off. "It's necessary." He walked to the door. "No one will know you're here."

"Thank you."

He paused, halfway out the door. "My brother is a sergeant with the police department. If you decide you want his help, you'll get it."

"My pride isn't worth risking my father's life," she replied.

His eyebrows flexed over those warm brown eyes again. "You really think she'd do it? Kill Norton?"

"No doubt in my mind. She's gotten her way from the moment she married my dad, probably years before that, too."

"All right. Relax. I'll be back with some gear to make this doable."

"Thanks," she called after him.

There was no point wondering what lies Regina was spreading about why Mia didn't make it home last night. Her father hadn't called to check in, so she knew it had to be bad. And there was no point involving anyone, not even a police officer, until she could be sure the truth would be seen *and* believed.

Only when Regina was effectively discredited could Mia come out of hiding.

When the sounds of the horse had faded, she cuddled Silas until he fell asleep. Confident he was safe and content, she ducked out to the car she'd hidden in the brush to take care of herself. She shouldn't trust Jarvis so easily, but something in his gaze put her at ease. Not when he'd looked at her as if they'd met before; they hadn't. She would've remembered a man with that perfect combination of hard body and kind eyes. No, it had been the way he'd looked at her son after she'd told him about Regina's threat.

He might be the first person to immediately take her side on the whole "wicked stepmother" situation. Not that she'd broadcast her frustrations everywhere. That would have backfired more than the occasional comments she made about Regina's spending habits.

Even her husband had encouraged her to ignore Regina's antics. A sickening thought occurred to her. What if Regina had seduced him, too? The highly unlikely but not impossible scenario was completely irrelevant now. She and Roderick were through and she was better for it. The divorce settlement had been generous and swift since he preferred to pay one lump sum to get rid of the child he never intended to meet and the wife who'd let him down.

She had a knack for disappointing the men she cared about most. That trend would stop now, with Silas. Nothing would keep her from being the mother he needed.

The real-estate endeavor wasn't precisely necessary right now, but she'd hoped to put the bulk of the divorce settlement into long-term investments. And despite loving motherhood—and Silas—more each and every day, her mind had been ready for a challenge.

Well, she had it now, didn't she?

She cleaned herself up a bit and finally changed into clean shorts and a soft tunic top that were better suited to the rustic conditions. There was a spark of hope that she'd get through this, and the only cause was Jarvis. How curious that one awkward and unsettling encounter with a handsome cowboy could make her feel a thousand times better during the lowest moment of her life.

She'd know soon enough if she'd made a mistake by trusting him, and while Silas napped, she set things up for a quick escape if it proved necessary.

* * *

Jarvis hoped like hell she'd still be there when he got back. His search for Isaiah's proof forgotten for tonight, he rode hard back to the stables and bunkhouse where he'd been living since Asher hired him.

His mental list of the things Mia would need to make her stay easier kept growing. Although *easier* would only be a marginal improvement. She needed running water, a real bathroom, a refrigerator. He couldn't make any of those things happen at the warming hut. She needed a lot more than she'd decided to settle for, he thought as the Colton mansion near the main entrance of the Rattlesnake Ridge Ranch came into view.

Her stepmother's ugly threats trailed after him as he rode straight up to the stable. It was a cruel person who threatened to kill an infant. He just couldn't wrap his head around how anyone could say such a thing. Not even Aunt Amelia, who'd reluctantly taken them in when their parents died, had been that cold.

No mother should have to hear that. He didn't care for the idea of Mia dealing with the threat on her own. The idea of bunking out there with her flitted through his head and he dismissed it quickly. While being in close proximity to the beautiful woman who had fascinated him through college appealed, he worried that standing guard for her would draw unwanted attention to her location.

Normally, he would personally tend to his horse's care after a long workday, but this evening, he handed the reins to one of the other men on duty. "He's had a full day," Jarvis said, scratching Duke's ears. "If we have any apples, he's earned it."

"Sure thing," Jimmy said. "Got a hot date?"

Jarvis laughed at the joke. He'd gained a reputation for being the one cowboy every girl in town wanted to flirt with when they went out. Not that he hooked up often. Usually, he danced, made a few women smile and headed back to his room alone. He'd tried to tell the others that a good sense of humor was the key, but they refused to believe him.

"Got a call for a last-minute supply run for morning. You need anything while I'm going?"

Jimmy shook his head. "Not this time around."

"All right. I'll be back in an hour or so." Add another hour or so for getting the supplies into Mia's hands, but he kept that detail to himself. "Thanks again for the assist with Duke."

Jarvis picked up his truck and left the ranch through the service gate. He could get most of the supplies Mia needed at the feedstore that was conveniently located between the ranch and Mustang Valley. No chance he'd bump into Regina or anyone who ran in the same circles as Selina and his Colton Oil cousins there.

With a case of bottled water, a battery-operated lantern and a couple of blankets in the cart, he stopped to compare sleeping bags. He chose one that included a ground tarp and an inflatable pillow. He turned down the next aisle and decided a camouflage net might do a better job of hiding her car from view. Waiting to check out, he added a selection of meal bars. A nursing mother needed to eat more and more often. At least, that was what he'd learned from caring for the livestock on the ranch. Probably better if he didn't tell her that was his theory.

Not perfect, but easier, he thought as he loaded the purchases into his truck. A few small comforts should help her relax and rest. Maybe then she would be thinking clearly enough to make a better long-term plan.

As he pulled out of the parking lot, he finally gave in and called his brother. "Hey, Spencer," he said as his brother answered. "I have a hypothetical question."

"If it's about getting your career back on track, shoot."

Jarvis was more than a little bit tired of the refrain. "No. I, um, well I overheard a threat," he said. "A death threat," he clarified. "If I gave you the details, would the police department do anything about it?"

"Seriously?"

"Yes," Jarvis said through gritted teeth. "At what point do you investigate that kind of thing?"

He heard his brother sigh, could picture him rolling his eyes. "Hell, Jarvis. There are too many unknowns in your hypothetical."

"Come on, Spencer." Nervous, Jarvis adjusted the air vents to blow all the cool, air-conditioned air at him. He didn't know Mia well, but if first impressions could be trusted, she'd be furious that he'd made this call. "What evidence or complaint would you need to take action if someone threatened to kill another person?"

"We can't take action before a crime occurs. Depending on the facts and situation, we might do some surveillance. Most people don't go from zero to killer in one fast leap. We'd look for other signs of smaller trouble. Who are you worried about?"

Surveillance wouldn't work in this situation. There was no way to keep an official eye on Mia and her son without her noticing. "All right. That is helpful." Except it wasn't.

He suddenly understood why Asher didn't want to

use his father as bait to draw out the person who'd shot Payne several months ago. He wouldn't feel right putting Mia in a killer's crosshairs and he'd just met her. Not to mention she would never take that kind of chance with her son.

"All right," he said again.

"Are you in trouble?" Spencer asked.

It felt like it, though the trouble he sensed didn't fall into a category his brother could deal with as a cop. "No one's threatening me," Jarvis replied. "I'm thinking it'll blow over soon enough. If it doesn't, I'll let you know."

"Do that."

"Is it a crime to have an extramarital affair?"

"What the hell is going on with you?"

"Just answer the question," Jarvis snapped. "Please."

"Well, yes, technically it is a crime in the state of Arizona. We don't make a habit out of hauling in offenders or tossing them in jail. We typically let the divorce lawyers deal with that stuff."

"Good to know." So Mia was wrong about that; Regina's affair was a criminal offense. "I'll see you soon," Jarvis said, ending the call before his brother could ask more questions.

He hit a drive-through and downed a burger and fries, his mind set on finding a way to help her. He'd hope that if his sister was in trouble, someone would go the extra mile for her. And the baby. He couldn't get the little guy out of his mind. The kid was so tiny. Vulnerable. Completely defenseless if someone wanted to make sure he didn't wake up from a nap. Whether or not Regina really did intend to commit murder, Mia believed she was capable of doing so and that was all that mattered right now.

He considered calling Spencer back, but his brother would need solid evidence, not a chain of text messages. Jarvis didn't care about the video proving Regina was unfaithful; he was more concerned with her threats to harm Silas and Norton.

Jarvis didn't usually worry over the welfare of anyone other than his siblings. He sure wasn't the ride-to-the-rescue type, yet here he was, charging in to help Mia. She was on his family's land, whether or not his grandfather's story held up. And if trouble followed her, he had to be ready for it.

Instead of driving up through the service entrance used by the Triple R crew and support staff, he circled around, looking for the road she must have taken to get to that warming hut. This end of the property wasn't neglected, but it wasn't well used right now, either. Mia had made a smart choice with her hiding spot, though she couldn't stay indefinitely.

The light was all but gone, the first stars winking into view overhead, when he found where she'd turned off the paved road and onto Triple R land. The access road was only a single lane wide. Not a high-traffic area, even when they were grazing herds up this way.

He still didn't understand how or why Mia even knew to come out here or that the shelter would be available. One of several questions he hoped to ask without spooking her when he dropped off these supplies.

His truck lumbered over the bumpy road, rutted from the last time they'd had serious rain. When his headlights flashed off the window of her car nestled into a dip in the landscape, he breathed a sigh of relief. She'd stayed. That small act of trust filled him up, smoothing out the parched sections of his soul he largely ignored.

He turned off his lights as he came around to the front of the weathered shelter and then cut the engine. His heart sped up, anticipating another view of her lush curves and sultry gaze. Not that she aimed that specific gaze his way in an inviting manner, but it was enough to remember it was possible. And yeah, certain parts of him were really into the idea of winning one of those famously seductive looks from her.

He left the cab and moved around the front end of the truck to open the passenger door and take out the gear and groceries. "It's Jarvis," he called softly so his voice wouldn't carry too far. "You can put down the stick."

He heard movement and a low exhale. Relief? Disappointment? A soft light flicked on inside the hut and Mia stepped out, her body a mouthwateringly curvy silhouette.

She'd changed from the dress to form-fitting shorts and a loose shirt. But the sneakers on her feet told a tale. She was ready to run at a moment's notice.

"How's the little guy?" he asked, hoping to put her at ease.

"Snoozing again." Her raspy voice and half smile made him wonder if he'd woken her up. "Come in," she said. "I didn't expect you to come back."

Best not to take that personally. She was clearly rattled and convinced that those dearest to her were in danger. "If my sister was in trouble, I'd hope someone would have the decency to help her." Did that sound as sappy to her as it did to him? "I brought bottled water, too," he said, setting the supplies in his arms down on the worn floor. "Give me just a second."

Walking back in with a pack of diapers stacked on top of the water bottles and the strap of the sleeping bag hooked around one finger, he saw her swiping a tear from her cheek.

"What is it? Did I get the wrong flavors?"

Those dark eyebrows flexed into a frown. "No, the snacks are perfect. Thanks."

"Good." He winked at her. "I should have asked. Are you allergic to anything?"

"No." Her mouth twitched.

"Great." He smiled. "You said you were stocked, but I hear there's no such thing as too many diapers."

She rubbed her arms as if chasing away a chill. "I wasn't aware the Triple R had a day care."

"Not exactly." He rocked back on his heels and shoved his hands into his pockets. If there was a protocol for helping a woman on the run survive an insufficient hideout, he didn't know it. "My boss has a baby under a year old and his fiancée has a day care center. I've picked up a few things."

She yawned, and though she tried to hide it, he could see weariness embarrassed her. "Go ahead and roll out the sleeping bag," he suggested.

"You're not leaving?" she asked in a rush. "You can't stay."

Again, he refused to be offended. "I won't stay unless you ask," he said. "I have a camouflage net for your car. Just another precaution," he assured her. "Once that's in place, I'll be out of your hair." For tonight.

She nodded and set to work on the sleeping bag. He dragged his eyes away from the enticing view of her long legs and curvy hips, away from the temptation to soothe or distract her. They didn't know each other, and while she'd trusted him with her story, he hadn't actually verified it. More than that, he'd set himself a task out here that was better done without an audience.

Working in the dark, he added the netting to the scrubby brush she'd used to hide her car. He could come back in the morning to make sure it was all intact and effective. She might think she was alone out here, but she wasn't. Not while he was on the property. She'd just have to get used to it.

Walking inside again, she had the lantern he'd purchased set up in a corner, giving off better light than the small flashlight she'd been using. The sleeping bag was unrolled, right next to the baby seat. "All set?"

"Yes, thanks."

"Is your cell phone charged?"

Another slight frown marred her brow. "It is. I've been running the car for a few minutes at a time."

Too primitive, he thought darkly. "Add my number to your contacts."

"That's really not necessary," she said, shying away from him.

"I can be here faster than any first responders because I know where I'm going. Do you have any kind of protection?" He eyed the stick near the doorway. "Besides the bat?"

She had the grace to smile. "Would it ease your mind to know I was the top hitter in softball three seasons running in high school?"

Squinting, he patted a hand around his neck. "Not much, no."

She laughed lightly. "Thanks for everything, Jarvis. Please don't worry. I've taken self-defense classes, too. We'll be out of your hair tomorrow. The day after at the latest."

"Don't leave without letting me know where you're headed," he pressed. "You said it yourself, your step-mom is resourceful."

"I think it's best if I reach out and offer to sign a non-disclosure agreement or something. There has to be a way to draw that up. To reassure her."

Or something? He didn't think a piece of paper would stop someone devious enough and mean enough to threaten a baby. "What if I found you a better place to hide?" Why couldn't his brain remember that her problems weren't his? The sooner she was off the ranch the better.

"We've talked about this," she said. "I can't go anywhere near the Colton house."

"I know." He took a step forward and drew up short. This was so strange, fighting himself to keep his distance. "There are two bunkhouses that we use now instead of this place if we have herds out this way. They aren't in use now," he added hastily. "No need for them really this time of year. But they're updated with power, freshwater wells and septic systems. You'd be more comfortable."

He'd be more comfortable. The bunkhouse he had in mind was farther off the beaten path of Triple R acreage. And if he loaned her his truck, no one would suspect a thing.

"Won't people notice the bunkhouse is in use?"

"People really don't come out here if the herds are grazing elsewhere," he assured her. He was willing her to take him up on the offer. "If anyone does notice, they'll assume it's a grad student taking soil samples."

"That happens often?"

"Not often. I've just heard others mention it. Seriously, it would be a better solution for you."

"Why does my solution matter so much to you?"

Seriously? Shouldn't it matter to anyone with common decency? A new mother and infant should *not* be in such primitive conditions. "It's a brother complex," he hedged. It had to be a sibling thing, because Jarvis didn't do involvement, romantic interest or relationships. Those ended badly.

Her gaze narrowed. "What did you do? Did you tell someone about me hiding here?"

"No." His denial didn't help matters at all. Her fingers curled into fists and her eyes blazed. If she had the stick, he'd be on the floor by now. "I haven't done anything to expose you, Mia. I just called my brother."

She muttered an oath under her breath and then bit down hard on her lower lip. "Let me guess—whiny stepdaughters can't file complaints with the police."

Granted, they'd only had two conversations, but he hadn't heard her whine once. "I was asking about how death threats might be reported." Damn it. Her brown eyes narrowed and her lips firmed. He kept saying the wrong thing. She was clearly ready to bolt. And then what? If she'd thought she was safe here, he needed to make sure she was safe here. "And adultery is a crime in Arizona," he added.

"Good grief." She rubbed her temples. "That's probably an accusation that carries more weight when the injured party files the complaint, not the stepdaughter of the unfaithful partner. Forget about me, Jarvis. I'll just go."

"Stay." His primary goal was to help her feel secure. Even here. He stepped forward and caught her hands, holding them loosely between their bodies. He rushed to full alert at the contact. Her skin was silky under his rough thumbs. He didn't crowd her, but he felt her pulse racing under his fingertips. "I'm saying this all wrong and I'm sorry for making you worry. I was trying to be transparent and reassure you."

She stared at her wrists, caged by his fingers. "That failed. Not that I want to be left in the dark, either. I've had enough surprise attacks for a lifetime."

"Noted. On both counts." A ghost of an amused smile slipped across her lips. "No one knows anything about you here. No one will. Not from me," he vowed.

"What about the rest of the crew?"

He'd manipulated the weekly schedule of responsibilities to accommodate his search. In his view, this was a happy coincidence, with her crisis and his search intersecting. "Won't be a problem. I'm the only one who is scheduled to be out this way."

She gently extricated herself from his grasp. "Okay."

He immediately missed the warmth of her skin. The wall she built between them was practically visible and plastered with no-trespassing warnings.

"I'd still prefer you move to the bunkhouse. Tomorrow," he added when she started to argue. The baby stirred, because of the conversation or because he had some other issue, Jarvis didn't know.

Mia sighed, scooping up her son before he could really work himself into a crying jag. She was lovely with or without the baby in her arms. That was one more strange new awareness in a day filled with oddities. Watching her struck a chord deep in his chest and resonated through his system. He'd developed a crush on her when she was modeling everything from swimsuits to eyeliner. Watching her devotion as a mother was like opening a safe expecting cash and finding a stash of priceless gems. This side of her was so unexpected, this facet of her beauty so raw and unpolished and alluring. Since when did he find mothers *alluring*?

He wasn't that kind of guy. He'd never wanted the hearth-and-home deal. Losing his parents was proof that life was too fragile and the world too fickle. Better to have some fun and move on before the good stuff got ripped away, leaving bloody knuckles, bruises and painful scars behind.

"Jarvis?"

She'd caught him staring like an idiot. "I'll, um, I'll keep watch tonight so you can rest easy." The statement made, it felt exactly right. How else would he make sure she didn't disappear without a trace? It was the practical thing to do, he argued with the voice in his head accusing him of being hopelessly infatuated.

"Stop it." She shook her head. "That will only draw more attention."

"From who? Nothing but coyotes and owls out here when the cattle are elsewhere."

Her lush lips twisted to one side. "I don't have much to fear from an owl, and a coyote has no reason to wander close enough to trouble me. Go home and get your own rest. I hear cowboys have to get up early."

"Just like mothers and models," he said. She rolled her eyes. "I live on the ranch," he added, hooking his thumbs in his pockets. "Call me if a coyote gets out of line."

"I promise."

Her smile was relaxed, natural, and the sparkle was back in her eye rather than frustration and fear. Promising he'd be back in the morning, he walked out of the warming hut and climbed into his truck. But he didn't go all the way back to the ranch. Instead, he retreated only so far as the service road and parked. Now he was effectively blocking anyone trying to take an established road toward her hiding place. It also meant he was less than a minute away if she *did* need him tonight.

As he adjusted the seat to get comfortable, he wondered which outcome would make him happier—an undisturbed night or one in which she called him for help. *What was wrong with him?* He didn't wish trouble on her or the baby. She'd been through too much already.

His brother would chide him for not verifying her story before siding with her. His sister would accuse him of being more interested in her face than her predicament. Although his siblings knew him best, neither of them would be entirely correct about this. Oh, he was plenty attracted to Mia and he hadn't vetted her claim with a source beyond her cell phone.

But he was running on his instincts and her reputation. That was more than enough to justify a few bucks in supplies and spending the night in his truck under the expansive sky.

Just as he was settling in, lightning slashed across the sky and a deep rumble of thunder chased it. So much for stretching out in the bed of his truck. Knowing rain was imminent, he cracked the windows and braced himself for a cramped and uncomfortable night.

Chapter 3

The sudden storm lashed at the warming hut and lightning revealed all of the gaps in the aged and weary structure. Mia rarely wallowed in regret. She'd invested years of effort and tears learning how to accept her strengths and her weaknesses equally. Right now, she wished she'd accepted Jarvis's generosity rather than resisting him due to her innate stubbornness and the fear Regina had planted in her heart.

Silas was restless, too, and she blamed either the weather or her own edgy energy. The combination definitely wasn't helping matters. She fed him, rocked him and changed him. She bundled him snug in a blanket and when that failed, she tried letting him rest in only his diaper.

Nothing worked. Her eyes were bleary and she was well beyond frazzled as she dealt with her son. In the parenting classes, they'd warned her there would come a time when nothing soothed the baby and she would want to pull out her hair. Like all the other parents in the room, Mia had chuckled nervously, not believing things would get bad enough to sap her patience and make her short-tempered with her child.

She believed it now.

If she'd thought consoling him had been a challenge when Jarvis found them, this was a whole new level of agony. Standing here when she had zero help nearby was a lousy time for a revelation. There was no one to trade off with, no option to walk away and take a breather, as the instructor had recommended.

"I'm trying, baby," she murmured, pacing as far from Silas as possible. "What is it you need?" She didn't want to let him work up another good cry. Not that she thought anyone would hear him over this storm.

Sitting on the sleeping bag, her legs crossed, she swayed gently side to side and watched his little face pinch, his body coiled for his next hearty wail. A good mother would be impressed by her son's lung capacity. Mia, feeling like a failure in every aspect of life, burst into tears herself.

"Oh, I'm sorry, baby. What was I thinking?" She tucked Silas into the security of his car seat and paced the three strides to the door of the hut. Swiping at her cheeks, she tried to pull herself away from the brink of a self-destructive meltdown. Nothing would improve if they were both sobbing.

How was it her father had been such an amazing single parent and role model after her mother had died? His commitment, patience and love had given her a solid foundation of confidence and self-worth, despite the grief and loss they were both coping with. He'd filled in and worked around that missing piece of her heart.

And then that foundation had been ripped away, thanks to Regina. The woman had entered their lives in a whirl of affection and companionship, things her father sorely missed after years as a widower. In short order, Regina began suggesting that Mia's resistance to a new mother figure proved she needed less attention from Norton and more independence. And Norton had fallen for it. Despite her stepmother's antics and efforts to drive them apart, her father's courageous example in the years prior had inspired Mia to raise her son alone.

It had been the right decision, the only logical solution, even knowing her husband wouldn't tolerate such a tectonic shift in their marriage dynamic.

On the other side of the weathered door, she could hear the wind changing and another swath of rain battering the hut. A leak in the roof splatted on one end of the sleeping bag Jarvis had delivered. She hurried to move things around the small space, while Silas continued to cry.

Steeling herself, she opened a bottle of water and indulged in a brief fantasy about ear plugs. As if she'd ever use them to blot out her son. She reminded herself that this was a moment, not forever. Her baby was safe even if he was currently unhappy. And she was a single parent by choice.

Roderick had been quick to remind her they'd agreed not to have children in order to better focus on their respective careers and the things they wanted to accomplish in the world. Of course, she hadn't gotten pregnant on her own; she'd been consistent and careful about preventive measures, and yet, by some miracle, she'd conceived. In her mind it was meant to be. Roderick saw it as a betrayal.

She'd been proud to leave modeling behind to be the wife and partner of a tech mogul with strong philanthropic values. They'd traveled, joined humanitarian projects around the world and she'd launched and managed his charitable foundation. They'd been happy and close and in love. Or so she'd thought. Why was she so easy to discard?

The better question was why she was rehashing all of this now. Her husband had stepped out of her life, or, more accurately, pushed her out of his with aloof efficiency. It was done. He'd run the numbers and projections of parenthood expenses, including college, against his anticipated income and basically written her a check to cover that amount. No one could fault him for shirking his responsibility. Though Silas would never know his father, she was sure it was better than growing up around a parent who would ignore him.

"Not my first hard day," she reminded herself. "Won't be the last." The only good news, she thought as she adjusted her belongings again to avoid another leak, was that Jarvis had left.

She couldn't imagine how crowded it would feel in here with him. His presence overpowered everything, including her good sense. The instant attraction had surprised her, once the distress of being found had worn off. Her pulse had fluttered and the ripple of temptation over her skin had scared her almost as much as the instinctive urge to trust him.

Mia hadn't trusted anyone other than herself in quite some time. She loved her father but questioned his decisions, which typically revolved around Regina's preferences. Although she'd accepted his feedback and advice about her new career options, going into real estate felt pretty foolish while she was hiding out in a leaky warming hut.

Had Regina set her up from the start? Was the scene at the country house an elaborate scheme to permanently force her out of her father's life?

The answer couldn't be yes. But Regina did gain from the stunt, which made her speculation seem more plausible than paranoid. With Mia gone, Regina would now be the sole woman in Norton's life. Mia was no longer there to defend herself from any of Regina's lies or to protect her father from his wife's lavish spending habits.

She shoved her hands into her hair, pulling out the tie and finger combing the long, thick waves back from her face. Clearly, the stress and lack of sleep were catching up to her. Regina was cunning, to be sure, but from day one she had avoided any action that could possibly cast her in a negative light. Why would she put her status as Mrs. Norton Graves at risk by having an affair?

Mia should have the upper hand, with the incriminating video saved on her phone as well as backed up to a secure cloud storage. But all the advantages in the world were useless while Regina had the leverage.

Half of the leverage, she thought, picking up Silas again. Her sweet boy was still crying, but she was calm enough to make another attempt to soothe him. She sat in the lone chair, which she considered a testament to good craftsmanship rather than too brittle to be useful, and rested Silas on her chest, heart to heart, hoping he'd calm down.

These parenting challenges would only become more complex as her son grew. Someday, she hoped to find someone willing to become her partner in this adventure so she wouldn't go through every day alone.

Those days were light-years away at the moment, but they could happen. She sang softly to Silas, stroking his dark, baby-soft curls while her mind drifted between the past and the future. Lasting love was more than fairy tale or fantasy. Motherhood confirmed that for her every day. Even the strident moments of motherhood underscored that soul-deep truth.

There *was* someone out there for her. A man who would treasure her for more than her connections. For more than the status of dating a former model. Someone who wanted to be both partner and father.

"We'll find the right someone," she whispered into Silas's hair. It was the same promise she made to him every day, in one way or another.

The roof sprang another leak and water dripped down, plinking on the floor close to the door. As much as she didn't want to move from this rustic little pocket of safety, the storm had made Jarvis's point. She didn't yet have a viable plan that would protect her father while she exposed Regina's infidelity. Until she had that plan, she needed a better place to hide.

"Momma will figure it out," she soothed as Silas's cries finally abated on a shuddering breath. "We'll go home. We'll be a family, just you and me." She'd figure out a career, with or without her father's support if necessary.

She just had to keep her son and father safe long enough to see that dream fulfilled.

Jarvis was up with the sun, grateful the rain had blown over. Less grateful for the stuffy cab of the truck and the kink in his neck. Other than the storm, there hadn't been any trouble through the night, which gave him confidence that Mia would be all right out here today. From this vantage point, he had to work to separate her car from the rolling hills and scrubby grasses and he knew exactly where to look. He should go on to work, trusting her to stay put and stay hidden. Instead, he started the engine and drove back to the hut to check on her and Silas.

Before he was out of the truck, the cabin door opened just a smidgen as Mia confirmed it was him. Her caution only slammed home exactly how nervous she was about her situation. Then she stepped out into the morning sunshine, the baby in her arms, and he thought she was prettier than a sunrise.

"Good morning," he said. He noticed the circles under her eyes and the tension pinching the corners of her mouth. He was almost afraid to ask, "How did it go last night?"

"The rain made your point about the accommodations," she replied. "There are a few leaks in the roof here."

"A few?" He stepped back and eyed the shed-style slope. "We really should just knock this thing down." He knew he should've insisted on moving her yesterday. "We don't keep up with the huts," he said. "I'm sorry."

"It's not your fault I can be too stubborn for my own good," she said, smothering a yawn. "Does the offer of moving still stand?"

The guilt in her voice, in her tired eyes, punched him in the heart. Just when he thought life had drummed out all the soft spots. "I can move you right now," he said.

"Oh?" Her eyebrows flexed into a frown. "Don't you need to get to work?"

"Not as much as you need reliable shelter. Come on. I'll help you load up."

"Jarvis, I can wait until…" Her voice trailed off, exhaustion clearly interfering with whatever she'd meant to say.

"Now is just fine, Mia. Let me help." He closed the distance, guiding her gently back into the little hut to help her pack. She didn't resist or give him any attitude and somehow that lack of fight worried him more.

Inside, he cringed. Signs of roof leaks were everywhere, her supplies clustered in the dry spots. The roof had apparently let in more rain than it kept out last night.

"What if you're late to work?" she asked.

"Don't worry about me. It's not like I'd pin the blame on you," he teased, rolling up the sleeping bag. "Did you get any rest last night?"

"A little." She tucked the baby into his seat, rolling her eyes when he started to fuss.

"Is he okay?"

"Just grumpy. I think the storm was unsettling."

"Makes sense," Jarvis said, though he had no idea if it did or not. "There's a shower at the bunkhouse I mentioned." He'd make sure it was operational before he drove in. "And hot water."

"Really?"

He smothered a laugh at the eagerness in her voice. "Really."

"You'll have to tell me who I owe for the utility expenses. When I'm gone, I can send money back."

Not this again. He stood, the sleeping bag under his

arm. "Let's wait and sort it out once you've had some sleep."

"Right." She buckled the baby into his car seat and wrestled to zip the diaper bag closed. "I should only need a few more days. A couple of people owe me favors. It's possible one of them will let my dad know what's going on without hurting him too much."

"There's no rush this time of year, I promise."

She started for her car, but he loaded up his truck instead. "If you can deal with being isolated until the end of the day, I'd rather you didn't move your car."

"Why? I'm not sure I'm comfortable with that," she said. "If something happens to the baby."

"You'll call me," he said. She frowned. He was running on instinct, unable to verbalize why her leaning on him was a positive thing for both of them.

"Without a car I'll feel trapped."

Right now she looked too exhausted to feel much of anything else. He hated to spell it out for her. "If someone does think to look for you here and they managed to find your car, it will look abandoned."

"How does that help me?"

He stowed her things in the truck bed while she got the car seat in place. Did she even realize she was arguing and cooperating at the same time? "Ditching the car should create the impression that you've already moved on."

"My car being here implies a connection," she pointed out.

"Connection to what? No one at the ranch has seen you. The assumption will be that you found another way out of town."

She spoke softly to the baby and then climbed into

the passenger seat. As Jarvis drove across the grassy pastures to the bunkhouse, he was torn between emphasizing the remoteness of the new location as a safety feature and ignoring it to prevent undue worry if she did have a crisis. He kept his thoughts to himself and Mia seemed content with that.

The baby, too. "He got quiet fast," Jarvis observed.

She snorted, apparently unimpressed. "He loves car rides," she explained. "And he was up all night. They warned me it would happen."

"It?" he queried.

"The inconsolable baby. It's a whole thing, but like any new mom, I thought I could handle it."

He pulled to a stop at the bunkhouse and cut the engine. "You did handle it," he pointed out.

"Possibly at the expense of my sanity. A chunk of brain cells at the very least." She flicked a hand toward the view through the windshield. There was nothing to mar the view from here to the mountains. "Beautiful," she said. "I see why you like it out here. It's peaceful. Or it would be if I wasn't more removed from any kind of help than before.

"I'm sorry." She rubbed her eyes. "Forgive me for being cranky. Once I get some sleep, I'll figure out a way to handle my stepmom and stop imposing on you."

"I'm sure you will."

He unloaded her things while she gathered up her son. Inside, the bunkhouse was stripped to the bare essentials, but it was clean and dry. Here, in addition to basic conveniences, she had a table and chairs, plus she could choose from four bunks. He turned on the power and the water pump, made sure things were running as they should, then propped the stick against the wall by the door.

"You'll call if you have any trouble?" he asked.

She started to nod, but the motion was cut short by another yawn.

"Want me to stay and, ah, babysit while you take a shower?" he offered, trying not to think of what she'd look like under a hot spray of water. Unfortunately, memories of her poses in swimsuits flashed across his mind. He moved toward the baby, away from her before he did something stupid.

"I should be offended, but that sounds like heaven," she said, her mouth tilted into a grin.

"All right. Take your time." He had no idea what babysitting an infant required. Silas was currently dozing in his seat, and with a little luck Jarvis wouldn't have to do much of anything. If the baby did need something, he'd look it up online and figure it out.

Practical problem-solving was one of his favorite parts of his job. He'd never expected to enjoy working outdoors or all of the unpredictable moments among the daily routines of ranch life.

"You should go on to work after my shower," Mia said. "Silas and I can manage."

"You're sure?"

"We've been managing just fine for a couple of months now." Her smile was softer, filled with affection as she watched her son.

"What happened to his dad?" It was a nosy question, but he was more curious if there might be a better, more secure place for her and the baby to hide.

"Silas's father isn't part of our lives." Her head

snapped up, her eyes flat, expression stern. "Go to work, Jarvis. You've helped enough today."

Okay, he'd crossed a line he hadn't even seen. He was about to apologize when his cell phone buzzed on his hip.

She shot him an I-told-you-so look as he stepped outside to take the call.

"Where are you?" Asher didn't usually bark out demands, but he'd been under some serious stress since his father had been shot by a still-unknown assailant. That came on the heels of upheaval at the Colton Oil offices, as the board dealt with accusations that Ace Colton, then-CEO, was not a biological Colton and thus an imposter. Seemed the grass wasn't as green on the Colton Oil side of the family tree as Jarvis had always imagined.

"I'm out driving the access roads after all that rain." At least, he would be as soon as he drove in.

"Oh. Yeah, that was smart," Asher allowed. "Look, Selina's in my face, needing something installed at her place. Has to be today. Can you handle it?"

Just hearing Selina's name explained everything about the call and Asher's agitation. Selina Barnes Colton remained a thorny presence in everyone's life as the vice president and public relations director at Colton Oil. Payne's current wife, Genevieve, and all six of his children despised Selina, yet somehow she'd negotiated a chunk of the Triple R just a quarter mile from the mansion she'd considered her own for the duration of her marriage.

Jarvis credited Selina's attorney with her posh, post-divorce settlement, but Asher and his siblings were convinced Selina had some unsavory leverage over their dad. Whatever the actual cause, the effect was Asher having to juggle schedules when Selina made noise about needing something on her part of the property repaired or demanded help with one project or another.

The whole situation was an odd echo of Mia's trouble. It seemed like both Selina and Regina might be unfaithful second wives whom their husbands' offspring hated. Women who manipulated people to maintain control.

Since Jarvis had been on the ranch, he'd been to Selina's home to unclog a sink, rip up carpeting for a flooring change, and install new blinds in her home office and a guest room. In general, she annoyed most of the crew Asher sent to help her. She couldn't seem to be polite and came at the men with either overdone flirty innuendo or flat-out dismissal.

Unlike his peers, Jarvis didn't mind taking on her calls. He used those opportunities to chat with her about the history of the ranch. So far, her information hadn't changed his search parameters, but he was gaining insight into the side of the family he'd never met. Although his boss didn't know his real reasons for not complaining about Selina, Asher definitely appreciated having a cowboy who didn't gripe about being her on-call handyman.

"Sure thing," Jarvis said. "I'll go straight over." Well, straight there after a stop at the warming hut and his own room for a shower and change of clothes. He could flirt with Selina to get the cup of coffee his system was craving.

"Thanks. Nothing out your way needs attention?"

Only his personal quest. "Everything is clear out here."

"Great. Let me know when you're done with my former stepmother," Asher said.

Silas let out a cry that filtered outside.

"What's that?" Asher asked.

As a dad, Asher was naturally dialed in to that sound. He and Willow were blending into a family of four with their baby girls, Harper and Luna.

"Radio," Jarvis improvised. "One of those vasectomy commercials."

Asher chuckled. "Those always get on my nerves."

"Kids or commercials?" Jarvis joked, as if he had any clue about the perils or rewards of fatherhood.

"Can't speak for all kids, but my girls are worth it every single day," Asher said, proudly. "If you hear Selina say anything useful, you'll let me know?"

That was one of the first cousin-to-cousin rules of handling jobs at Selina's place. If she mentioned anything Asher could use to get her off the Triple R and out of his life, he wanted to hear it. "Always, boss."

"Thanks."

Mia had quieted Silas once again and she waved at him from the doorway. He promised he'd be back to check on her this evening, reminded her to call if she had any trouble and then went to deal with Selina.

It would be a day working from the truck rather than on horseback as he'd come to prefer, but every day on the ranch beat a day in the office. Convinced Mia's car was still hidden after the rain, he did what he could to cover the tire tracks to the bunkhouse before heading toward his place. He felt a bit more human after his lightning-quick shower, but he wasn't looking forward to Selina knowing he'd kept her waiting.

The woman was hot when he arrived, her toe tapping and her face sharp with a frown when she opened the door.

"Oh, Jarvis." Her entire demeanor seemed to soften without even moving a muscle. "*You* are always worth the wait." Her eyes cruised over his body, lingering on his chest and south of his belt before she lifted her gaze to his face once more. "The fresh-scrubbed look is good on you."

He wouldn't be surprised if she asked him to work shirtless one of these days.

"Thanks." He resisted the urge to curl his lip in distaste, or pluck his shirt from his chest. He only now regretted pulling his clothing on over still-damp skin. "I figured you'd prefer fresh scrubbed to muddy."

"Hmm." This time the long perusal of his body ended with a fast lick of her lips. "I suppose muddy could be appealing. In the right circumstances."

She was too obvious in her bids for attention, but Jarvis considered her mostly harmless. She flirted and talked a good game, but he doubted she'd back up that bold, sexy bluster by actually getting muddy in any way, shape or form with a simple cowboy.

Jarvis was well aware that she considered him eye candy, which might be flattering from another woman. From Selina, it felt sticky. From the start, he'd chosen to play along—with extreme caution—so she'd keep talking to him.

He smiled, employing the easygoing charm that had won over many a person in boardrooms and out here on the ranch. "What is it I can help with today?"

"You are such a treat." A catlike grin spread over her face, and her blue eyes sparkled. Her hair was down, the red-gold waves flowing over her shoulders. She stepped away from the door so he could walk inside. "The problem is back this way."

He followed her through the house. She was an attractive woman and her casual sundress played up her best features. Surely, she'd tempted many a man on or off the ranch into her bed. Jarvis focused on the newest additions to her luxurious decor rather than the woman herself. She was always changing something. Yeah, her attorney had been superb, but she still struck him as lonely. To his relief, today's trouble wasn't near her bedroom, but outside, where she kept making improvements to her deck and outdoor kitchen. Selina loved to entertain.

"I ordered new fixtures for the sinks and a better wine cooler. Take the old one if you want it."

What was he going to do with a wine cooler? He could hear the crap he'd take from the other ranch hands if he put it in his room. "We'll see," he said, eyeing the various boxes. The thing might be of some use to Mia out at the bunkhouse or even his sister, Bella.

"It impresses women when men are prepared," Selina said suggestively.

He arched an eyebrow. "Prepared to serve wine properly?"

"Boy Scouts have a stellar reputation for a reason," she demurred.

He laughed, unable to temper the reaction. She sucked in a breath. "What's so funny about that?"

"You'd be bored with the Boy Scout–type in about thirty seconds flat."

She folded her arms under her breasts, boosting them a little. He kept his eyes locked with hers, refusing to take the bait. She pouted. "Fine. You might be right."

Sauntering closer, she dragged a finger across his shoulders. "Rugged and rough is *much* more to my liking."

Today, maybe. Selina wasn't the type that stayed content. Hell, she'd had it all with Payne and seemingly tossed it aside to chase younger men. Of course, she'd landed on her feet. Ignoring her attempts to distract him or bait him into something physical, he focused on the fixtures.

"I need to let Asher know I'll be here awhile." Looked like his search for confirmation of Isaiah's story would be pushed back another day.

"You do that," she said. "We can make a day of it."

"Sure." It would be a day of crawling around, squeezing under counters and twisting himself into tight spaces while Selina eyed him like a prize.

She drifted away on a cloud of expensive perfume and he shut off the water at the valve that served her outdoor entertaining space. At the breaker box, he cut the power to the outdoor appliances, just to be safe.

Normally, he had no opinion about how Selina lived. Her choices weren't his concern. But today it bothered him. She had so much luxurious space, all of it protected by a security system, big fences and a crowd of people who helped her even when they didn't enjoy the task. Mia, on the other hand, was barely making do with her son in a basic cabin. From his perspective, he was sure both women were lonely with their circumstances, but Selina struck him as sad underneath all of that. Mia was afraid of the threats, overwhelmed and uncertain, but somehow she gave off a ray of hope.

He shook off the weird thoughts. The talk-show shrink routine only proved he needed real sleep in his bed rather than the truck. And it wouldn't hurt to have something else to think about besides the mother and baby he'd left stranded on the opposite side of the ranch.

If only he could convince Mia to move to the main house until she sorted out the problem with her step-mom. Mia would rightfully throttle him if he exposed her that way. She'd been adamant that Regina was too close to both Genevieve Colton and Selina to take that chance. He couldn't argue it, having no real clue about the people the Colton Oil side of the family called friends.

Pushing all of that to the back of his mind, Jarvis set to work on the new plumbing fixtures. The sooner he knocked this out, the more daylight he'd have for his own agenda. To his surprise, Selina didn't hover over him. She took a couple of business calls from a lounger on the other side of the outdoor kitchen. Around noon she even offered to pick up lunch for both of them. He took her up on that since he'd missed breakfast.

But when she wanted him to linger over the food with her at the shaded table, he politely declined. Even though Asher would want him to chat her up, he was too tired and achy to guide the conversation without being obvious.

"Are you thinking you're too good for me, Jarvis?"

"Hardly," he said with a sincere smile this time. "We shouldn't leave your wine suffering at the wrong temperature."

He didn't have to like Selina to respect her talent for negotiation. Though the Coltons openly wished she'd leave the ranch and Colton Oil, she stuck hard and kept her head high despite her mistakes. Whether that was some unsavory blackmail or just her nature didn't make much difference to him. It took tenacity to pull off the life she'd carved out for herself.

"No, we wouldn't want the wine to suffer." This time when she chuckled, the sound seemed more genuine than calculating. Walking over to the brand-new faucet, she stroked the spigot with great affection. And just like that, Selina the seductress was back. "The oil-rubbed bronze is perfect," she mused, peering at him from under her lashes. "I should've gone with it from the beginning."

He wasn't about to fall into her games. "It fits the vibe you've got out here," he said, keeping his tone neutral.

She pursed her lips, as if deciding how best to come at him next, when her cell phone rang. Checking the screen, she gave him a flirty wave of her fingers and walked toward the house.

"Regina!" she gushed. "I was just thinking of you. Tell me everything new."

It was logical that Selina might know more than one Regina, but Jarvis didn't believe in coincidence. Did Selina suspect Mia was hiding on the ranch somewhere? Did Regina?

Mia's warning came back to him, complete with an icy trickle of dread down his spine. Selina and Regina were too alike not to be friends, or at least well-connected enemies. A moment ago, Jarvis had wanted to get out of Selina's reach as fast as possible; now he needed to drag things out just in case this conversation could be of help to Mia.

He turned the water on again and tested the seals and flow on each fixture. Taking far more time than the task required, he racked his brain for an excuse to get into the house and closer to Selina's office.

Gathering up trash and old fixtures, he caught a break to hear that she'd stopped in the kitchen. "What's the occasion?" Selina paused, listening. "Aren't you thoughtful? Norton will *love* that."

The comment dashed any hope that Selina wasn't speaking with Mia's stepmother. "Why isn't Mia helping? I know the baby is still so new—"

Selina went quiet. Regina must have interrupted.

"Well, I suppose the silver lining is you won't have to see her flaunting all that baby weight as if it's a badge of honor. That's just the worst." She added, "As if I'm in the wrong because I chose to take care of my body. After all those years modeling, I expected her to have more pride than that." Regina's reply brought out Selina's catty laughter.

Jarvis had a sister and, though his aunt and mother had died, he was aware of how some women could act toward one another. Mia's fuller figure was beautiful and real, whether or not she was still carrying baby weight. He bristled with an inexplicable urge to defend Mia. And if he did, she'd be in more trouble.

"Do you think her ex wrote that in to the prenup?" Selina queried under her breath. "What? He never wanted kids? So all those rumors about his brilliance are true," she muttered. "There's a man with my kind of priorities."

Grinding his teeth, he continued with his work. Two by two, he carried wine from the outside cooler into the kitchen, avoiding eye contact with Selina. She didn't seem the least bit perturbed that he could hear her end of the call. At least this uncomfortable scene would help him reassure Mia that her stepmother wasn't onto her current location.

When the wine was out of the way, he disconnected the old cooler and pulled it out of the space. While he was unboxing the new appliance, he heard Selina return, her call apparently over.

"Jarvis?"

He didn't turn around, his hands full as he carefully lifted the wine cooler out of the protective packaging. "Selina?" he mimicked her tone.

"Turns out I need a bit more help. From you."

"How's that?"

"My friend has an important gathering coming up. Important to her, anyway. I could use a date with a handsome cowboy. How about you?"

He pretended to read the installation manual. "Cowgirls are more my type," he replied.

With an amused giggle, she came around to help with the clingy packaging on the wine cooler. "What about *this* cowgirl? I need a date hot enough to make Regina Graves weep with envy."

He didn't think a woman who could threaten a baby could cry real tears. "That's quite a compliment," he said. "Who is Regina Graves?"

"Just another second wife, though she's still married to her musty old wallet," Selina said.

"You mean old man?"

"Semantics. I mean she's still earning her keep. It's a lot of work making a man believe you're in love with him. She's stuck and I'm free to date without any worries."

Jarvis barely kept his opinion locked down. "As long as your date makes her jealous."

"Especially on this occasion. Come on, Jarvis. You're a *man*." She licked her lips. "You don't need to understand the female mind in this instance. This can't be the first time someone asked you out because of that jawline or those shoulders. Not to mention…" Her gaze ventured south. She didn't need to finish the sentence.

"You don't think your friend is happy in the marriage?"

"How would I know? I don't even care." But the expression on her face said she knew all too well that love and devotion weren't Regina's motives for staying married. "What is wrong with you today? Have you met someone?"

"No," he replied. "I'm as free to date as you are."

"Then stop being a prude about this and say yes." Selina hopped up on the counter and crossed her slender legs at the knee. "Norton Graves has money growing out of his hairy ears and Regina loves to flaunt it. She's throwing a party next week and I could use a date. A *really hot* date. Say yes and I'll owe you."

Jarvis eyed her. It felt like a trap. The last time he'd seen Norton Graves, speaking at a luncheon before he'd left his career for ranching, the man's ears had been perfectly normal. Maybe Selina was right and guys didn't notice those details.

"Oh, don't get too excited there, cowboy. This is a one-night-only deal. I don't do relationships."

Jarvis did a mental eye roll to avoid getting lambasted. Again. He didn't want to go anywhere with Selina if he could prevent it. A night with her pawing at him and selling an attraction he didn't feel wasn't his idea of a good time. "I'll have to check my calendar," he said.

"Your calendar." Selina cackled. "Jarvis, you sound like a real Colton."

Thankfully, he wasn't in a position where she could see his face. He *was* a real Colton, even if Payne had refused to acknowledge the truth. In that moment, he decided he'd kick Selina out of her precious house if it did turn out Triple R belonged to him and his siblings.

He managed to make the connections without cussing her out or wrenching his arm out of the socket. Kneeling, he scooted the wine cooler back inch by inch into the space. Sitting back on his heels, he eyed the appliance and started to adjust it to level.

"Say something," Selina demanded. "Seriously, Jarvis. Don't be coy. You're the hottest thing out here. Help me out."

Thing. He took his time rooting around in his toolbox for the small level. He didn't do relationships, either, but he hoped like hell he'd never treated a woman with as much disregard as Selina did him. "Not sure I can swing it," he said. "I have a lot on my plate out here and a date goes over and above my usual tasks."

"This would be vaguely personal," she said. "You forget how much I know about this place. Asher gives you plenty of time off. I need to show up with the hottest man in town. Only the *best* eye candy is worth rubbing in Regina's face," Selina confessed.

"Sounds like some friend," he muttered. He set the level in place and then purposely missed the mark just to keep her talking.

"She's not all bad, but she is in a class by herself. Think about what you'll gain, rubbing elbows with wealthy businessmen who could help you get your career back on track."

"My career is on the perfect track," he said.

She swore. "What will it take to convince you to help me out?"

"When is it?" He made incremental adjustments until the wine cooler was perfectly level. Selina didn't tolerate anything less than perfection.

She gave him the date and time. "I'd need you to pick me up. And it'll be dressy."

"I'll check my calendar," he repeated.

She hopped down from the counter, arms crossed under her breasts. "While you're checking the calendar, I'll be checking with other available men."

He smiled, stretching his arms wide, giving her a good view and oozing the charm she expected from him. "You won't." Dropping his arms back to his sides, he pulled out his phone and checked the ranch schedule. "I'd hate for you to show up to such an important event with the second-best eye candy."

"Can you even do evening attire?" she demanded. "I can pop for a suit if you need it."

He rubbed his hand on his shirt, pulling the fabric tight. Predictably, her eyes glazed and her lips parted. He politely ignored her practiced response. "I know how to clean up when necessary."

She leaned back, her assessing gaze drifting across his body once more. "I bet you do. Put me out of my misery, cowboy. Just say yes."

He scanned the calendar and confirmed he was not on duty that evening. It would've been nice to discuss this with Mia before giving in to Selina's demand. Canceling on Selina would create more problems and make her a bigger nightmare than ever. Technically, he didn't owe Mia anything, and maybe a little up-close recon of Regina would help Mia decide what to do next.

"Invitations like this one aren't easy to get," she pushed. Her hands on her hips now, she stared him down.

"You're making it sound better and better," he drawled. "Irresistible, really. You need a date, you've got one." He ticked off the pertinent points on his fingers. "I'll dress appropriately. I will pick you up. I will converse appropriately. I will *not* expect any relationship nonsense."

"Mmm-hmm." She tapped a fingertip to her lips. "Do you have a gray suit?"

"Charcoal," he replied, more amused than offended at this point.

"Good, good." she purred. "I can work with charcoal. Do you have a decent car?"

"Just my truck."

"You'll drive my sports car," she declared.

"That will be an experience," he admitted.

"But you can't put the top down on the way to the party."

"Scout's honor," he agreed with a wink.

"And you won't drink." Her blue gaze turned hard and serious. "I want to enjoy myself."

"All right." Maybe if she got tipsy he could squeeze her for more details about the ranch history or whatever she might be using against Payne and his children.

He packed up his toolbox and then wedged the old wine cooler into the new cooler's box to protect the glass front. "I'll just pull my truck around to get all this out of here."

She caught his elbow. "In a minute. At the party, if anyone asks, you are totally into me."

"Of course I am, sweetheart."

She tilted her head, a sneaky smile on her face. "You've done this before."

"Feigned avid interest in a pointless conversation? Yes. Yes, I have."

She smacked him lightly on the shoulder, then bit her lip. He guessed she thought the rehearsed expression was sexy and appealing. Maybe it was for other men. For him, Selina was too obvious for her own good. "Stop."

"You first," he said. "There's a lot of ranch to cover and I should get out there. Unless you have more rules and requirements? Have a little faith. Everyone there will see that you have me wrapped around your little finger."

"Do I?"

"Selina." He picked up his toolbox and treated her to one of those long, obnoxious looks. "We both know you'd toss me out the minute you believed that." She was pretty and she'd kept herself in shape, she just didn't spark his interest beyond a basic appreciation for the packaging. He winked at her. "Until next week."

"Fine." She sniffed. "How long until the new cooler is ready to go?"

"Give it two more hours," he suggested.

He walked away from her lovely, entertaining space, taking the long way rather than cutting through her house to get to his truck. He supposed his truck out front served as solid groundwork for their "date" next week. Anyone in or around the main house would notice his personal truck and wonder who'd stopped by. She would definitely make up a detailed story that painted her in the best possible light. He didn't care. Let her say whatever made her happy. A happy Selina posed fewer problems for Asher and the rest of the crew.

Grimacing at the hours he'd spent with Selina, he sent a text update to Asher and then went out to see how he could best help the crew make the most of the day. Assuming they didn't run into any trouble, he might get some time for his search after all.

Chapter 4

Mia wasn't the least bit ashamed about the waves of gratitude that had been flowing through her all day. At this point, those buoyant feelings were probably the only thing keeping her upright. Silas had been fussy all day, despite the vast improvement in both weather and their accommodations.

The bunkhouse must have been remodeled and updated sometime in the past few years. The building was an excellent use of a simple rectangular layout, with four bunk beds at one end, a bathroom and kitchenette on the other end, and a square oak table in between. Big windows let in plenty of light and she even had a decent internet connection. Jarvis had been right on point about how much easier life was with running water and power. For Mia, this modest building might as well have been the luxurious sprawling country house she was supposed to be selling for her father.

Her shower earlier had cleared her mind and given her a wonderful boost, but she needed sleep. So far, Silas had only slept if she rocked him, despite being up all night long. Whenever she tried to put him down so she could nap, too, he wailed. And the wailing meant more worries, since her son's cries had exposed her original hiding place. Although Jarvis hadn't been joking about the remote location. Surrounded by acres of fallow fields and a clear view to the horizon, there was no chance of anyone surprising her out here.

Though the parenting books and classes had assured her this would happen, she fretted over every detail, worried he was running a fever or coping with colic. His temperature was normal and his food was staying down. His tummy felt normal rather than distended. She stripped him to his diaper and confirmed his clothing wasn't the problem. She changed her hold as she rocked him and tried the pacifier. Nothing helped.

Since she had electricity and her phone was charged up, she reached out to her pediatrician via online chat. The professionals concluded that her baby was perfectly healthy, just in a foul mood.

Well, that made two of them.

During the discussion, she was encouraged to let Silas cry a bit. In Mia's mind, two months seemed far too young to expect a baby to self-soothe, but she supposed the suggestion was more about giving her some space and a measure of peace than for her son.

Choosing to believe Jarvis's claim that they wouldn't be found, Mia buckled Silas into his car seat and stepped outside. She set her cell phone timer for ten minutes and focused on the stunning mountains in the distance while her son's miserable cries nearly broke her heart.

It was the worst ten minutes of her life. She rushed back to him and cuddled him close, murmuring nonsensical apologies. Neither she nor her son were any happier for the experiment, but no one could accuse her of not complying with professional guidance.

Swaying side to side with Silas in the crook of her arm, she picked up her phone to call Tamara. *No, no, no.* That call would leave Tamara in the awkward position of lying if Regina asked about Mia and Silas. Babies and mothers had been surviving moments like this since the beginning of time. It wasn't pretty or fun, but they would get through.

She paced outside, wishing for a cool breeze, but nature didn't cooperate, just gave her more of the still afternoon heat. If they'd been home, in her suite at her father's house, she would've had Silas's swing or bath seat. She would've had the option to relax outside in the glider swing under the shade tree, where she'd grown up chatting with her mother about anything and everything.

Everything but the emptiness that death would leave. She hadn't known to ask about that. After moving back in, that glider was where she'd first talked to Silas about the grandmother he would never know. That special place had been where she dreamed about a yard of her own with a swing set, sandbox and a baby pool for her son.

Her father had mentioned creating a space for his grandson with all of those things in his yard, whether or not she stayed. He'd wanted to have everything that would keep Silas happy when they visited. Thanks to

Regina, that grand plan was wrecked. Mia had been shoved out of her father's life until she found a viable solution. Regina would never accept Mia's promise to keep quiet about what she'd seen, which meant Silas would never be safe at their home. Gone was her hope for family dinners and frequent visits with Grandpa, reminiscing over the past and imagining the future. It hurt her heart to think Silas would grow up without his grandpa and they'd never enjoy those strong family connections.

Rehashing all those unpleasant and bleak thoughts wouldn't do her any good. While Silas fussed, sweat dampening his downy-soft baby curls, she sang to him, praying that something would break this wretched cycle they seemed to be mired in.

"You're so tired, baby," she said, tears of exhaustion welling up in her eyes. "It's okay to sleep. We're safe." Was she convincing him or herself? It didn't make much difference. If he relaxed, she could do the same.

Growing desperate, she carried him inside and straight to the bathroom. Removing his onesie and her T-shirt and shorts, Mia turned on the shower. Picking up her son, she stepped under the spray, keeping the water lukewarm. The water put a halt to their combined tears as the fine spray hit her skin and misted around his tiny form. The sudden quiet was such a relief, even if he wasn't asleep.

The blissful reprieve lasted while she toweled them both off. Wrapped in a towel, she curled up on the bunk and fed him until he dozed off. Confident he was sleeping, she gently laid him down on a folded blanket on the floor and inched away, holding her breath.

His limbs twitched and he sighed, but he didn't cry.

She counted it a victory when she was able to get her clothing on without interruption.

Though her eyelids were heavy and her energy gone, she resisted the urge to stretch out and sleep. She opened her laptop and used her mobile hot spot to connect to the internet, looking for any signs that her father might have reached out in concern, or that Regina had been slinging mud against her.

It didn't take long to find her stepmother's comments on Mia's most recent social media posts. There was the inquiry about getting back to work with a link to an article on working-mom solutions, as well as a gushing comment about seeing the "sweet grandbaby" soon. Though the wording was correct and polite, Mia read the underlying sneer behind them.

She noticed a picture of centerpieces on Regina's time line, along with a comment about an upcoming gathering to honor her "amazing husband" in which she expressed high hopes that the whole family would be there.

Mia choked on the water she was sipping, smothering the sounds so she wouldn't wake Silas. As if she'd bring her baby to an event hosted by that crocodile. Yes, she wanted desperately to see her father, to speak with him privately, but not with the threats against Silas ringing in her ears.

But then another dreadful thought crossed her mind. What if Regina meant to hurt Norton at the party? It would give her the perfect alibi: a hundred or so close friends milling about, all of them witnesses to the tragically premature death of her beloved, wealthy, investment-banker husband.

Mia rubbed her gritty eyes. She should go to the

party, if only to protect her father. It wasn't exactly party-crashing after Regina's public comments on social media. If she didn't attend, she'd be setting herself up for criticism from everyone else in town, but if she did go, who would protect Silas?

There was the small problem that she didn't have anything to wear. The dress she'd been wearing the day she'd caught Regina cheating wasn't dressy enough for the evening. She hadn't been thinking about formal wear when she'd packed in a rush to get her son to safety. Mia pushed to her feet and started to pace. Worrying about a dress wasn't the priority.

She'd never regretted moving back into the suite at her father's house more than she did right this minute. Going back meant leaving herself and her son vulnerable to attack. She couldn't watch Silas and Regina every single minute, not without help, anyway.

Her relationship with Regina had been fraught from their first introduction, but she'd never expected it to devolve into murderous threats. Mia had been a teenager and not the least bit interested in a replacement mother. Good thing, too. Regina hadn't been interested in anything resembling maternal affection. That rough start had grown over with thorny vines and choked with spiky weeds.

Their mutual dislike had escalated into cutting sarcasm through the years as Regina successfully pushed Mia out of the nest. Her concerns had been interpreted—thanks to Regina whispering in Norton's ear—as the antics of a spoiled girl who didn't want to share her daddy.

Looking back, Mia could see where she'd gone wrong with her constant griping about the unfairness of life in general and her stepmother in particular. By the time she'd learned to keep her thoughts to herself, Regina had complete control of Norton's affection and opinions. When Mia had discovered her college fund was empty and confronted her father and stepmother, it shouldn't have been a shock that her father believed his wife's lies over his daughter's truth.

Another battle lost to her father's blind love for the viper he'd married. She'd vowed that would be the last battle, choosing to make her own way, using what she knew and the natural abilities and strengths at her disposal.

Modeling had covered tuition and expenses. She'd built up her professional network and cultivated friendships outside of her father's sphere of influence and therefore out of Regina's grasping reach.

And now she was locked in another battle. Alone. Her father would never believe his wife had threatened his grandson. He'd been slowly convinced Mia was a perpetual problem, always in need of help, especially after the pregnancy ended her marriage. She never should've accepted his offer to move back in. Her father meant well and she'd been feeling vulnerable enough to go for it. Shame on her for believing things might be different now that she and Regina were adults. The house was big enough that they could have easily avoided each other.

Mia had been willing to let the past lie, but obviously Regina had felt threatened. In hindsight, Mia suspected that Regina had always worried about Mia catching her sleeping around.

Well, she'd done that.

Her mind spinning, Mia tried to push that disgusting picture out of her head. Knowing Regina's tendency to take what she wanted, whenever she wanted, Mia didn't believe that had been the first time. She doubted her stepmother had bothered to hide her affairs at the country house before Mia had moved back in. Not that it mattered.

She sat down again and closed the laptop, dropping her head to her folded arms on the table. Her thoughts were sluggish and she couldn't pin down the perfect way to tell on Regina without causing anyone else harm.

If she didn't tell…if she did…if she didn't…

The only thing that interrupted the futile cycle was Silas crying again.

Mia didn't bother checking the time. She simply gathered up her baby and moved through the motions of care, praying he'd eventually sleep off whatever was upsetting his system. As she tucked Silas into the sling that kept him close to her body, he subsided into general fussiness, which felt like a vast improvement over the constant crying. Her stomach growled and she was rooting through the grocery bag for a snack when she heard an engine rumbling closer.

Her immediate tension caused Silas to give a start, but he didn't wail. Maybe his throat was as tired as her ears. With one hand on the stick Jarvis had brought along from the warming hut, she peeked through the window and was immediately rewarded with a view of Jarvis swinging out of his truck. The man had an excellent, fantasy-inducing body. If she ever got to sleep again, she was sure her dreams would be memorable. Tantalizing. She soaked up the way he moved, his long stride and the easy smile on his face as he approached.

She opened the door for him, enjoying the sparkle

of amusement in his deep brown eyes as he stopped at the threshold.

"Hey," he said.

"Hi." She'd never been shy a day in her life, yet Jarvis managed to scatter her thoughts with a smile and she wasn't sure sleep would fix it. Something about him just slid right past the defenses she'd built up against charming men. "Come on in."

He dipped his chin toward the baby squirming in the sling. "Did I catch you at a bad time? Is he hungry again?"

"I wish it was that simple." She suddenly felt disheveled and frumpy despite the shower and better conditions. He'd left her in a fully equipped cabin and she was more of a mess than she'd been this morning. "Our long night turned into a longer day." She swept her bangs to the side. "We're fine, really. It's just that nothing is making him happy," she said.

"He's not sick, is he?" Jarvis set a bag on the table, his amusement gone and the sparkle in his eyes replaced with concern. "Do you need a doctor? You should've called me."

"No, no. We're fine," she repeated. "But thank you." She went to rub the crick in her neck and discovered the clip holding her hair up had drooped to the side. No wonder he'd been amused when he walked up. She must look a mess. "I did an online chat with his pediatrician."

Silas stretched his limbs, one tiny foot kicking her diaphragm. The sling was great, until it felt like pregnancy again. She shifted him for her comfort and he started to cry again. She swore under her breath, immediately feeling guilty. She couldn't make that a habit or his first words would be embarrassing and completely inappropriate.

"Pardon me. As I said, we've just had one of those days."

"On top of a rough night," he observed.

"Parenting." She shrugged, bouncing gently in an effort to soothe her son. "It happens."

"Guess so." His mouth curved into a smile. "This gives me a new perspective. I suddenly have way more respect for how my parents handled this in triplicate."

She couldn't have heard him right. "Triplicate?"

"Yup. They wound up with two boys and a girl all at once without even trying."

"You're kidding. Wow." She patted Silas's back. She really couldn't imagine dealing with three of him. "I hope you tell your mom and dad they're incredible every time you see them."

"I wish I could. They were awesome." His gaze was on Silas and his voice went soft. "They died when we were ten."

"Jarvis, I'm so sorry. Losing my mother was devastating." To lose both parents at once was inconceivable.

"It was a long time ago," he muttered. "We got through."

She knew getting through wasn't always enough. Restless, Silas pushed against her again, bringing her full attention back to the present. "I really thought the separation thing would be a few years coming."

She unwound the sling and realized he needed a clean diaper. Taking care of that calmed him for a few minutes, but he resisted when she tried to hold him again so she laid him down on the blanket on the floor so he could stretch and kick and fuss to his heart's content.

"I brought you a hot sandwich and a salad," Jarvis said. "Have you eaten?"

She opened her mouth and snapped it closed again, uncertain. "I must have," she said. "I was about to have a snack when you pulled up."

"Have a meal instead." He placed a bottle of water next to the to-go containers.

Her backside had barely met the chair when Silas erupted again. She stood, but Jarvis waved her back into the chair. "I wanted to talk about something, but it can wait. You look like you could use a relief pitcher. Eat."

She wasn't sure she could manage a coherent conversation right now. As he approached Silas, she started to ask how much experience he had with babies and stopped herself. He was only helping out while she was right here in the room, not applying for a position as a nanny. He certainly couldn't do any worse than she'd done today.

Mia popped the lid off the salad container, watching as Jarvis crouched on one knee by her son, his strong, tanned hand looking enormous as he let Silas kick at his palm.

"Don't you like cabins, little man?" he asked. "Is it too quiet out here for you?"

Silas's fussing eased and his big eyes followed the sound of Jarvis's voice.

"I didn't think about that." Mia felt dumbstruck. Of course Silas was more accustomed to background noise in and around her father's house. Out here on the ranch, things were so still. "I've tried talking and—" she gave in to a yawn "—and singing. It just hasn't been enough."

She wasn't enough. The thought steamrolled right over her and tears threatened to ruin the wonderful food

Jarvis had brought. She stabbed her fork into the salad, refusing to give in to the nonsensical emotions. She'd feel better after some sleep. Assuming Silas would eventually allow that.

"Would you mind if I held him?" Jarvis asked. "I could take him for a walk and you could take a nap."

"Oh." It was a generous offer and yet she hesitated. She was supposed to be doing this parenting thing on her own. Every time he was nice to her, she was filled with a weird, indescribable blend of feeling grateful and inept. "That isn't necessary."

He was already picking up the sling. "I think it is." His brow furrowed as he studied how it should work and where it would adjust to his frame rather than hers.

"Here," she began, reaching across the table for the fabric. "But you shouldn't feel like you have to do anything more. You've done so much for us already."

"You're supposed to be eating," he scolded with an easy grin on his face. "I can do this. With an online assist."

She watched him as he scowled into his phone and smothered a laugh when she heard a tutorial video start to play. She'd had to watch that video herself a few times.

Not Jarvis. He got it in one. He had the sling on and the baby snuggled close, a pacifier in hand. "We'll take a walk," he announced. "You eat up and then take a nap."

He was doing what? "You're too hot." She felt the heat of embarrassment climbing from her neck into her face, searing her cheeks. "I mean, the weather. It's too hot. Outside. You don't have to do this," she repeated.

Jarvis's gentle, knowing smile brought her rambling to a stop. "We won't go far."

"He might get hungry."

"Then you'll be right here. Take a nap, Mia."

"Do you know about—"

"Mia. Whatever I don't know, I'll look up." He raised his phone. "We'll manage. I promise."

Silas didn't fight Jarvis the way he'd shoved and kicked her. His eyes were wide as he quietly stared up at the cowboy, his mouth working on the pacifier. Oh, she would not be jealous that her son preferred a stranger over her on his worst day. She had to respect Silas's taste in strangers. Like her son, she felt better when she stared at Jarvis, too.

"It's weird," she admitted. "Taking a nap while you're out with him. I mean, I trust you."

"Mmm-hmm."

"But what if—"

"Try. Just try to sleep." He walked over to her, looking for all the world like he did this kind of thing all the time.

Maybe he did. She didn't know him. "Do you have kids?" she asked, horrified that she might be keeping him from his family.

"No. Quit stalling and finish eating so you can sleep." He patted Silas. "Tell your momma goodbye. We have man things to discuss."

She leaned in close to kiss her son's downy head and was met with the heady combination of Jarvis's warm and masculine scent mingling with the sweetness of her baby. That was dangerous territory. Edging away before she jumped him, she hoped her burst of hormones and attraction weren't too obvious. "Have a good time," she said.

"We will." Tipping his tan cowboy hat and giving her a sexy wink, Jarvis walked out. With her baby.

Instinctively, she jerked forward to follow. Scolding herself, she took another bite of salad and tried to appreciate the flavors. Jarvis had proven himself trustworthy time and again. If he'd shared her location, she would've heard about it by now. He wasn't running off with her child, her heart. He seemed genuinely respectful of her desire for secrecy. Another yawn seized her and she knew she'd be a fool to waste this opportunity. She needed rest more than food. After stowing the take-out containers in the small refrigerator, she flopped down on the bunk and pulled the edge of the sleeping bag over her legs.

Jarvis walked well away from the bunkhouse before he started talking to the baby. He didn't want Mia to have any reason to follow them or worry that he was in over his head. He was, but he would figure it out. Kids were *not* his thing and he'd never taken much interest, knowing they wouldn't be part of his future. He'd always resisted the burdens that came with choices like commitment and family. His siblings had recently opened themselves to that kind of thing, but Jarvis planned to keep holding out. Why give fate a chance to steal one more person he loved the way his parents and grandfather had been snatched away? It would be hard enough to cope when his siblings inevitably died.

Every family needed a fun-loving uncle. Maybe if they'd had one, they wouldn't have been saddled with a kid-hating aunt. *Families* sounded stable and reliable, and he sincerely hoped that for his siblings, that would be how it turned out. Most of the time, family sucked. Being right here on this ranch was all the reminder he needed. Generations ago, two Coltons had screwed each other over, and Payne's side of the family prospered while Jarvis's had floundered.

He looked down at the baby and knew that if his brother or sister needed him to step up as a guardian, he would do it. And he'd do it with far more affection and attention than they'd received from Aunt Amelia. By all accounts, she'd been a pleasant, approachable woman until losing her husband. "That's my role," he said to the baby. "Fun uncle. I'm good with it. No sense doing something that would make me that kind of sad and bitter.

"You've been running your momma ragged, little man," he said to the infant. The dark circles under her eyes had been more pronounced than this morning and he was worried about her.

Tiny fingers curled into the fabric of his T-shirt and the baby's head rested heavy against his chest. He'd been as surprised as Mia by Silas's reaction to his voice. "Kids won't be in my future," he said. "Frankly, your efforts this past twenty-four hours aren't changing my mind."

Feeling rude, even though he knew the baby would never remember this conversation, he backtracked a bit. "Not that you aren't adorable in your way. Loud and opinionated can be good traits. Like, if you grow into a coach," he mused. "Or a stockbroker. Definitely need to be loud and decisive for that job."

The baby shifted and sighed, and Jarvis looked down

to see he was fast asleep. His lashes were dark crescents on his chubby cheeks. "Way to go, little man."

Maybe if Mia and Silas both got some good rest at the same time, it would serve as a healthy reset. He wasn't sure how long Mia needed to stay, but he was determined she'd have the time and safe space that she needed.

He should tell Asher about Mia before the foreman found out about her presence and revealed it by accident. Jarvis was happy to cover her expenses if she did actually need money for a hotel or a rental car. She'd claimed money wasn't an issue, but she'd also implied her stepmom could track her down by following her credit card purchases. He was better off finding a solution for Mia off the ranch. There just wasn't a good way to inform Asher without breaking Mia's trust. The reverse was just as true. Asher wouldn't see this solely as an exercise in hospitality or charity. The man was compassionate, sure, but this was crossing a line.

Then again, maybe it wasn't Asher's decision, assuming Jarvis found Isaiah's mystery box soon and the contents of the box were accurate and useful. He hadn't spent a minute on his search today, despite having plenty of daylight after the work was done. He'd wanted to get out here to see Mia, and not with Selina's perfume clinging to his hair and clothing. So he'd squandered the daylight with a hot shower and some research into the Graves family before picking up food for Mia's dinner.

"Your grandpa Norton is a pretty big deal," he said to the sleeping baby. "Your momma, too. Your dad is smart as hell, but way too glossy. Just my opinion." The pictures online of Mia with her husband at various events were almost blindingly beautiful. Tech mogul

Roderick Hodges could've made a career modeling, as well. "Good genes, though," Jarvis admitted. "And he's wildly successful. Still, if your mom left him, you can be sure it was for the best." He wondered what it would take for Mia to tell him that story.

He'd skimmed through several early articles on Norton Graves. He'd read archived reports on the man's financial strategies, his interviews and theories on investing and even a graduation speech or two. Jarvis had found pictures of Norton with Dalinda, his first wife, who was from Jamaica. The biography claimed the two had fallen in love at first sight during a professional conference. Mia had inherited her mother's almond eyes, flawless skin, sumptuous curves and brilliant smile.

"A shame you won't know Mia's mom. As grandmas go, she probably would've been amazing."

From all accounts, they'd been a normal family until her death. There wasn't much in the way of personal news on Norton and Mia until she'd started modeling. Norton had done an excellent job protecting his daughter's privacy. Then as her career blossomed and her smile became known worldwide, reporters covering her industry and her father's looked for any crossover they could find. The media seemed to believe Norton had pulled strings to get her into the right agencies and on the right assignments, but no one found any evidence.

"I don't think so. Your momma's tough and determined enough to get what she wants when she wants it. Except maybe sleep," he said, patting the baby's back.

Silas snored lightly and Jarvis smiled at the sweet sound. It was more than a little disconcerting how right it felt to be walking over a field with a baby strapped to his chest.

"Right or wrong, this is a short-term gig," he said aloud. Reminding himself or informing the baby? "Families can be good when they work. For as long as they work." And when something broke down, families were an unending source of disappointment and pain. "The trouble with families is that people are involved." Regina was a prime example. "I hope for you and your mom it works, little man."

However Mia decided to proceed, Jarvis thought Regina should do hard time just for threatening harm to this innocent little boy. It infuriated him that the woman thought it was reasonable to put Mia and Silas in jeopardy for getting caught in her own mistakes. It was easy, out here with the sun sinking low on the horizon, to understand why Mia had chosen to hide rather than confront her stepmother head-on or give in to the woman's demands.

Pausing to soak up the stunning sunset in front of him, Jarvis swayed side to side, lost in his thoughts as the evening breeze stirred the gray-green grasses. He understood Mia's panicked reaction better with every encounter. His own bone-deep need to protect the baby and the mother were impossible to ignore. He could only imagine how much more intensely Mia felt about protecting her son.

When Jarvis and his siblings had been orphaned, they'd relied on each other to muddle through the grief and loss. Their parents hadn't had much in the way of money or assets, and the family court had dumped the three of them on the closest relative's doorstep.

Aunt Amelia wasn't cut out for mothering. Any maternal instinct was noticeably absent in the way she treated them like short adults. "We were left to handle ourselves," he said to Silas. "She was a wasp, impatient and sharp. Man, I couldn't wait to get out of school and out of that house."

And then she'd died. Suddenly. Proving that people were fragile and relationships were fleeting. They'd been twenty-one and it shouldn't have mattered overmuch to any of them. But Bella had cried and cried at the news. Spencer had been shell-shocked. Jarvis had dealt with the funeral arrangements, alternating between numb detachment and blazing fury over being abandoned again.

No more family for those "poor Colton triplets," as they'd been known in school and around the neighborhood. Oh, sure they'd had their grandpa, but Isaiah wasn't what anyone could call stable, dealing with alcoholism and early-onset dementia. Jarvis had cleaned out Amelia's house. He'd sold the place and split the money among the three of them.

He'd gone through the expected motions of life, finishing college, finding a great job and throwing himself into it. Dates, girlfriends, poker nights with friends and holidays with his siblings. All of it had been just a little out of sync until he'd come to the Triple R.

This felt right, with or without Isaiah's stories and the potential fortune at stake. He could breathe out here, heal. He could push himself when necessary and relax when it wasn't. Early on, all of those right feelings had made him mad, too. Resentful that Payne Colton's greed and pride had kept the triplets away from this amazing place.

Even with Mia's son in his arms, this twilight sky, the panoramic fields and the deep blue shadows of the mountains felt right.

The baby shifted but didn't wake. Jarvis stroked the vulnerable spine. He had the sickening feeling that Mia's will stated Silas should be raised by Norton if anything happened to her. Who else would it be since she was an only child? If the worst happened, would Regina step into the motherhood role or simply dispose of the inconvenient infant? A chill raised the hair on the back of his neck as he turned toward the bunkhouse.

"It's your momma's business, but I hope she's smarter than that." The woman needed a partner to help her with days like this one. Not him, obviously. His heart was too hard to take this on full time. He was done taking chances on people and leaving himself open to the inevitable pain. But capable as she was, motherhood was tough and Mia needed someone she could trust standing with *her*.

The idea of another man walking with Silas and partnering Mia put a bitter taste in Jarvis's mouth. Dumb but true. "A nanny," he said. "She needs a reliable, kind nanny."

He reached the bunkhouse as the sky deepened and the first evening star twinkled overhead. He paused, singing "Twinkle, Twinkle Little Star" to the baby even though Silas was sound asleep.

The light over the kitchenette was on and Jarvis was pleased to find Mia in her sleeping bag. She was curled on her side, one hand tucked under her chin, her breathing deep and even.

He debated unwinding the sling and decided not to mess up the one thing that was working. Since coming to the ranch, he'd pulled his share of all-nighters. Most of those had occurred during calving season, but there had been other reasons, as well.

He eased himself down into one of the chairs at the table and propped his legs on a second chair. Pulling out his phone, he opened the app he used to track his search for the Triple R ownership evidence Isaiah claimed was buried out here. He studied the landmarks he had pinned on his custom map, comparing those points to the log of coordinates where he'd searched already. It would be smart to get back and finish that attempt near the warming hut. First thing tomorrow, before he got busy with the normal ranch schedule, he promised himself.

The baby scooched around inside the sling and Jarvis held his breath. When the little guy sighed, working that pacifier, he relaxed again. If he could keep the kid asleep all night, it would be ideal for Mia.

He stared at the dark curls covering Silas's head. How old were babies when they started sleeping through the night? Asher didn't complain of short nights or interrupted sleep these days, so his girls must sleep all night most of the time.

He searched the topic on his phone and found answers with a wide enough age range to be annoying rather than helpful. As a milestone, sleeping all night seemed to involve some mysterious baby X factor that was unique to each individual child. How did parents manage this stuff?

He went back to looking up Regina Graves. Most of the news he found related directly to her marriage to Norton. Doing the math and skimming the old publicity photos, he figured Mia must have been a teenager when her father remarried. Though she smiled in her father's wedding photos, her eyes were flat and a little sad.

That led him to the pictures online of Mia's modeling career and eventual wedding. On that happy day, she wore ivory lace that flattered her skin, her eyes sparkled and her smile was the brightest he'd ever seen as she linked hands with her groom, Roderick. Jarvis studied the man again. Her ex was well over six feet tall and powerfully built. For a man known to push the envelope with computers and tech, his thick blond hair, blue eyes and chiseled features were Hollywood worthy.

Jarvis studied the baby resting contentedly in the sling. Silas didn't resemble his father at all, only Mia. Maybe Jarvis was biased, but he hoped it stayed that way. For everyone involved.

The baby snuffled, hiking up his hips and rubbing his face on Jarvis's chest. The pacifier came loose and Jarvis started singing, his voice low and gentle as he nudged the pacifier back in place.

It worked for a few minutes, then he squirmed again. Jarvis stood up and carefully unwrapped the sling, still singing. Every minute he could give Mia had to help her. Nestled in the crook of his arm, Silas went back to sleep. Jarvis kept singing and swaying.

Mia came awake to the mellow sound of a baritone voice singing softly. It was "Home on the Range," she realized as the melody registered in her sleepy mind. Feeling refreshed, she let herself be lulled by Jarvis's efforts to keep her son quiet.

It was the sweetest sound and she didn't want to move and spoil the moment. From under her lashes, she watched him sway gently, silhouetted by the pale light over the sink. She'd never seen a more devoted picture of fatherhood, unless she thought of her own father. She tried to imagine Roderick tending to his son this way and the pieces wouldn't fit.

There was a picture similar to this one in her baby album. Her mom had caught her dad in the act of singing her to sleep one night. Dalinda had been adamant about creating and keeping memories. After her death, Mia was doubly grateful for her commitment. The album of her first year was in her father's study at home and she'd planned to share it with Silas one day, to use it as a model for his baby book. Would she ever see that precious scrapbook again?

Right now she used an online journal to keep up with Silas's baby milestones. The program allowed her to share the online pages with friends and relatives and she could order prints of the pages. But her recent days had been so bad that she hadn't wanted to revisit them—until this moment, as she watched Jarvis with her son.

Stretching slowly so the mattress wouldn't squeak in the frame, she eased up to a sitting position. Jarvis didn't stop singing until he reached the end of his verse. When he finally looked up, the intensity of his gaze stole her breath.

Her body heated in an instant and hormones she barely recognized sat up and begged. For Jarvis. A taste, a kiss, a touch. Any tangible connection he'd allow, she'd gladly accept. What would those hardworking hands feel like on her skin? Her fingertips positively itched to feel the rasp of the whiskers on his square jaw.

She tried to smile, focusing on other reactions and signals. She needed the bathroom and based on the fullness in her breasts, her son would soon need to nurse. Much safer to address those needs instead of this sudden longing for a man who was simply kind enough to help a stranger.

She hurried to the bathroom and took care of herself,

splashing water on her face to cool down her heated cheeks. Silas was fussing again when she emerged, but it wasn't anything like it had been.

Or maybe it was just as bad, but sleep had blunted the sharp edge.

Jarvis was on the floor again, changing her son's diaper, a more bizarre sight than watching him sing a lullaby. He glanced at her and a grin spread over his handsome features. "Feeling better?"

"Much. Thanks to you." She picked up Silas and started to nurse while Jarvis disposed of the diaper and washed his hands.

It should feel awkward, but didn't. She blamed the illusion of normalcy on the late hour. Since giving birth, she'd discovered that two in the morning gave her a false sense of being separate and distant from real-world constraints. She could think and say things in this hour that no one else would ever hear. It was liberating. Especially after nearly six solid hours of uninterrupted sleep.

"How did you get him to sleep for so long?"

Jarvis shrugged. "Ask him. I didn't do much at all."

"You sang to him."

He tapped his phone. "Just applying advice I found online. Every cowboy knows that song."

She shook her head at his deflection. "*Thank you*, Jarvis. You have no idea how much I needed the break." She brushed fingertips over her son's head. "We both needed this. You're a natural."

"That's, *um*... No. I don't think that fits."

Maybe this rare hour was only soothing and restorative for her. "Easy, cowboy. It's a compliment, not a commitment."

He sat down across from her, his lips tilted sheepishly as he kept his gaze averted. "Noted. Do you want me to stay?"

Yes. "Since you're the hero of the hour, you can do as you please," she said. "Just be warned, he might not go another six hours."

He scrubbed at his face. "I'll stay. If I go back now, it's likely to raise more questions than if I'm out all night," he explained.

She'd visited the Triple R several times for various events and never once given a thought to where or how the crew lived. "You live on the ranch?"

He nodded, a challenge glinting in his gaze. "Is that a problem?"

"Are you kidding?" Even if it was, why did her opinion matter? "I just never thought about that aspect of the operation at a ranch this size."

"No one does. Not even me. Living here isn't required, but I like it. Plus, it's convenient."

"I bet." She paused to burp Silas. "Thanks again. I feel like a new woman."

"Happy to help." His gaze warmed and his smile sent tingles all through her system.

Shocked by her raw responses, she averted her gaze. "How can I repay you? There has to be something I can do."

"Do you rope cattle or ride fences?" he joked.

"I can *walk* fences," she volunteered quickly. "I do have a wealth of skills beyond mothering." That might be overstating it, but she was a quick learner and she enjoyed learning new things.

"If only we needed a swimsuit model."

She rolled her eyes. "You looked me up."

"Didn't have to," he said. "We studied your career in my business classes."

"You what? That's…" She shook her head. "No. No way. How old are you?"

"Relax." He chuckled. "I'm thirty-one. It was right after your first swimsuit-edition cover. We were studying how you'd branded yourself."

"It wasn't easy." She looked at Silas. "Dad wasn't amused by my decision. Furious is more accurate. He didn't want me 'flaunting myself,' as he put it, but I needed the money to get through school."

"Your dad didn't help with your education?"

"It would be more accurate to say that my stepmother helped herself to my college fund. She had a better story than the truth when I discovered the problem."

"Your dad believed Regina?"

"Yes." Jarvis's dumbfounded expression was such a comfort. For him to side with her without needing any proof was a balm to her battered heart. Silas, his tummy full, was starting to doze off again. That was miraculous. She wanted to gush and thank Jarvis all over again, but she thought that might embarrass him, so she kept the words inside. "They say love is blind. In Dad's case, they're right."

She missed the rocking chair from the nursery, but she managed to mimic the gentle motion. It soothed her as much as her son as her mind drifted back to those grim days. "I can't say there's a single day that I ever liked my stepmom." She could talk about it now without too much animosity or grief. "From the start, she struck me as fake."

"Spoiler alert, it seems like you were right."

"Well, she's been good to my dad and I can't deny that he's happier. He was crushed when Mom died."

"If Regina's been good to your dad, why do you think she'd follow through on the threat to hurt him?"

Mia snorted softly. "The woman is after his money. Any thoughtful gesture or kind effort she's made has carried her closer to gaining control of his fortune and more influence in his professional circles."

"But she was never in banking. Not like your dad."

Mia glanced up from her son's sweet face to catch the furrowed brow on Jarvis's face. "Someone's been doing his homework."

"Protecting the ranch, remember?"

She started to laugh, caught herself before she woke the baby. When she had Silas wrapped snug and settled into his car seat, she rocked it a bit with her toe. "You've been researching all of us."

"Only to a point."

She didn't know why it was funny. It should be offensive or off-putting at least. Instead, she wanted to give him a high five. Or a hug. A kiss. Please, yes, a kiss. Her gaze dropped to his lips and she pressed her own together—hard—to stop her runaway thoughts about how he would taste and feel.

"Regina is ruthless. Manipulative. She says one thing and does another all the time."

"With your college fund."

She nodded. "And her marriage vows. I'm not sure she expected to deal with Dad for decades. As far as I know, she only has control of her accounts, not his. And I'm pretty sure she hasn't convinced him to cut me out of the will, though she is his primary beneficiary. After this incident, though, if she can keep me away and spin it right, there's no reason to keep him around."

"Mia."

The tenderness in his voice nearly broke her. Serious talks in the wee hours were perilous. Worse were the questions she burned to ask *him* about his past, his choices, and if he might be willing to have an affair with her. Nothing permanent. No obligations.

"I really should get some sleep before he wakes up again," she said.

"Yeah. I'll be out of here by sunrise." He waited for her to crawl into the bunk, with Silas in his seat tucked between her and the wall. Then he turned out the light and stretched out on the bunk opposite hers.

For the longest time, she listened to his breath, imagining how it would be to have all that strength wrapped around her. Sleeping alone had been the biggest adjustment when she'd left Roderick. It had been such a strange sensation not having his solid body to curl into, to reach for in the night.

Thank goodness the bunks were narrow or she might have embarrassed herself by asking Jarvis to spoon her. Her imagination took over and she shifted restlessly, willing herself to sleep.

"Mia?"

"Mmm?" It was nice to know he wasn't asleep, either. Could it be because he wanted her, too?

"Why did you marry Roderick?"

Her sex-fantasy bubble burst. "Love." That had only been part of the equation. "Love and money," she admitted. She rolled over to face him, her back pressed close to the hard side of the car seat. "I'm not ashamed of that."

"I wouldn't say you should be."

"We had an understanding about life and goals. He was a good match for me in several areas—we were both ambitious. And he was hot," she joked.

"Obviously." Jarvis chuckled softly. "You were a stunning couple."

She groaned. "I hate the internet." She didn't, really. It was one more tool she'd used to her advantage even after her prime modeling years. "I mean, thanks."

His bunk creaked as he shook with smothered laughter. "You should sleep," he whispered when he caught his breath.

"Same goes, my friend," she replied. "Thank you for everything today," she said quietly. "If we're not up when you leave, have a good day tomorrow."

"You, too. Remember to call me if there's trouble."

"There won't be," she said. She was too cozy, too safe here in this moment for any trouble to touch her.

"I'll bring out a truck and some dinner tomorrow night."

"Mmm. Sounds good."

She shouldn't let him keep helping her, but she enjoyed his company. He gave her something wonderful to anticipate, a happy thought that shot like a sunbeam through the clouds of uncertainty and fear in her mind.

Chapter 5

When his phone beeped with the morning alarm, Jarvis rolled out of the bunk, more rested than he expected after the short night. As quietly and quickly as possible, he made use of the tidy bathroom and dressed again in the same clothes from yesterday.

The baby and Mia slept through it all. Her dark hair spilled across the pillow and one hand was tucked next to her son's knee while he slept in the car seat. He hoped they had a much better day today.

It was all he could do not to kiss her goodbye before leaving the bunkhouse in search of strong coffee. If she needed to stay on, needed more time to make a plan, it would be smart to keep an overnight bag here. Not that he was so eager to move in, but so it was less obvious he was spending nights away from the ranch.

Early sunlight washed over the paddocks near the

main stable and filled him up with positive energy. Maybe that energized feeling was more about Mia than the clear day, but either way, he'd take it. Gladly. He picked up his task list for the day, more than a little relieved there weren't any work orders at Selina's place.

He needed to find a way to talk to Mia about the party. Selina had texted him a couple of pictures late last night in various dresses. He wasn't sure what he was supposed to do with the information and he responded as vaguely as possible. Whatever she wore, he'd be in his best suit. Coordinating colors seemed more suited to a high school prom than an adult occasion, but maybe her social set put more stock into that kind of thing.

He'd worked through the various chores inside the barn and moved on to cleaning and repairing cattle trailers when Asher found him. Even with his hat shading his face, Jarvis could see the Triple R foreman was in a somber mood.

"Walk with me?" Asher asked.

He could've made it an order, but he hadn't. Curious, Jarvis turned off the hose he'd been using and fell into step beside him. "What's up?"

Asher paused, watching a few horses in the close paddock, then moved out farther still. Whatever he had to say, he clearly didn't want to be overheard. A slippery coil of dread settled at the base of Jarvis's gut.

"Word is you haven't been in your room the past couple of nights."

Jarvis didn't try to deny it. "That's true." He rubbed a smear of dirt from his hands before looking Asher in the eyes. "When you hired me, you didn't say anything about bed checks."

Asher swore. "That's not what this is."

Jarvis waited.

Leaning his forearms on the top rail of the fence, Asher hooked one booted foot on the lower rail. "You can have a place in town, you know that. But if you're planning to walk off the job, tell me straight up."

Jarvis relaxed. "I don't have any plans to leave," Jarvis said. "I like it out here." He couldn't leave until he found Isaiah's evidence. If that find went his way, he was definitely staying. Forever.

"Then where have you been?"

"Why does it matter? If there's a problem, say so. Do I need an alibi or an attorney?"

Asher winced. "Depends on where you've been."

He knew Asher wasn't kidding. "I've got nothing to hide." Nothing but a frightened woman and baby who were in serious danger if Regina found them. "What's your real question?"

"Are you sleeping with Selina?"

"No." Jarvis wouldn't have been more shocked if his boss had thrown a sucker punch. Still, Asher looked downright sick to his stomach. Pretty much how Jarvis felt when Selina flirted too hard. He shook his head, trying to clear the random images. "No," he said again. "I only go over there when you tell me I have to."

"The rumor mill is that you're taking her to some fancy party next week."

"Well, yeah." Jarvis searched for the right explanation. "I was going to run it by you." He could hardly tell his boss he was going so he could do some recon for Mia and possibly warn Norton about Regina. "She took a call from a friend yesterday and then pretty much harangued me into being her date. I can't say I'm looking forward to it."

"Then why did you agree?"

That was an easier question than where he'd spent his last two nights. "Hell, I don't know." That was complete honesty. "Mainly, I agreed to shut her up. You know how she is. I'm not going along so I can schmooze around for a new job, though she did toss that out as a carrot. She doesn't believe I prefer the ranch over an office."

Asher nodded as if that made total sense to him. "Do you prefer the ranch? I'm worried you're bored."

"Not a bit," Jarvis said. "This is the best work I've had, barring the days when Selina snaps her fingers."

"So you're not into her?"

Jarvis just stared down that question.

"Good." Asher rubbed his forehead. "All right." He took a deep breath, his gaze on the horses ambling across the paddock. "Now I need to ask a favor."

Again, Jarvis waited. It was a tactic he'd learned in the business world, but even among less-than-chatty cowboys, silence often proved the most effective way to get information.

"When you're out with her," Asher began, "would you please keep an eye on her? I've seen her at parties and she likes to indulge. The more expensive the champagne or the more open the bar, the happier she is."

"Regardless of whether or not I like her, it's not my nature to ditch a date when she's drunk."

"I'm asking more than that, man." He tipped back his hat. "I need you to stick close. Let her flirt and let her ramble. She doesn't censor herself when she's drinking. If she gets to talking, if you can keep her talking, I want to know if she says anything about shooting Payne."

Jarvis whistled. "You think *she's* the shooter?" This just got more and more interesting.

"Doubtful. No one knows who shot my dad. Yet. We will find out, one way or another." He glared out across the landscape. "I'm not sure she's capable of pulling the trigger, but she might hire it done. I can't see how taking him out helps her, but then again, I'm not a criminal."

Jarvis reeled. As far as he'd heard, there were still no leads about the attack on Payne Colton. He figured there were plenty of suspects. The man had money and land, but he hadn't won any popularity contests in the area.

"The woman got a house and a seat on the Colton Oil board," Asher said, his voice a low growl. "Whether or not she's the shooter, she must have been blackmailing him. That's the only way to explain how he caved to her demands when they divorced. Maybe he threatened to stop cooperating."

Jarvis didn't know Payne the way Asher did, hadn't seen the fallout of what sounded like a rocky marriage on the best of days. "I'll stay alert."

"Thanks. Just stick close. Pay attention to who she talks to and listen for anything helpful. Maybe she'll get tipsy and start bragging."

He thought he and his siblings had been treated poorly by Payne, but the longer he worked here with his cousin the less he envied the way Payne's children had been raised and all the advantages they'd enjoyed. Those benefits clearly had come at a price.

"Can't be easy to be Payne's son," Jarvis said.

"Can't say it is. I know my dad's a jerk, but whatever his opinion, you're a cousin to me. I'm asking as family, to protect family."

How strange to hear those words from one of the Colton Oil Coltons. Jarvis had groomed himself to dislike them nearly all of his life, considering them the snooty side of the family tree, too aloof to bother with him. But as his own family died out, snipping his roots out from under him, a small, childlike piece of his heart had longed for a connection.

Ridiculous. That piece of him needed to sit down and shut up. The last thing any piece of him needed was another emotional beatdown. He could help Asher, but he had his own reasons for wanting Selina to open up. To that end, he'd make sure she had a drink in her hand all night long.

"I'm a good listener," he said. "Per her orders, I'm driving, so I have even more reason to stay sober. You'll get a full report."

"Great." Asher relaxed, removing his hat and combing a hand through his hair. "I appreciate it more than I can say."

"Best save that appreciation until I actually have something." The men started back toward the barns. "Would you have asked me for this if I'd said I was involved with her?"

Asher laughed and clapped him on the shoulder. "Not a chance," he admitted. A grin creased his face. "If I thought you were seriously into her I would've fired you."

Jarvis believed him. "I would've deserved it," he said. Asher had made it clear from the start he expected loyalty to run alongside hard work.

A strange morning, complicated by a lack of sleep, but he got through the rest of his assignments with willpower and focus.

Once he was done, everything extra came down on him like a ton of bricks. He'd needed to speak with Mia about the Graves party and he'd been half tempted to give her his real reasons. Now he had the extra excuse of helping Asher. If he was lucky, she would immediately trust him not to reveal her hiding place.

Before he headed out to continue his search for Isaiah's mystery box, Jarvis took some time and chatted with a few of the other hands. He'd thought he'd made some friends, but it seemed he'd held back just enough to be considered gossip fodder. Maybe if he cultivated those relationships, the rumors about him and Selina would slow down.

When he finally got back to the location near the warming hut, his focus was divided between his search and Mia's continued safety. It troubled him that she'd had to rely on an online chat instead of taking her baby to the doctor. Yesterday hadn't been anything serious, but it wasn't fair to make her wait for him if a real problem did crop up.

He needed to figure out a way to get Mia a vehicle, something she could use if there was an emergency. Moving her car to the bunkhouse was one option, but doing that meant Regina might spot her easily if the woman visited the Triple R or if Mia had to drive into town.

He could probably give her access to a ranch truck, but most of those were equipped with a GPS tracker. He didn't want anyone revealing her hiding place because they were confused about a vehicle left sitting at a remote bunkhouse near currently unused grazing fields.

For the first time, Jarvis regretted the immense size of Rattlesnake Ridge Ranch. It wasn't as simple as driving a truck out to her and hiking back.

Not in the afternoon heat, anyway. He supposed he could handle the vehicle swap at night. If he picked her up at the bunkhouse and she rode to the ranch with him, she could drive a ranch truck back to her hiding place.

That still didn't leave him with an explanation for Asher about the location of that truck. He let transportation issues simmer in the back of his mind, returning to the place he'd been digging when he'd first heard Silas's cries.

He grimaced at the hole he'd left behind. After his previous attempts to find the evidence supposedly buried on this ranch, he'd carefully covered his trail. Here, in a hurry to find the crying baby, he'd made a glaring error. Anyone who happened upon this would wonder who was digging and why. Those were questions he wasn't ready to answer.

As with all of his previous sites, this one, too, was a big fat no-go. When he'd finished filling in this hole, he leaned on his shovel and stared out across the grazing land. "Maybe Granddad's brain was playing tricks on him. Could be he was making stuff up or getting old stories confused. Everyone else thinks so." It felt a whole lot better when he had these one-sided conversations with his horse. Thankfully, no one was out here to witness his lack of common sense as he addressed his truck.

He tossed the shovel into the bed and settled behind the wheel. Turning on the engine, he cranked the air-conditioning as cold as it would go. Making the note on his search app, he put the truck in gear and headed back toward his assigned room.

He showered off the workday, put on clean jeans and a better shirt and opted for tennis shoes rather than boots tonight. He packed up a few things, just in case he didn't make it back, and then went to join the majority of the crew for supper. With rumors flying, it was better if he met those head-on rather than let them fester. Personal lives were always juicy gossip in a small town and this wasn't the first time Jarvis had been a prime target. Just the first time here at the Triple R.

Over the meal, he fielded questions about what Selina had needed and what she'd been saying about him. Amid the heartfelt thanks tossed at him from the men who appreciated him "taking care of her," he realized he'd given her carte blanche to say anything about their status as a couple. She sure was taking him up on that, based on the nonsense flying around about their intense affair and his "new" prospects in Mustang Valley. The woman was a mess in Jarvis's mind, but he couldn't call her a liar without losing a valuable opportunity to help Asher and Mia.

As soon as he was able, he extricated himself from the conversation and an invitation to go out for a beer. He wanted to get some hot food out to Mia as soon as possible. He didn't think she'd heard his promise to bring a meal back tonight and the shock on her face when he pulled up to the bunkhouse confirmed it.

"I wasn't expecting you back tonight." She'd brought a chair outside and was sitting with Silas resting on her thighs. She wore shorts and a loose top with a scoop neck. Her feet were bare.

She had pretty feet, which had to be the first time he'd ever had *that* thought. Her toenails were polished with a soft pink color that emphasized the warm color in her darker skin. He ached all over, wanting to kiss her, to have that privilege.

"I picked up a burger for you. Cheese, bacon, pickles and mayo. You can dress it your way."

The wariness fell from her gaze, replaced by anticipation. "Please don't tell me you learned that online."

"No. I figured you needed something fresh and hearty, so I took a chance." He reached into the truck for the drink carrier. "And something sweet sounded good, too."

"Burgers and milkshakes?"

He nodded. "Your choice of chocolate or strawberry. Unless you're allergic or something."

"No allergies. Oh, I could kiss you." She waved him closer. "One perk of pregnancy was not obsessing over every calorie."

He traded the burger bag for the baby, pleased beyond reason when the little guy gazed up at him with wide, dark eyes. "I take it today was a better day?"

"Absolutely a perfect day." She unwrapped a straw and stuck it into the top of the chocolate shake. "Thanks to you." She repeated the process with the strawberry shake, handing it to him.

Jarvis shifted the baby easily and took a long pull of the cold, creamy treat. "You want me to take another walk?"

"Stay." She smiled up at him and something went loose and gooey in his chest. "I could use some adult time and age-appropriate conversation."

He could think of a thousand inappropriate ways to be an adult with Mia. But he did need to speak with her about Selina, the party and her plans... She moaned as she bit into the burger and his thoughts simply vaporized.

"Jarvis." She licked a smudge of mayo from her thumb. "I don't know how you knew, but this was exactly the right thing."

"Glad to help." He cleared his throat, swaying a bit with Silas. "I said I'd bring you some transportation, too. Y'know, in case you or the baby have some trouble and I can't be here quickly."

Her gaze scanned the area, tracking back toward the warming hut. "There isn't really a good place to hide my car."

"I had the same thought. I was thinking I'd leave you my truck and keys."

"What? No. That's silly. I can't take your truck."

He leaned against one of the support posts for the roof that covered the narrow porch. "I don't like the idea of you being stranded out here. It doesn't have to be an argument," he added when her gaze narrowed.

She took another bite of the burger and closed her eyes while she chewed. Swallowed. She swiped a bit of sauce from her lip with her tongue and he nearly lost track of the entire reason he was out here.

"I want you to be safe. And to have options," he said, his voice rough. "The ranch trucks have GPS and some-one might wonder why a truck is out here by itself."

"GPS?"

"It's a big ranch."

"True." She grinned. "Lucky for me."

"In my truck, you can get away if you need to, go to town or whatever."

Her dark eyebrows drew together. "Town feels like a risk no matter what vehicle I'm driving, but you can't baby me forever."

A voice in his head wanted to promise her that very thing.

What a bizarre idea, that Jarvis Colton would baby Mia Graves. Except he wanted to bring her surprise milkshakes and help with *her* baby, and otherwise spoil her the way she deserved. They could share meals and laughter and talk each other to sleep at night. He'd be honored to shelter her from a wicked stepmother and help her restore her relationship with her dad.

All of that was way outside the realm of reality— *his* reality. He was a single ranch hand, and he liked it that way.

"It's better to have the option," he pressed. Giving her the option to leave was the strongest argument he had. He couldn't guarantee he'd be close if something did happen to her or the baby.

"I'd rather come up with a true exit strategy."

No. Thankfully, he kept the reaction locked down. He was just getting to know her. To like her. He wasn't ready for her to make an exit. Where was all this ridiculous need coming from? It felt bigger than infatuation, but this was hardly the time or place to start dating. Besides, the sooner she was out of here, the sooner he could get back to his search. Turned out a working ranch didn't leave quite enough time for two secret side projects, and he wouldn't abandon his grandfather's last dream.

"About that," he said when she finished eating. The baby was dozing in his arms, looking like an angel. "Something came up and maybe I can help you brainstorm a way out of your predicament." *Predicament* made her situation sound almost palatable.

She froze, staring up at him. "What came up?"

"Your stepmother is hosting a party and I've been invited. Aggressively invited." He'd thought this would be fine, that he could explain without hurting her, but the crushed look on her face stopped him short.

Her gaze darted all around, as if expecting her stepmom to jump out and attack her son. She crossed the porch and plucked Silas right out of his arms, holding the baby close to her heart.

"Regina invited you to a party?" Her lips parted and then closed into a flat line. "You said you didn't know her."

"I don't." His arms empty, he didn't know what to do with his hands. He shoved them into his pockets. "She didn't invite me, Selina did. Aggressively, like I said. When she gets her teeth into an idea, it's hard to distract her. You told me those two run in the same circles. Selina got a call from Regina. About the party."

Mia's dark eyes narrowed, making him feel smaller than a bug under a microscope. "Go on."

"Part of the gig at the Triple R is jumping whenever Selina snaps her fingers. Drives Asher nuts," he added. "The rest of the guys, too. She's a huge flirt and sometimes gets a little too familiar."

"What?"

"Doesn't matter. My point is Asher sent me to her place to install new fixtures in her outdoor kitchen."

"Why does she even live on the Triple R?"

"The views and proximity to the Colton Oil offices," Jarvis replied. "That's what she tells us, anyway."

"The views." Her tone was snarly and her gaze raked over him rather than the nearby mountains. "She has no right to touch you or anyone without permission."

She studied her son as if imagining him subjected to Selina's unwelcome advances. It was a strange glimpse into that theory that mothers always saw their children as babies. Not that he had any experience of an adult relationship with a mother figure, having lost his own mom, Christy Colton, when he was still a baby-faced kid.

"She got off the phone with Regina and came at me, pretty much demanding I take her to the party."

"Why you?"

He didn't blame her for being suspicious. "She wants eye candy—her words—to flaunt in Regina's face. For friends, they seem to be ultracompetitive in a nasty way."

"They are." Mia rolled her eyes. "That actually makes sense."

"I only said yes to get close to your dad. I could warn him, or try to catch Regina making a threat." And if he was super lucky, Selina would spill more details about the generations of history of the landownership or how he might get his hands on the original deeds from the late 1800s.

"You can't confront her," Mia protested. "You're just as likely to put yourself and us in danger if you do that."

Was she kidding? "Didn't you hear me? I can get a message to your dad. She'd never know. Someone has to stand up for you. You're out here alone and scared and—"

"I'm *not* helpless," she snapped, cutting him off. "I'll leave the ranch tomorrow morning. Tonight, if you drive me back to my car."

He groaned and pushed a hand through his hair. At least the stick was out of her reach while she was looking so murderous. "I don't want to drive you away, I want to *help*." Hadn't that been obvious from the start?

"Confronting Regina is the opposite of helpful," she said, keeping her voice low for the baby's sake. "I did my own due diligence on you today, Jarvis Colton."

"What are you talking about?" He crossed his arms over his chest.

"I assumed with a name like Colton you might have a share in the ranch. Especially from the way you talk about it."

His blood turned cold. "That matters to you?" Of course it did.

She came from money and surely expected the people around her to be in the same league. By all reports, she'd earned a fortune herself during her modeling years. Just last night, she'd openly confessed that she'd appreciated her ex-husband's financial success, which had added to her net worth by marriage. Naturally, a man like him, a typical working cowboy with a middle-class bank balance, wasn't good enough.

"I couldn't figure out why I've never heard of you or seen you with your cousins," she said, dodging his question.

Their blood relation was not even close enough for the triplets to be called distant cousins, according to Payne.

"Why would you have heard of me?" Her stratospheric social circle wasn't even within sight of his. He resented the old hurt and sense of inadequacy that came bubbling to the surface. He'd really thought he was past this.

"Mustang Valley is a relatively small town." She peered at him through her lashes. "It's not like being a Smith with an address in Los Angeles or New York City."

"I'll have to take your word." He wasn't well traveled; aside from a wild weekend in Cabo San Lucas, he hadn't been anywhere more exotic than Las Vegas.

"We're only a couple of years apart."

"Make your point, Mia." He couldn't take much

more. Wanting a woman who was making it crystal clear she'd never have lowered herself to speak with him under normal circumstances. He'd been infatuated, instantly attracted and she'd merely been in need. He was dangerously close to beating himself with that stick she kept by the door. He'd liked the woman he'd met in the warming hut, but maybe that just wasn't the real Mia Graves.

She settled back on the chair, the baby resting on her shoulder. "Why did you change careers so drastically?"

"It was time for a change." He forced the words through clenched teeth and gracelessly changed the subject. "Once it's dark, I'll hike back to your car and use that for as long as you choose to stay here."

"Why, Jarvis?"

"Because you need transportation," he said, purposely misunderstanding her question. He didn't owe her his life story or detailed explanations. Maybe once people saw him in Mia's car, Regina would be pushed to do something to incriminate herself.

Mia glared at him. He didn't think she realized how sexy that expression was. She definitely didn't know how it heated his blood. "You'll have the truck whether you like it or not," he added. "It's the smart move."

She patted the baby's back gently while she sipped at her milkshake. "What about Selina? You can't take her to a party at my father's house in my car."

"She told me I'm driving her car."

"Told you…" Mia cocked her head, then burst into merry laughter. The baby flailed his hands happily in response. They were the cutest pair. And cute had never been one of his goals or interests.

"I won't go if it bothers you," he said. Irritated as he

was, he wouldn't like himself if he purposely did something to upset her.

"I'd think it would bother you to be objectified and used," she said.

"Says the supermodel."

"*Former* less-than-super model," she corrected him. "Who knows what she's talking about."

"I don't care what Selina or Regina or anyone else thinks of me. If I go, I'll be *in* the house. I can talk to your stepmom, search for something useful, warn your dad. Whatever you need."

"And if Regina catches you, you're in danger."

"I'm not as fragile as I look," he joked. Humor was his safe zone during sticky conversations. Better to joke than let out any ugly or real feelings. "Take your time and think about it. I can cancel."

"Not if you want any peace," Mia pointed out.

"Let me worry about it." He picked up his milkshake and turned to watch the horizon. "I can handle Selina better than most."

"I bet you can," Mia quipped. "She'd probably enjoy it if you handled her." In Selina's shoes, Mia would delight in being handled by Jarvis. Good grief, she had to get a handle on these wayward thoughts and hormones. She hadn't felt this kind of wild, uncontrollable attraction in…ever.

He shot her another annoyed glance, as if he had hard things to say and he didn't think she could bear to hear them. She'd offended him somehow. Unable to pinpoint her error, she didn't know exactly how to smooth it over. She really should let him be the one to worry about that shark in designer clothing. There were more important people for her to worry about. She finished off her milkshake and tried to find a lighter topic of conversation while Silas dozed in her lap.

The weather was trite and she didn't know enough about cattle to carry that subject. "You should go to the party," she said, cycling back to pertinent matters. "I'll think about it and let you know where to look for anything incriminating in the house. Though, if Selina's agenda is to rub you in Regina's face, she likely won't let go of you all night."

"Not fragile." He knocked his fist lightly to his chest and her eyes drank in the motion.

No, the man didn't look the least bit fragile. He was as firm and sturdy as the ground beneath them. Of course, the ground itself had proven vulnerable during the earthquake a few months ago. A philosopher might find some correlation there, that the world and everyone in it was subject to life-altering change at any moment. Completely breakable under the right pressure and circumstance.

She was tired of feeling weak and unsettled. Tired of Regina applying pressure that forced this awkward circumstance. Mia would much rather find a way to explore Jarvis's considerable strength and the tenderness underneath it. Every kindness he showed her, every time he held her son, she felt drawn in, as if he pulled her by an invisible string. Worse, she liked the sensation.

Because it was new, or because it was him? The two were inextricably intertwined. Jarvis was new in her life but what he made her feel was tantalizing, uncharted terrain. She wanted to dig in and find the source of the hot sizzle in her bloodstream when she merely *thought* about him. Her marriage hadn't been passionless, but it hadn't had *this*. Jarvis wasn't out here with her because it made him look better. He wasn't looking for an inside track to her father. He looked at *her*, at her son, with a fresh sincerity she hadn't realized her life had been missing.

"More than searching for dirt on Regina, I'd feel better if you can confirm that my dad's all right."

"Consider it done," he promised. As he moved closer, the last rays of sunlight set the sky on fire behind him. "Do you want me to give him the video?"

She couldn't even imagine how that would be possible. Regina knew how to keep her father isolated, even in a crowded room. Always at his ear, hovering while whispering endearments, hanging on his arm and his every word. "We have time to think about it," she said, avoiding that ugly minefield for tonight.

"You really miss your dad."

How did Jarvis, basically a stranger, see right through her? She smiled down at her baby, too raw to look at the man crouched at her side. "I've missed him for years. Having a child of my own only makes it harder to understand why he chooses her over me every time. It wasn't like this with my mom. They were a team, sure, they were the authority, but I was part of it. Included, even when I didn't get my way. I admit I struggled with the adjustment when he brought Regina home. I was a brat."

"You were a kid," Jarvis soothed.

"A bratty kid," she said, compromising. "Yes, it hurt seeing another woman where my mom used to be. Worse was that he wouldn't talk to me like a miniature adult anymore. I didn't want to break them up. Not really. I was fighting against being cut out." She sniffled, tracing the shape of her son's tiny fist. "And it happened, anyway. Fighting so hard only brought it on faster. This entire situation is just the latest battle in a war for my father's attention and affection."

"Based on what I've heard from you and Selina, Regina is warring with you for Norton's influence and money," Jarvis said. "And she fights dirty."

"You're right," Mia allowed. "Maybe that's why I keep losing ground." She shook her head, embarrassment creeping in. "I didn't mean to dump all of that on you. Sorry. And I thought pregnancy hormones were bad," she joked. "I'm learning motherhood is full of pitfalls." She stroked Silas's perfect ear. "I look at him and can't imagine putting him second to anyone."

"Because you're a good mother," Jarvis said, his tone gentle. He brushed a tear from her cheek.

"My dad was a good father," she countered. His tune had changed when Regina showed up and twisted all of her childish mistakes into character flaws that disappointed him. "He provided and nurtured. He gave me a head for business and urged me to use it."

"You did that."

She sniffled again. "Pardon me." She blinked rapidly, willing this meltdown to stop before she lost all control.

Jarvis walked into the bunkhouse, returning with a packet of tissues from the diaper bag.

"Thanks." She blotted her eyes and runny nose, wishing she could recapture the cool, self-assured inner strength she'd enjoyed before her pregnancy. "I'm not always such a mess."

To her relief, he didn't offer an opinion on that. How could he? They'd known each other for only a few strange days.

"There has to be a way to make Regina pay for this mess she created," he said. "Between the two of us, we'll figure it out."

She believed him and couldn't decide if that belief was rooted more in fantasy or desperation. "Why did you walk away from your career to come work here?"

Jarvis's chest rose and fell on a deep sigh. Sitting down, he leaned back against the pillar and stretched out his long legs, crossing them at the ankles.

It wasn't a particularly sexy pose, but to her he was temptation personified. She could hardly blame Selina for insisting on a date. Mia had found Jarvis's headshot as well as pictures of him in a suit for a community fund-raiser kickoff in town. Selina had chosen superb eye candy for Regina's party.

"Several reasons, starting with a need for change," he was saying. "I was doing well enough, but it was the same old thing day after day. Meetings and conference calls, maintaining an image that didn't feel right."

The words sounded rehearsed and she wasn't buying it. "You could've done anything, but you came to this specific ranch. A Colton ranch," she said, pointedly.

"True. And I leaned on the connection, used my last name to win over Asher. Payne likes to pretend the three of us aren't actually related to him and his kids. His children aren't as bad, though."

"That's silly. You are related." His gaze locked with hers. Oops. She hadn't meant to reveal just how personal her search had become. "Small town," she said as breezily as possible. "Both your family and his have deep roots. Any other conclusion is impractical."

"Well, Payne's an arrogant jerk," Jarvis said.

The cavalier response wasn't as convincing as he

probably intended. This issue of family mattered to him. "Being excluded hurts," she said.

"What hurt more was being dumped with an aunt who didn't want anything to do with us."

"So you came here to get under Payne's skin?"

"In a way." He slid one palm across the other as if testing the calluses. "Not that he's noticed me. I showed up here to prove Payne doesn't know everything about me or my siblings, and discovered that I enjoy the work."

"I get that," she said.

"You do?"

His furrowed brow was as appealing as everything else. "Sure. I went into modeling because I needed a speedy fix for my financial crisis and discovered I enjoyed it. No, no," she said when he opened his mouth. "You won't divert me this time. You might love the work, but there's more to it."

He chuckled and the sound made her want to stretch and purr. Did he know how he affected her? How could he not? She assumed he'd seen his reflection recently. His body was formed by the work he did, rather than hours in a climate-controlled gym with precise exercises and supervision. The resulting differences had never been so clear to her.

And she really had no business comparing Jarvis to her ex-husband.

"Mia?"

She blinked and heat washed over her face, down her throat as she got caught staring at him.

"If you're tired, go in and rest," he suggested.

"I'm fine. Adult conversation, remember? Keep talking. I've been open with you. Give me whatever you're holding back."

He only smiled, the expression slow and indulgent. She pressed her knees together against the quivering response at her core and shifted her attention to the gentle slope of Silas's nose.

"How about a story?" he asked.

"As long as it's real."

"I can only tell you what's real to me," he replied. "My grandpa used to tell us that we should be as wealthy as Payne and his kids. He told me that back in the 1800s, his grandfather's brother, on the Colton Oil side of the family tree, stole the ranch from our side of the family."

"Your grandfather, Isaiah Colton, told you this?"

His casual expression turned razor sharp. "I'm starting to hate the internet too," he groused. "What do you know about it?"

She motioned for him to keep talking. "Tell me more."

He raked a hand through his thick hair. "No one in the family believed Isaiah's tall tales. He talked about gunfights and feuds that started generations ago between Colton brothers. He claimed that trickled down and is the reason Payne pretends we aren't related."

"Why didn't anyone believe him?"

"It was Isaiah. He was half-drunk more often than he was stone-cold sober. I loved those stories of generations long gone. Stories about poker games, cattle rustling and shoot-outs as the area was settled, stolen and settled again. It was a lark, really. But when the dementia set in near the end of his life, he got agitated and vocal about it. And detailed. He talked to me more, insisting that I listen to what he called the facts. Granddad was convinced the Triple R belonged to us and he wanted me to find the proof and take it back."

She was on the edge of her seat, literally, leaning forward to hear more. "Have you verified his story?"

"I've done some research into dementia and confabulation. It's entirely possible he's twisted up old Western movie plots and family rifts."

"But you became a cowboy, anyway."

"I did. With dementia, sometimes the oldest memories are the truest. And his details, Mia—they convinced me to try. That's why I'm here. Near the end of his life, he told me the proof of rightful ownership of the Triple R is buried here on the ranch.

"The legend, according to Isaiah, goes that his granddad, Herman Colton, lost a chunk of prime acreage in a poker game. Herman swore to anyone who would listen that he was cheated in that game. Enough people believed him that his brother, Eugene, agreed to buy back the land for him. Isaiah told me the brothers struck the deal, but then for some reason Eugene refused to sign the acreage over to Herman. He kept it in the family, passing it down the line."

"Kept it and kept adding to it," she said.

"Yes. Isaiah said Herman had a signed letter of the agreement between him and Eugene, proof of the poker game stakes, and even a confession from the man who cheated to win."

"Herman is the one who tossed the land into the pot."

"Haven't you ever done anything impulsive?" he challenged.

"Sure." She'd been having plenty of impulsive thoughts about Jarvis, but she wasn't about to drive her only ally away by jumping him.

"Herman's fault." He thunked his head back against the post. "I don't blame you for thinking it. Growing up,

I heard ghost stories of how Herman cursed our branch of the family tree. It wasn't until he was dying that Isaiah gave me actionable details."

"Such as?"

"He described a metal box with Herman's initials scratched into the top of it. Told me that inside the box, in addition to the proof about who should own the land, there was more family history Payne couldn't ignore. One way or another, Payne would have to acknowledge us. Herman buried that box on the land that he felt was rightfully his and urged his sons to take it back once Eugene was dead."

"Why wait?"

"Granddad said Herman spent years searching for the card cheat, waiting to get a confession out of him. Distracted, he relied on his family to manage the smaller plot of land, while he burned through any ready cash following a gambler around the territories. Eventually, one bad season followed by another forced them to sell out."

"To Eugene's sons?" she asked, certain of the answer.

He nodded. "Got it in one."

"Wow." The story was preposterous and plausible at the same time. In his shoes, she, too, would have been hard-pressed to let it go as an old man's rambling. "Takes courage to follow through the way you have. Does either Asher or Payne know what you're up to?"

"No." His chin came up, as if he dared her to contradict the tale or threaten to blow his cowboy cover. "I'm aware dementia can do strange things to the mind," he admitted softly. "But Isaiah talked about landmarks. So many details…" Jarvis's voice trailed off as his gaze drifted toward the darkening mountain range. "On a spread of this size and searching by myself, I have to be realistic that even if the story is true, I might never find one small box."

A fresh excitement twinkled through her system, like the stars popping into view overhead. She loved learning new things. "That's why you were out there the day you found me," she said.

"You mean, the day you were channeling Babe Ruth?" He grinned. "I was out there riding fence first and searching second. Asher's a good man and a fair boss. If he was a jerk like his dad I might shirk the workload, but I respect him too much."

"So you'll work here until you find Herman's box and can stake your claim?" She looked out over the acreage shrouded in darkness. Landmarks or not, there was too much ground for one man to cover.

"In a perfect world, yes. It would be a blast to march into Payne's office, looking for his wife, Genevieve, and demand a fair current price on the land."

"That's a deal I could broker for you," she teased. "You'd be rich in an instant."

He snorted. "Rich divided three ways, plus your commission." He winked. "At this point it would be just as satisfying to see Spencer and Bella react. They'd be shocked to learn that I bought into this family myth. Truth is, I feel better about the work I do here, rich or not, than I ever did at the office."

"You loved your grandpa," she whispered. "I want Silas to know his grandpa, to make lasting memories. Regina is bent on preventing that." Her dad was all Silas had. Roderick's parents had shown zero interest in being part of their grandson's life. Anger rose up high and fast, unhindered by the choking fear of her stepmother's threats. Something about Jarvis being around gave her hope and courage that she could find a solution Regina wouldn't slither out of.

Silas started squirming and fretting, and she checked his diaper. "It's that time again," she brushed her nose to her son's. "We'll be back."

. But Jarvis followed her, pausing just inside the doorway. She heard him laugh and glanced over to find him eyeing the heavy stick she kept propped by the door.

"Always prepared," he observed.

"Mothers and the Boy Scouts," she said. Once Silas was in a clean diaper, she curled into a corner of the bunk, giving him a chance to nurse while she mulled over Jarvis's story. It made her happy that he'd shared it, that he trusted her not to betray him. It felt good to be on even ground with their shared secrets and concerns. "Have you done any research into the records of sale for this property?"

"I did visit the records office," he replied. "The documents on file match what everyone has accepted as truth. Per those official documents, Payne's side of the Colton family tree bought the land generations back and built a thriving cattle operation."

"Mmm. Okay." Her mind was spinning, happily distracted by his search over her own problems. "You didn't find the box out by the warming hut, so where will you look next? How do you decide where to search?"

"I've been working off the landmarks Isaiah described and I keep track of the locations with a geocaching type of app."

That sounded fascinating. "Do you think I could help?"

"Why would you want to?" he asked.

She shrugged, hoping the nonchalance would hide

her intense curiosity about the quest. More than anything, she wanted to thank him for helping her. Well, that was a lie. She wanted to keep seeing him. "It's better than my current agenda of convincing potential clients to list their property for sale with a shiny new real-estate agent they can't meet in person."

"Yet," he said. "We'll figure out a way around your stepmom. I didn't anticipate any help with the search, but if you feel like it, I'll gladly accept."

"Good." Her spirit soared. "Tell me more about the landmarks."

He pulled out his phone. "I'll just send you everything I have. What's your email?"

She gave him the information. A moment later, her phone chimed with the incoming message. "This will be fun," she said, mostly to the baby. Her phone chimed again and she did a double take, checking the alert on the screen. The first message wasn't from Jarvis at all. In fact, it looked like an email from her ex-husband. "What the hell?"

Jarvis was beside her in an instant. "More trouble?"

"I—I don't know yet," she admitted. She wouldn't deal with anything negative while nursing her son. The first part of protecting Silas was putting his needs first. "It's from my ex. He hasn't contacted me since the divorce was finalized."

"Not even when Silas was born?"

"Of course not," she said.

"But you said he's the father."

"He is." She deliberately kept her tone bright to remind Jarvis this wasn't the time for a stressful conversation.

He held up a hand and backed away. "I get it. All of that can wait."

She shot him a grateful smile. "He'll be out soon. We might even get through a second night in a row."

Jarvis sat down on the bunk across from her, an odd expression on his face. She wasn't sure she wanted to know what was going through his head. He didn't avoid looking at her as she fed her son, but he didn't ogle her or stare in an awkward way.

At last her baby's bottomless pit of a stomach was content and quiet. Once he was tucked into the car seat that currently served double duty as his bed, she picked up her phone and headed to the table. The email from Roderick was as succinct as it was jarring. Her knees went weak and she wobbled into the first available support, which happened to be Jarvis.

His arms came around her and he eased her into a chair at the table. Her fingers trembled as she read through the full message again. "I can't believe this."

Thankfully, Jarvis took the phone and read the message himself. "He's asking for a custody hearing?"

She pressed a hand to her stomach, wishing now she'd skipped the milkshake. "He relinquished his rights before I delivered. The divorce settlement covered everything." She swallowed a panicked sob. This couldn't be happening. "He got everything he wanted. So did I."

"Meaning?"

"Roderick wanted complete and total freedom. Forever. No visitation, no obligation to be a father. He agreed to set up a fund for Silas's college expenses and he had to pay me half of the value for our house. The alimony payments were calculated and once we agreed on a number, he paid me in full so he didn't have to think about me ever again."

Jarvis touched her gently, his hand warm at the nape of her neck, his fingers circling gently over the knotted muscles. "I don't want to be a dad, but I can't imagine walking away from my wife if we got pregnant. I didn't know my parents for long, but I remember how in love they were. Committed to each other and us as a family, through thick and thin."

"My husband was furious when I told him I was pregnant."

Jarvis's hands stilled. "Why would he demand a custody hearing now?"

"Because the universe is laughing at me? Maybe his mom decided she was ready to be a grandmother after all." She curled over, resting her head on her hands on the tabletop. Jarvis just kept kneading her neck. The man was a saint. "Mia Graves, so sure she could be mother of the year all by herself."

Behind her, Jarvis snickered.

"Don't laugh at me. There's a mug and everything."

"Sweetheart, you're the best mom I've seen in ages."

She opened her mouth to argue and a low moan came out instead. Jarvis cleared his throat and she knew she should move out of his reach. But it felt so damned good to be touched this way. He was only being a friend— a caregiver, really, but she wasn't strong enough to resist this.

"Your hands are miraculous." It had been so long since anyone had touched her like a woman; medical professionals didn't count.

"This says you have to appear tomorrow. Your husband has serious clout to get a hearing in family court so fast," he said.

"Ex-husband," she corrected.

"Right." His fingers changed directions, spearing into her hair and massaging her scalp. She could happily melt into a puddle of not caring about anything outside of this bunkhouse.

"This doesn't make any sense," she said. "What could have changed that he wants to exert a paternal claim now?"

"Usually, that kind of pull is reserved for emergencies," he added. "When we were orphaned, it took a week for them to get everyone into the court at the same time."

His voice was as soothing as his hands. Floating somewhere just shy of bliss, she let go, listening and surrendering.

"We stayed with Isaiah that week, but he couldn't run herd on the three of us and he didn't have the money to hire help. The court decided to dump us on our aunt. Amelia complained bitterly from that day forward about the burden of three children she never wanted."

"Have things improved with her since you're all grown up?" Mia asked.

"She died when we were twenty-one."

She sat up now, twisting to catch his hand in hers. "I'm sorry."

He frowned at their joined hands. "Don't be. The four of us did little more than survive those years. My siblings and I were as relieved to cut loose at eighteen as she was to see us go. Why was your ex mad about the pregnancy?"

"He never wanted kids. We agreed not to have children before we married, so he felt betrayed. He reminded me he married a model and expected me to stay in photogenic form."

"So he married you because you were hot, too." Jarvis's eyebrows jumped up and down in a comical innuendo. "Can't fault him for that."

The man could make her laugh, even while her ears burned at the compliment. "And my money," she agreed. Reaching for a bottle of water, she took a long drink. She crossed to the bag of supplies on the counter and pulled out her vitamins. Silas needed her to stay healthy and strong. And calm. "Our marriage wasn't as cold as it sounds. We did care about each other." She paused for another sip of water. "I thought it was love. A good and solid love that would last."

"Until you got pregnant."

"Yes." Her gaze went to Silas. "We were both shocked, but I saw it as a miracle and he saw it as a problem. So we parted ways. If it wasn't amicable, it was civil."

"You miss him."

She sighed in defeat. "Not as much as I should."

"Come sit down." Jarvis pulled out the chair for her again. When she sat, he started massaging her shoulders. "Read the message again."

Her laptop was closer, so she used that instead, regretting the loss when his hands fell away for a moment. He stood behind her, somehow without looming, as she opened the email. "Hang on." She looked closer. "This isn't his primary email address. There's a dot here when it should be all one word."

"Then let's assume that link to the court calendar isn't valid, either."

She used the track pad to hover the cursor over the

link without clicking it. "One way to check." Opening a new tab on her browser, she entered the family court into the search bar. As she compared the links, it was clear someone was trying to fool her.

It was chilling that anyone would attempt this. Not anyone. "Regina," she said with a hiss as a new wave of fury blasted through her system. She pushed back from the table, pacing back and forth across the bunkhouse. "I don't know how she did it, but it has to be her."

"Agreed."

"I would've gone," she said as disappointment in herself chased the temper. "I would've rushed Silas right into her trap."

"What happens to Silas if, um, if something were to happen to you?"

She met his gaze and saw a flash of the wounded little boy he'd once been. "My will stipulates management of his college fund to his legal guardian along with his daily expenses. Naturally, I left him a trust fund, too, that he can access when he's twenty-one."

"Who's the guardian?"

"Melody Williams, my best friend from college. She loves kids and we have similar values and philosophies," she added. "She was my labor coach and she stayed with me at the house for the first couple of weeks. She's done video chats with us since she had to go back home."

Jarvis frowned. "Why hide in the warming hut instead of with her?"

"I couldn't put her in the line of fire too," she countered.

"Fair point." Jarvis held his hands up in surrender. "I'm staying again tonight."

Guilt weighed her down, sapping the benefits of the massage. "You should be in your own bed."

"I'll sleep there all I want later," he said.

"Spoken like a man without kids."

He smiled at her and tugged her up from the chair. "Tomorrow, I'll scoot out of here early and take your car into town. Maybe I'll even drive by the courthouse."

"You shouldn't do that." If Regina did see him, she'd harass him at the very least.

"Of course I should. My brother's a cop and I haven't dropped in on him in a while. Trust me." He wrapped one loose tendril of hair around his fingertip. "Please?"

"One condition," she said. He smiled and she momentarily lost her train of thought. "Let me help you figure out where to search for Herman's box of proof."

She didn't like how he dismissed her suggestion with an eye roll. "You've done more for me in the past few days than anyone has done in years. It'll be fun for me, I promise."

"Fine," he relented. "As long as you're discreet."

She leaned back. "Please. I'm a model. Discretion is my middle name. The things I could tell you about… Well, never mind."

He grinned. "You are a tease."

His playful tone made her want to be. "I've been called worse."

"Tell me a secret. Not about any one model. I mean a trade secret."

"Hmm." She tapped a finger to her lips and her mouth went dry as his gaze locked onto that spot. A delicious heat shimmered through her bloodstream. Would a kiss be such a big mistake? "In the preshoot prep, nearly every model looks like the girl next door. Plain. Mundane."

"Like I'd fall for that one," he said, his lips tilted into a grin. His hands slid to her elbows, holding her in place. "Nothing about you is mundane or plain."

His fingers gripped firmly, drawing them together. Her breasts brushed up against his chest. She wanted to plaster herself to him, to discover exactly how firm those muscles were.

"Please kiss me." The words fell from her lips and she couldn't muster any shame. He was the most genuine person she'd met in ages. Since her father had written her off as too spoiled to try to mend fences.

Jarvis tempted her, roused a desire she hadn't known existed. Oh, she'd wanted her husband, had enjoyed a healthy sex life in those early years. But longing? She wasn't sure she'd ever felt this intense pull. More than a little afraid she'd break down and beg, she felt her heart race as he leaned close.

At last his lips brushed over hers. Featherlight and full of promises, with a hint of challenge. She kissed him back, let herself sink into his scent and taste as her hands molded his shoulders, stroked up the column of his throat. She laced her fingers behind his neck and held on, letting the heat, the sweet, sizzling contact, burn away every unpleasantness.

His hands came around her, gliding up her spine, down to her hips, urging her closer still. The kiss filled her with a lightness, an unrivaled joy. Here in his embrace, she found a piece of herself she hadn't known was missing.

That discovery rocked her emotionally, left her gasping as she pulled back. For a brief eternity they stood there, staring at each other. Her heart pounded so loudly in her ears she couldn't think.

"I, ah, I won't stay," he said into the charged silence.

She wanted to argue, but she was too fizzy from the aftershocks of that kiss. "Probably for the best," she managed.

He stepped back, his fingers still twined with hers. The next step parted them completely. She locked her knees, braced one hand on the chair for balance.

"Text me if you need anything from town."

She nodded. If she tried to talk, she'd beg him to stay, beg him for more than a kiss.

She wasn't sure how long she stood there, lips tingling, body humming, wishing for him to stride back in and overwhelm her again.

That was her first postdivorce kiss. While she was pregnant with Silas, rebound dating hadn't been a priority. Did every woman have that bone-melting reaction? She was probably just dumping every random emotion on Jarvis's broad shoulders.

Those shoulders could take it.

She moved to turn out the lights and crawl into her bed when she saw the glint of keys on the table. He had left her his truck. Which meant he was crossing serious acreage on foot, in the dark. She dashed off a quick text message.

Let me know when you're home safe.

The reply came back within a few seconds.

I'm safe. Go to sleep.

Suspicious, she went to the window. Sure enough, Jarvis was in his truck, the glow from his cell phone highlighting his handsome face.

Relieved that he wasn't crossing the ranch alone in the dark, she went to bed without inviting him back inside. She curled into her sleeping bag, hoping to dream of Jarvis and his talented hands and mouth.

Chapter 6

Jarvis left Mia's hideout in the soft gray before dawn. The landscape blurred as he jogged toward the warming hut where her car was hidden. This might have been the worst idea he'd ever had.

Second worst, if he counted that kiss.

No. No, that was all wrong. That kiss didn't belong in a negative category of any kind. It had been the *best* kiss of his life and though he'd slept lightly, Mia had been the star of his dreams.

Kissing her was better in real life than any fantasy he'd had in college. No matter how he tried to scold himself for crossing that line, he didn't regret it. Her big brown eyes had been glazed over with longing when he walked out, beautiful and tempting. He wasn't sure where he'd found the willpower to sleep outside when he could've slept with her.

The most important factor, far more important than slaking his desire, was that he wanted to help her. And as long as she needed his help, he should probably keep his hands and his lips to himself. Neither of them needed more complications right now.

When he reached the old warming hut, he dug her car out from under the various layers hiding the vehicle, grateful when it started immediately. He was already second-guessing his plan to drive it to town later this morning, but it would definitely get him to work on time.

In his room, he showered and changed and started plowing through the day's task list. As time for the false court appearance neared, Jarvis tracked down Asher and asked for a couple hours off for an errand in town. He also offered to bring anything back for the ranch.

Armed with a short list for a stop at the feedstore, he swapped his dusty T-shirt and boots for a button-down shirt, his good belt and a clean pair of boots. He headed out through the back gate, just to avoid anyone near the main house who might recognize Mia's car.

The ten-mile drive into Mustang Valley was uneventful, not that he'd expected trouble. Regina had no reason to think Mia was on the Triple R. Jarvis parked behind the courthouse with thirty minutes to spare before the fake hearing, so he decided to drop in on his brother at the police station.

Spencer was just walking out and did a double take when he saw Jarvis. "Look who came home from the range." He gave Jarvis a one-armed hug. "Bella and I were about to grab lunch down at Bubba's Diner. She'll be happy to see you."

"I need to take a rain check," Jarvis said. He suddenly didn't know how to explain himself. He'd wanted to ask Spencer for advice, maybe cajole him into hanging around the courthouse for an hour or so. He had no idea what to do if he was right and Regina showed up with the intention of trapping Mia and Silas.

"A rain check?" Spencer froze. "What's going on with you? Did you—" His cell phone rang from his pocket, cutting off the query. "It's the US Marshals office. Let me take this."

Jarvis was grateful for the reprieve. He wasn't in the mood for another lecture on what Spencer and Bella called his delusions of cowboy glory. Without Mia's permission, he couldn't give any details about why he was in town. So he stood there, listening to his brother's end of the call.

"No record at all?" Spencer scowled at the street in general while he listened. "What about the other name, Luella Smith?" A pause. "Yes, I know what witness protection means. And I'm sure you know what interagency cooperation means."

Jarvis tried not to listen too closely while he watched for any sign of Regina.

His brother shook his head, frustration stamped on his face as he ended the call. He shoved his phone into his pocket. "Don't repeat this," he said, donning his sunglasses. "I'm working to verify what I suspect is a bogus line Micheline Anderson fed me."

Jarvis recognized the name. Anderson had founded the Affirmation Alliance Group and transformed a ranch near town into a retreat with a self-help focus. Rumors were swelling that the AAG was actually a cult, bilking members out of their money instead of offering a beneficial service. So far Spencer hadn't found anything definitive, but for Jarvis, his brother's suspicions was more than enough confirmation.

Spencer nodded, his brow puckered over the sunglasses. "She's doing all the right things and the group has been a big help in the community, especially after the earthquake. But I have a bad feeling."

"Then something's wrong," Jarvis said. His brother's instincts were as dependable as Boris, his chocolate Lab K-9 partner. "Did you learn anything helpful?" he asked.

Spencer knew Jarvis would never blab about anything. Though the parts of the conversation he'd overheard raised questions, he wouldn't press. The triplets shared a unique and innate trust. One more reason why he felt awkward keeping Mia's dilemma to himself.

"I hope so," Spencer replied. "Time will tell. Positive thinking is great, but I still can't make the pieces of the AAG fit together into a wholly legitimate business model." He clapped Jarvis on the shoulder. "Come on. Bella will chew me out if I'm late, unless you distract her. Get her talking about wedding stuff."

Jarvis chuckled. "Not this time. I have my own crazy to-do list today."

Spencer eyed him with an expression Jarvis figured he'd learned at the police academy. "Asher sure is leaning on you."

"I'm reliable," Jarvis said with a smile and a wave. He jogged backward a few paces. "Tell Bella I'll call."

He circled around to the side door of the courthouse, wondering what in the hell he'd say if he ran into Regina. Nothing, obviously. Although he could recognize her from local publicity as Norton's wife and the videos Mia had shared, Jarvis was a stranger to her. And what were the odds she was even here? From what Mia had shared, he supposed Regina was bold enough to ambush Mia directly, but he didn't know.

His stomach knotted. In about a week he was going to walk into a party hosted by the very woman he was spying on today. Suddenly, this felt like the dumbest idea in the world. If she noticed him here and then recognized him at her party, it would be a short leap for her to guess Mia was hiding at the Triple R.

His bravado drained away, leaving him with a void that quickly filled with uncertainty. This wasn't some lark. A woman's life was on the line, and the future of her baby, too. But he was here and committed to the effort. He had to follow through.

He took the stairs to the second floor toward the courtroom specified in the email. There was no sign of Mia's ex, or anyone else. The hallways were way too quiet for any court to be in session. The pervasive hush was worse than in a library. He turned a corner, following the only sound—a low, impatient voice. Her body was silhouetted against the light pouring through the window at the other end of the hall, making it impossible to verify that it was Regina.

Sitting on a bench near an open office door, Jarvis pulled out his phone, pretending to text while the woman fumed aloud in hushed tones as she paced the width of the hallway.

"Keep looking," she said. "Yes, I'm sure that's her car. I told you she is *not* up here." She paused, rushed back to the window, her high heels clicking across the marble floor. "What do you mean, it's not there? There's a bracket thing. In the back seat."

She'd snarled those last words and Jarvis knew he was watching and listening to Regina. As they'd thought, this custody hearing was a trap for Mia. He kept his head down, angling his hat to hide his face. Not that Regina would've registered anything outside of her current tantrum.

"She didn't just disappear."

Oh, but she had, he thought once the sound of her heels faded. He walked toward the window where Regina had been and looked down at the parking lot. He couldn't see anyone showing too much interest in Mia's car. But the rear tire was flat on the driver's side. A hot spike of temper slammed through him. Regina was showing every sign of being too desperate. Spencer would call this "escalating."

Pressing the panic button on Mia's key fob, he was quickly rewarded as Regina's glossy updo rushed into view. Following her movements, he identified the person who was most likely helping her by the car while Regina had been on the lookout up here.

Though Jarvis wasn't eager to take another look at the indiscretion Mia had caught on video, he would have to so they could verify if the man down in the parking lot was the same man Regina had been with at the country house. In the meantime, he had to do something about Mia's car. And he needed a lift back to the ranch, by way of the feedstore. Thankfully, he knew exactly where to find his sister and brother.

He hurried down the street to the diner, pleased to find Bella and Spencer still at lunch at a table near the window. He ordered a sandwich to go so he wouldn't delay their meal and then sweet-talked his sister into driving him back out to the Triple R.

"Only if you're buying," Bella said, though she couldn't suppress her smile.

"Deal," Jarvis agreed.

"What happened to your truck?" Spencer asked.

"I was borrowing a friend's car, but it has a flat. The garage is taking care of that and I'll get a ride into town after work to pick it up." He was sure one of his siblings would call him out on the fib, but Spencer was distracted by someone or something outside.

Bella and Jarvis exchanged a look. When Spencer was in cop mode it was hard to break through with normal conversation. While they waited for his sandwich, he dutifully admired her sparkling engagement ring and urged her to fill him in on her fiancé, Holden, and the initial wedding plans.

"It's still weird to think of you getting married." He raised his chin toward Spencer. "Both of you."

Spencer continued to be preoccupied, but Bella wiggled her eyebrows. "Maybe we'll rub off on you."

Jarvis laughed. "Not a chance. Cowboys don't get married, we just ride off into the sunset with the woman of the moment."

Bella elbowed him, hard. "Have you seen Ainsley around the ranch?"

"Not much," he said. "It's a working ranch. I'm not there to plan a family reunion."

Bella slumped in her seat, deflated, and he felt like a jerk. His sister had always longed to be closer to their Colton Oil cousins and had recently bonded with Marlowe over her newborn. Payne's dismissive remarks about their parents and grandparents never seemed to faze her. Probably because she'd been saddled with two ornery brothers and a fractured home life. He could tell her the grass wasn't really greener on the Colton Oil side of the family tree, but why wreck her fantasy of having cousins who'd always cared? "Marlowe, Ainsley and Asher are all right," he said. "They've never treated me like a leech. Maybe you should reach out."

"Are you well?" She pressed the back of her hand to his forehead and he swatted it away. "Sorry," she said, though she clearly wasn't. "You're not sounding like you."

Admittedly, Mia was rubbing off on him more than his siblings. Watching her cope with an unthinkable scenario on her own made him face uncomfortable facts. Bella and Spencer had partners and love now, and assuming all went well, they had someone to lean on in tough times. Despite all they'd been through, it would be natural and right for their spouses to come before him. It didn't mean he wanted a wife and kids, just that he should probably cultivate friendships with people other than his sister and brother. Eventually. Today his plate was full enough.

On a low grumble, Spencer shoved out of the booth. "Excuse me a second."

"And that's lunch," Bella said, shaking her head. "Remember to leave a good tip." She patted Jarvis's cheek and followed Spencer.

Jarvis took care of the bill, tipping well like his sister would do, and then grabbed his take-out bag. Bella had followed Spencer, standing a few paces away while he spoke with Micheline and her assistant, Leigh Dennings. The pair were finishing lunch at an outdoor table at the bistro across the street. Considering the phone call he'd overheard, he assumed spotting the women had diverted Spencer's attention.

"What do we do?" Bella asked under her breath.

"What we do best." He winked at her. "Stick together." He strode right into the conversation, greeting both Micheline and Leigh with his best smile as he propped a hip on the railing that framed the outdoor seating area. His sister followed suit and soon the five of them were conversing.

"Jarvis Colton." Leigh sighed. "I haven't seen you around town lately," she said. A blush flowed over her cheeks at the admission and Jarvis heard his sister snort. Leigh and Bella had competed in the Ms. Mustang Valley pageant recently while Bella was researching a story on pageant culture. Leigh, as the winner, still seemed to shine with the victory.

"I've been busy on the Triple R," he explained. "The cowboy life works better for me."

She fanned herself. "It does work. You look great."

Jarvis inched closer to Bella, using her as a conversational shield. On his other side, Spencer angled himself to block Micheline from the chatter, though Jarvis could still hear them clearly enough.

"I've made some calls, Micheline. You probably won't be surprised that the US Marshals Service doesn't have any record of you or Luella Smith as protected witnesses," Spencer said.

Jarvis struggled not to react to that while he kept up the conversation with Leigh and Bella. During his investigation, Spencer had learned that the person "Micheline Anderson" had only begun to exist at the same time that Luella Smith, the woman who switched her baby for the real Ace Colton, disappeared.

"Well, of course they wouldn't tell you anything," Micheline said after the waitress picked up the bill and her credit card. "That would defeat the purpose. Not that any of it pertains to me, though I appreciate your thorough concern."

Jarvis caught Spencer's scowl and knew Micheline had struck a nerve. He continued to distract Leigh, with Bella's help, even as he listened to his brother. "I'd like it if you would make time to speak with me."

"For private coaching, just call Leigh and set up an appointment," Micheline said, her tone warm and smooth as honey as she handed him a business card. "We'll be happy to help you find your most productive mind-set."

Spencer accepted the card, responding in kind. "A few minutes at the station would put my mind at ease about recent events that intersect with you and the AAG."

"This is bordering on harassment, Sergeant Colton," she added with more bite than barbed wire. She signed the receipt and shoved her copy into her purse. "If you'll excuse us." Micheline stood and urged Leigh to do the same. "We must be going."

"Where to?" Spencer asked.

Leigh hefted a full tote over her shoulder. "Micheline is delivering our popular *Be Your Best Self* seminar to the local chapter of the Arizona Insurance Council," Leigh gushed. "Those events are life and career changing."

Jarvis could only marvel at the pride rolling off the young assistant. Her cow-eyed devotion was a bit unnerving.

"It was a pleasure to see you, Jarvis." Leigh fluttered her fingers and scampered away.

Behind him, he heard Bella snickering. "Stop," he muttered under his breath.

"Hey, Micheline!" Spencer called out. Both women turned. "Is AAG a cult?"

Jarvis whistled softly. His brother was clearly frustrated with Micheline's convenient answers for everything. The investigation must be taking some worrisome turns to push him to such an aggressive tactic.

Leigh gasped and pressed her fingers to her mouth. Micheline smiled, the expression brittle and cold. "Of course not, Sergeant. Good day." She turned on her heel and marched down the block, Leigh trailing after her.

"You okay?" Bella asked.

"I don't know," Spencer said, his gaze still locked on the two women. "I'm missing something."

"You'll figure it out," Jarvis assured him. "You always do."

All day long Mia had ridden the high of that kiss, reliving the feel and taste of Jarvis's mouth. Her dreams had been delightful, if a bit unsatisfying. It was a shock how one intense embrace could give her this renewed sense of self as a woman apart from motherhood.

She'd gone out to offer him breakfast and found the truck empty. But the text message that came through informing her he'd picked up her car reassured her that he hadn't walked all the way back to the ranch.

The second text message he'd sent was no comfort at all.

Custody hearing was a trap. Your car has been towed due to a flat tire. More later.

She'd thanked him by text and spent the next hour stewing over what to do about Regina before taking Silas out for a long walk to clear her head.

As much as she enjoyed the ranch, she couldn't stay

out here indefinitely. She was basically squatting on Colton property—not a great look for an aspiring real-estate agent. More than that, she was already too fond of Jarvis.

Fond. What a flimsy word for all the things he made her feel.

He'd taken care of her without undermining or minimizing her concerns. He'd given her a peaceful sense of safety and security she hadn't experienced in years. She'd always seen herself as the bold one, going out and striving for her goals. She'd never realized how much she enjoyed solitude or how much she missed it after Regina had stormed into her life.

Self-assessment could be a pain.

She rubbed Silas's back as she walked along, her stride parallel with the mountain range in the distance. Emotionally, in her heart, she'd been a mother the moment the pregnancy test showed positive. Roderick had asked her to end the pregnancy. Ending the marriage had been the only solution.

Divorce had meant facing more disappointment in her father's eyes, but once she started to show, his excitement over being a grandfather had eclipsed everything else. Silas's arrival had rebuilt a bridge that Regina had nearly destroyed with her manipulative nature. Mia had never expected to be in this position a second time, isolated from family and a trustworthy support network. Of course, with Regina around, anything was possible.

Once more, Mia debated putting the video out there. Sending it directly to her father would cut him to the core. If he even saw it. Mia had no doubt Regina was screening Norton's email. Through the years, several emails and text messages to her father had gone missing before he'd read them, causing all sorts of communication issues that made Mia look like a problem child.

The family court email only proved Regina must have had skills or expert help to twist Mia's next attempt at making contact into whatever form suited her stepmother. Silas was safe in her arms, but her father was not. Until she was sure her father could be protected, she couldn't expose Regina's infidelity to the world. They were still at an impasse.

Returning to the bunkhouse, Mia tucked her sleeping son into his car seat and then opened her laptop. She started a file, writing down everything she recalled from her conversation with Jarvis, eager to explore how she might help *him*. She found it sweet and a bit curious that he believed so strongly in the validity of his grandfather's stories. If she could help him sort out his search, it would make her feel like the scales were closer to even.

She started with the easy stuff, details he probably already had, locating online birth records for Jarvis and his siblings. From there, she easily traced his family tree to Isaiah. The further back she went, the closer to Isaiah's grandfather, Herman Colton, the murkier the official documentation got. Fortunately, the publications in and around Mustang Valley had been scanned and enhanced online. In those websites, she searched for family notes and random articles about the people of the era. Some mentioned Herman's brother Eugene; others called the two men cousins.

Which was it? Jarvis would need to know. A tighter family relationship might give him a better chance to make a claim to the ranch, no matter what evidence Herman had buried out here. Her real-estate classes covered a bit about inheriting and selling properties, but he would definitely need an attorney if he planned to go up against Payne and his family.

After the next predictable interruption from Silas, she started to backtrack through the land sale records. She worked her way from the most current tax records until she reached older documents that had been scanned into the system. It would be nice to see these in person, but she did her best to decipher the increasingly faded handwriting and drawings of the land parcels involved on each deed.

She came across a registered deed of sale between Herman Colton and a T. Ainsley. Payne's first wife had been Tessa Ainsley. It was entirely possible the Ainsley on the deed was one of *her* ancestors. Wouldn't that be something, for Payne to have married a descendant of the family who'd had ownership of the property generations ago?

The sale covered more than half of Herman's acreage and all of his livestock at the time. Maybe dementia ran in the family and Herman had forgotten or been confused. That didn't explain the poker game or the deal between Herman and Eugene. Maybe Eugene had forged Herman's signature. She pressed her fingers to her temples. Anything was possible while this part of the country was being settled and developed.

Mia took a screenshot to share with Jarvis later and leaned back in her chair. Without knowing which year the poker game occurred, she couldn't be sure if this information validated Isaiah's story or affirmed Payne's ownership of the land. Assuming the registered sale was legitimate, she might have just eliminated any reason for Jarvis to keep looking for confirmation of his grandfather's story. Would he give up?

She didn't think so. His dark eyes had been bright with curiosity and intent as he told her the story. She'd been honored that he shared it with her. Jarvis didn't seem the type to open up with just anyone.

"And who would I tell anyway?" she said to Silas, brushing her nose to his.

She kept digging. Eugene and Herman had started with parcels that had shared a border, each man expanding as successful seasons allowed. It would be interesting if she could track down the livestock records, as well.

With the original property borders in mind, and the information Jarvis had shared, she shifted her focus one more time to try to narrow down his search parameters. Naturally, he'd been working off Isaiah's story, supposedly passed down from Herman himself. She thought that was odd, in and of itself.

By the time Jarvis sent a text that he was on his way over with dinner, she had what she thought were two excellent target areas.

Surely, a possible treasure hunt was why she was so excited when she heard a truck approaching. Yeah, right. Why did she even try to lie to herself? Jarvis was the reason butterflies were performing complicated aerial maneuvers in her stomach.

"How's it going?" he asked, striding up to the bunkhouse, a big smile on his face.

She'd known her car had been the only casualty at the courthouse, and still a rush of relief poured through her that Regina hadn't hurt him. His presence filled her with a beautiful happiness. His scent wound around her, mingling with something savory in the bag he carried. Even Silas kicked his legs happily, his face turning toward Jarvis's voice.

"We've been productive," she said.

"No nasty texts or emails?"

"All clear on that front."

"That's good." He paused and she wished he'd kiss her. "If a little surprising," he said as he unpacked the food.

She agreed. After Jarvis foiled Regina's plans at the courthouse, she'd expected a barrage of threats, either directly from Regina or from her fake family court template.

"Where'd you get the truck?" she asked.

"It's a loaner from the ranch."

"But you said—"

Jarvis smiled and tickled Silas's bare foot. "This one is so low-tech no one cares where it is. It was never GPS tagged." His eyes met hers. "I triple-checked."

She peered past him through the open doorway. The truck was in rough shape, with a dent behind the passenger door and spots of rust around the wheel wells. "You'll leave me that one?" she asked.

"No. Keep my truck for now. There will be fewer questions if I'm using the old model." At the table he unpacked the meal. "The garage called to let me know the tire was replaced today, but they can hold on to the car for you. I wish we could've taken it to the police station for evidence collection."

"You brought enough food for an army," she observed. There was no sense repeating herself about why they shouldn't involve the police yet. Until she had something more substantial than the classic bitter-stepdaughter story, she would keep the threats under wraps.

Jarvis pegged his hat on a hook by the door. "I wanted to eat with you tonight. Unless you need me on sway duty."

It took her a second to register the meaning, and then she laughed. "We're all set here. He just ate."

Jarvis's warm gaze drifted over her and a slow smile curled his sinfully sexy mouth. "Then we should catch up."

He'd brought barbecue and corn bread, along with fresh salad and steamed veggies. "I wasn't sure what you liked, so I loaded up a bit of everything."

"It's perfect. Now stop stalling and tell me all about what happened at the courthouse."

His brow furrowed. "I'm glad you didn't go." He shoved his fork into the pile of shredded meat but didn't lift the bite to his mouth. "Whatever she had in mind, I doubt it was pleasant." He paused long enough to gulp down a bite of the barbecue. "She was waiting for you outside the courtroom, at the window that overlooks the parking lot. Someone else was down there, keeping her informed." He pulled his phone from his back pocket. "I think this is the guy."

Mia wiped her fingers on a napkin and picked up the device. She enlarged the picture as far as it would go. "That looks a lot like the man she was with at the country house."

"Thought it might be," Jarvis muttered. "Assuming he was invited, we can't go after him for trespassing."

"Correct." She poked at her salad. "You're sure she didn't see you?"

He spread his arms wide and grinned. "She was

looking for you and the baby, not a random cowboy. She completely ignored my existence."

She appreciated the way he made her laugh, despite the fear rattling her nerves. "This really is above and beyond the call of cowboy assistance."

"I'm not so sure," he said.

Seeing the kissable smirk on his lips made it tough to stay on her side of the table. When would she find her perspective? She couldn't keep turning one errant kiss into something significant. He'd initially helped her for the sake of the ranch and now he felt obligated to see it through. It didn't exactly make for a level playing field.

"Maybe you should bail on the party," she suggested.

"No." He shook his head. "I'm more curious than ever, and you want an eyes-on report about your dad."

"If she gets suspicious, you could be in trouble. I should go and force her hand."

"Judging by what I saw today, that woman was born calculating and mean," he stated. "Her suspicions are the least of my worries. I promise I'll look good enough that Selina won't let me out of her sight and so different from a working cowboy that Regina will have no idea that she passed me in the courthouse today."

He looked pretty damn hot right now, but she kept the observation to herself. She had to believe in him. "I added the video file to my cloud folder at my attorney's office." She hadn't meant to bring that up, but someone trustworthy should know. "Along with the fake custody email that came through last night."

"Does your attorney check that folder? Will he take action?"

"Only if I request it. I just wanted you to know so if **something happens…**"

"Nothing will happen." His voice rumbled through the cabin like thunder. "At the party I'll speak with your dad and make sure he's feeling well and sounds like himself. If I can gather any more information, I'll do that, too. Then we'll make a plan to get you out of here and safely back to your life."

She was sure he didn't mean to hurt her feelings, but she felt as if he was pushing her away, nudging her along like a willful steer. Chances were good she was too sensitive and too lonely out here to accurately interpret what Jarvis did or didn't mean by every other word. He'd helped her and she'd done something to help him, as well.

"Speaking of plans," she began, pausing to snag another piece of the corn bread. "I worked my way through the land records and have some suggestions about where you might want to search."

"Tell me you found a land survey with an *X* on it, signed by Herman."

She laughed. "If it were that easy, you'd have found it without my help." She told him her theories on the landmarks and how they might have changed through the years. As well as where the original boundary had probably been.

He drummed his fingers on the table, repeating the pattern when Silas turned toward the sound. She melted a little at the effortless way he engaged with her baby. A string of "if onlys" raced through her mind and she yanked herself back to reality. Jarvis wasn't her Mr. Right just because he was within reach and kissed her senseless. He wasn't going to fall in love with her because they'd traded secrets and family drama.

Determined to be as good a friend to him as he'd

been to her, she told him about the registered sale between Herman and T. Ainsley.

"How can both be true?" he wondered. "If Herman sold the land, why pass on the story about it being stolen?"

"Bad blood between the brothers? Signatures were hardly verified back then the way they are now."

"A forgery?" A frown creased his brow. "Yeah, I guess that's possible."

He went quiet, lost in his thoughts while she cleaned up the remnants of their dinner and bagged the trash.

"I'll keep looking."

She startled at the sound of his voice and they both chuckled. "I thought you'd say that. I'm glad." She wanted to ask if he'd keep kissing her, too, but her typical bravery failed her.

"It's always been a bit of wild-goose chase, but if I stop now I'll have to find something else to keep my shoulders in shape."

His shoulders looked perfect to her.

"Will you be okay out here tonight?"

"Of course."

He studied her face, and then shocked her by reaching out and nudging her chin up. "No circles under your eyes." She might believe it was a clinical assessment if not for the heat in his gaze. "And it looks like you got some sun today."

She should move out of his reach, but her body refused to cooperate. "We went for a walk, not far, but fresh air helps him nap."

"I could stay." He released her chin. "You might need a break overnight."

If he stayed, she'd want to spend every spare minute

awake, in his arms, learning what pleased him and savoring every pleasure his sexy mouth and strong hands could create. "It sounds almost like you enjoy being with my son."

"He's cute." Jarvis hooked his thumbs in his pockets. "I enjoy you more," he said, his voice loaded with charm. "You're beautiful, Mia." He touched his lips to hers in a soft, fleeting kiss that left her feeling cheated.

She caught his shirt and drew him close. "Want to give that one more try?"

"I want to do more than try," he confessed, his rasping tone scraping away any pretense. He covered her mouth with his, his tongue sliding with hers in a hot caress that shot tingles straight to her toes, hitting all points in between.

It had been years since she'd felt an all-consuming desire like this. She and Roderick had fallen into a nice and predictable pattern. Enjoyable enough. Or so she'd thought.

She let herself loose, willing to cede control to Jarvis while her knees trembled and her heart raced. This was something altogether new and exciting. She dropped her head back as his lips traced her jaw, kissing, nipping and soothing a path down her throat.

"Mia," he whispered her name against the pulse throbbing at the base of her neck and she shivered. "You feel… I want… This is crazy."

"The best kind," she agreed. "Don't stop." Her breasts ached as desire arced through her like an electrical current. She pressed closer to the hard wall of his chest and moaned at the contact, relishing the sweet friction.

His hands molded to her hips, eased higher over her rib cage. One of his hot palms cupped her breast, stroking and teasing her through her T-shirt and bra. It was enough to bring her right to the edge.

"Please, Jarvis." She kissed him again and worked his shirt free of his jeans. Her reward was the incomparable feel of warm skin and crisp hair over slabs of mouthwatering muscle.

He trapped her hand, his breathing ragged as he retreated. "We can't."

She opened her eyes to find him watching her too closely. She arched an eyebrow in query.

"We shouldn't," he amended. "Seriously." He looked around, his gaze as hot and bewildered as she felt. That was a small consolation that she wasn't in this alone, but it steadied her.

"The baby," he said desperately.

"Is asleep," she pointed out. She reached up and smoothed a hand over his cheek, loving the feel of his whiskers against her palm. She loved every nuance and discovery Jarvis allowed. He had so many textures and layers beneath that rough-and-ready exterior. "And he's too young to remember anything he might see."

She clamped her lips shut and didn't protest when he stepped back. Pride would not allow her to beg for the connection or passion he wasn't ready to give.

"Mia." He pushed a hand through his hair, his chest expanding on a deep inhale. "I want you, but I don't think it's smart. For you."

"Uh-huh." She crossed her arms, reflexively preventing her heart from leaping into his hands. "Do you always lie to yourself?"

"Hang on." He scowled at her. "I'm not *lying* to anyone. Being with me isn't a smart move. It would be fun, unforgettable, no doubt. But I don't buy into the whole family dynamic. You do. I—I'm more like your ex."

Please. He could toss out all the excuses he wanted; she'd seen his reaction when she told him about Roderick's response to her pregnancy. "You think having a baby ruined my body?"

"What?" His gaze raked over her, leaving her feeling scalded. "Hell no."

"Then you're nothing like my ex." She recognized fear and uncertainty, having seen it often enough in the mirror lately. "I didn't ask you for a ring or even a promise, Jarvis." She had no idea how she was keeping her cool. "To be blunt, I'm attracted to you. I'm woman enough to say I'd like to follow that attraction to its logical conclusion. Just healthy sex, no strings."

He didn't need to know her emotions were surging all over the place. That was her problem, her responsibility. She could keep her mushy feelings well away from the need blazing between them. It was entirely possible this blaze would burn that emotion to cinders, anyway.

"That sounds cold." He stalked over to the door but didn't leave. On an oath, he turned back and she saw his arousal straining against the fly of his jeans. There was nothing emotional about her response to that view. Her mouth watered and heat pooled between her thighs.

"You wanted poetry?" she asked. "Being coy has never been my strong suit."

"I'm just a messed-up cowboy." He pushed a hand through his hair. "You're a model."

"I'm a woman. If you're messed up, I'm a wreck," she said. "But I'm honest. I want you."

"You deserve the best, Mia." He sounded so sincere.

"You deserve rings and promises from a man who believes family is a functional institution."

The pain underscoring his words was like a knife in her chest. "What do you mean?"

"I barely remember what a healthy family looks like. The three of us were dumped on an aunt who was forced to step up because that's what 'family' does. She didn't want to call us hers any more than Payne Colton wants to claim us. Family is obligation and responsibility and I can't—I can't give you that."

"Jarvis. Whatever you're thinking, stop and hear me." She took a cautious step closer. "When you kiss me, I feel like *me* again. When you touch me, I don't feel afraid or frumpy. That's a gift, a treasure. And right now, that's plenty. It's probably all I can handle. I'm not going to fall in love over a kiss and demand an exclusive, permanent relationship."

She was fairly sure that *was* a lie. She had the sense that Jarvis would be easy to love, either on the rebound or for forever. Thank goodness she'd learned to control her facial expressions during her modeling career.

He dropped his head back, staring at the ceiling. "I didn't mean to insult you or overreact or whatever the hell it is I'm doing."

She moved around the table and pulled a bottle of water from the refrigerator. "Stay if you want. I won't attack you in your sleep."

"Same."

She heard his boots against the floor as he walked away from the door. "I feel weird kissing you, knowing I'm going out with Selina in a few days."

That admission might be closer to the real issue, but she sensed there was more, something twisted up with his pessimistic views about family. She hadn't expected dating as a single mother to be easy. Hadn't anticipated that she would be this intensely attracted to any man so soon. Maybe Jarvis could help her more by giving her a reality check about her hopes for her future.

"Not that it means anything." He slid into a chair at the table. "She was very clear that my only purpose is to look good and be into her, so she can make Regina jealous. As if I'd be tempted to stick around." His nose wrinkled and his lip curled as if he'd tasted something sour.

Mia laughed at his absurd expression and the baby jerked in his sleep but relaxed again. She sat opposite him, doing her best not to stare. "Your charm and flirtation skills must be off the charts."

"I have my strengths." He winked and her belly quivered.

"You do," she agreed. It was a challenge to sit and talk when only minutes ago he had her body throbbing and speechless, but this seemed to be what he needed. And she wasn't ready to be alone.

"Being around Selina is like trying to walk a rattlesnake." His amusement turned somber. "There's a woman who made the right choice by not having kids."

"It must have been terrifying for you when your parents died," she murmured. "I'm sorry." She stretched out a hand, offering comfort without pushing it on him.

He lifted his gaze, his dark eyes shaded by his furrowed brow. "I don't remember anyone saying that," he said. He touched his fingers to hers. "I'm sure they did. They must have?"

"Probably," she said. "I remember hearing it. I can't imagine how you and your brother and sister suffered.

My world wasn't ripped apart like yours. I still had Dad. I didn't have to move." She laced her fingers through his. "Losing someone you love is always devastating, no matter when it happens. I wasn't sure Dad would ever smile again after Mom died. There was an invisible cloud that followed me around everywhere, a shroud over everything. Sunlight, bright colors, flavors and feelings, all of it was dim for a long time. Grief takes time to wade through and the effects linger."

She hoped not forever. Jarvis was too good a person to spend his life afraid of living deeply and completely. She understood abandonment, even if her experiences differed from his. Her dad had essentially walked away from her, withdrawing his support and confidence in her. At the first curveball, her husband had chosen his idea of the perfect couple over adapting along with her and becoming a family.

"My brother and sister are moving on," Jarvis said. "It's good. They'll both be married soon." He withdrew his hand, leaning back in the chair. "Probably with kids."

"And you'll be the cowboy uncle."

"Absolutely." A hint of a grin tilted his mouth. "All of the fun, none of the pressure. The traditional path isn't the right fit for me."

"Isn't searching for proof of Isaiah's stories a way of moving on?" she pressed. She refused to mention that kissing her could qualify, too.

"The search started as a weird way to connect with our past and, if Isaiah's information is right, the result might be a better future for the three of us."

She sipped her water. "In my book that sounds like

a man who knows exactly how to value, work for and honor his family."

He shrugged off the compliment. "At this point, I think I'm just too stubborn to quit."

"Stubborn doesn't have to be a weakness. Being willing to fight and adapt is also a good family trait. Your list of strengths is getting longer."

"Stop it," he said without any real heat.

"Why?" She turned the ring on her thumb. "Families are as different as the people who make them up. I had family with Mom and Dad. I had a family of friends in college. Now, with Silas, I have a new family. Just because it doesn't resemble some gooey holiday commercial doesn't make it less valid."

"I hear you, Mia. But I just can't give anyone that much power to hurt me again. I've dealt with enough pain for one lifetime. And the flip side is I don't want to risk hurting anyone, either. Not the way I was hurt as a kid."

Her heart ached for him, for cutting himself off from the world. Loneliness was a pain unto itself. She wished she could make him see that. Taking a deep breath, she gave him her award-winning smile. "That's understandable. Trust me when I say I'm not looking forward to the moments when Silas and I hurt each other. Life won't be perfect. One of us already shows signs of a strong and unquenchable temper."

Jarvis laughed. "At least one of you."

She ignored the jab. "You're talking to a woman who's cleared her own path more than once. Going it alone is exhausting," she admitted. "Without you, I probably would've given in to Regina or flat-out run away and changed my name by now."

"Not likely, with your famously beautiful face."

She soaked up the sweet words, the heat in his eyes as he said them. "I can do wonders with makeup," she teased. "Yes, the person you love most is also the person who can hurt you the deepest. I still want to have love in my life."

"After what happened with your husband, I'd think you'd be done taking those chances."

"I'm not. The fact that it was easy to walk away from Roderick only confirmed that what we had wasn't as deep as it should've been. And when I said that, I was actually thinking of my dad."

"The man who put his new wife ahead of his daughter." He shook his head. "Doesn't that prove the wisdom of keeping part of yourself protected from that kind of rejection?"

She wondered if he heard the brokenhearted little boy in his voice. "At the risk of sounding like a shrink, I'll remind you that the loss of your parents when you were so young had a lasting impact. Compounding that when you lost your aunt—"

He shoved roughly to his feet, the chair scraping across the plank floor. "Her death wasn't the same at all."

"The same or different, it was another loss," she soothed.

"More like a burden lifted." He scrubbed at his face. "She didn't want us, we didn't want to be with her. More family dysfunction." He sighed. "How did we get on this topic, anyway?"

"You stopped kissing me."

"Well, call me a fool," he said with a wry grin.

"I'm not asking for more than you want to give," she

reminded him. "I'm only suggesting you allow yourself to think about what you need to take."

"From you?"

She rolled her eyes. "From anyone, Jarvis. You're a good man. One of the best men I've met. You said all that about what I deserve, but you deserve happiness, too. Peace. Family. Love. However, *you* choose to define any of those things."

"Right." He grabbed his hat. "I'll be back tomorrow. Text me if something comes up or you're low on anything."

"I will. Thanks." It took every ounce of willpower to stay in her chair, to keep her mouth shut.

He paused, the door halfway open. "I'm not angry."

"Me, neither." Halfway in love with a man who didn't believe in the concept, but not angry. "See you tomorrow."

With a curt nod, he was gone. A moment later the truck engine rumbled and faded as he drove away. Obviously, she'd said too much. She didn't regret it and wouldn't retract a word. The world needed more good men like Jarvis, and he needed more good from the world.

Chapter 7

The intense conversation with Mia simmered in the back of Jarvis's mind for days. He'd been annoyed as hell that first night. Had even considered not going back. Couldn't do it. She needed someone keeping an eye out for her, even in the updated bunkhouse. It wasn't safe for her to go into town, not while Regina still held so much leverage.

. So he manned up and went back day after day, determined to keep his distance physically and emotionally. It wasn't easy; the woman left him wanting, but he managed. They found a routine and kept conversations on the lighter end of the spectrum or locked onto his search pattern. There were more kisses, yet by some tacit agreement they kept those lighter, too. He made sure she had what she needed, including a few minutes to herself every time he stopped by.

Still, her challenge haunted him, forced him to think about things he'd always pushed down or ignored. How did he define happiness? He was completely at peace and content with his opinions on family and love and his future role as the fun-loving uncle. But happiness? That should probably involve more than a career, more than time with his siblings.

Spencer and Bella were happier with their newfound soul mates than he'd ever seen them. After all they'd lost, that kind of leap into commitment and love seemed like too big a risk. One of them had to stay sane and logical. If he was okay as the family backstop, why did it matter what Mia thought about his choices?

He was still searching for a good answer for that.

He did enjoy spending time with her son far more than he wanted to admit even to himself. He wouldn't call himself attached; he was just more curious about how the baby soaked up the sights, sounds and smells each day. Jarvis had come by on his horse one afternoon and he swore the little guy smiled when Mia guided his tiny hand through the mane.

All of those relaxed and easy moments made tonight more difficult. Putting on a suit and heading out to a party with a different woman felt all kinds of wrong. Selina and Mia might run in the same social circles, but they were on opposite ends of the personality scale, in Jarvis's opinion. Selina was cold and sleek and calculating, and Mia was everything warm and kind and beautiful. Both women had tremendous strength, but he preferred Mia's easygoing glow over Selina's sharp edges and pushy manner.

He couldn't accurately term the time he spent with Mia as dating, but it was definitely more fun than the myriad roles he had to play tonight. Spying for Asher. Bolstering Selina's pride. Assessing Norton's health for Mia. Not to mention the variations on those themes that included giving Norton a message or finding something incriminating on Regina. He didn't want to let Asher or Mia down, and disappointing Selina would backfire in the worst way on the ranch.

Per Selina's last text message, he parked behind her house so the ranch truck wouldn't mar her home's perfect curb appeal or alter the impression that someone wealthy was escorting her to Regina's event. Smoothing his tie and checking his cuff links, he strolled up the walkway, admiring the flawless landscaping the ranch crew maintained for her. He rang the bell and waited, trying not to wish the evening over before it began.

Selina opened the door and he was momentarily struck mute. Her dress hugged her body like a second gleaming skin. Gold sparkled in the black fabric, catching the light and winking in and out as she moved. Gold bangles slithered up and down her wrist as she invited him in.

"You look great," he said, choosing a bland compliment.

Her gaze narrowed. "My, my." She walked a circle around him and he sympathized with a fresh side of beef in a butcher shop. "You do clean up nicely, cowboy."

"Thanks." He gave her a slower appraisal this time, adding enough heat until her eyes twinkled.

"That's what I'm after," she said with a sassy giggle.

He had to admit she was an attractive woman, even if she wasn't his type. Thanks to Mia, he found himself wondering if Selina believed in family. Probably not, considering she might have cheated on Payne, clearly resented his kids and had carved out a chunk of his estate for herself in the divorce.

"This is going to be epic."

"I'm glad you approve." He knew she believed his sole purpose this evening was to send Regina into a fit of jealousy. He'd play his part, hopeful that an "epic" distraction would be enough for her to slip up about the situation with Mia.

"We'll be the talk of the party." She tossed him a set of keys. "You aren't going to wimp out over a little gossip, are you?"

He smiled. "It'll be a pleasure."

She sucked in a tiny breath and petted his shoulder. "Keep that up and you might get to hang around more often."

He guided her fingers down to curl around his elbow and escorted her out to the sleek sports car waiting in her driveway. "I didn't know you had a Jaguar."

"One more perk of being a Colton ex-wife," she said, her tone low and sly. "Coma or not, Payne will never say no to me."

After opening the door and helping her into the passenger seat, he rounded the hood and sank into the supple leather upholstery. He rested his hands on the steering wheel, admiring the gleaming walnut accents, before adjusting the seat and mirrors to suit him.

Selina snickered. "When we get to the party, can you aim a little of that passionate infatuation my way?" She put the address into the car's navigation app and sat back again.

"I promise." He glanced over. "When I was in college, we used to daydream about status cars. Some of the guys went out and took test drives."

"Not you?"

"Not me." While the test drives motivated others, Jarvis knew that getting a taste of what he couldn't yet afford would've only frustrated him. "I had plenty of time for that once the money was in the bank to back it up."

"Oh, that's right. I forgot you put yourself through college and landed a real job before you signed on here," she said. "Are you really thrilled about riding a horse these days instead of driving a Jaguar?"

A few weeks ago, he might have bristled or felt defensive at the sly dig. After finding Mia and especially after their talk, he chose to take the comment at face value. "They're both temperamental," he joked. "Turns out the ranch is an excellent fit for me. I get to drive a horse *and* a Jag."

"Just for tonight," she reminded him, coolly. Her perfectly manicured nails dug into the small purse on her lap. "Listen. Even if Payne survives, I'm sure he won't ever admit that your tenacity and independence impressed him."

That hit harder than the reminders that they were from two different worlds. "I don't know why." He cleared his throat. "We were just three orphans who coincidentally shared his last name and hometown."

Selina scoffed. "Whatever he says, I think he's always been impressed by you."

He shot her a quick look. That was a surprising reveal and he wasn't sure what she gained by sharing it. Selina was impossible to figure out. He pulled away from the Triple R, taking the turn with care and minding the speed limit.

"Oh, open her up," Selina said. "I'll cover any speeding ticket."

She didn't have to tell him twice. He forgot the strife and ghosts lurking in his family tree and drove toward a less-traveled stretch of road where he could let the Jag loose. The engine responded with a throaty growl and they were suddenly flying low through the twilight, the speedometer edging toward ninety, then ninety-five, miles per hour.

Selina made a sound that landed somewhere between a squeal and a laugh. Jarvis didn't take his eyes off the road, even as he eased off the accelerator and brought the car back to a normal, law-abiding speed.

"That was exhilarating!"

He glanced over and caught Selina's wide grin and bright eyes. She had color in her cheeks that made her look remarkably youthful and carefree. Right now, it was easy to see why Payne had fallen for her, and possibly, why he'd been convinced to keep her close both at Colton Oil and at the Triple R.

Darkness swept over the valley as they drove to the exclusive gated neighborhood where the Graves family lived. The pale stucco homes and red tile roofs were set well apart from each other and the landscaping, highlighted by low lights and streetlamps, seemed to be coordinated from the entrance to each individual drive.

Mia had grown up here. It was impossible not to picture her as a little girl learning to ride a bike or as a teen lounging away the summers with a pack of friends around a backyard pool. He'd done those things, too, but across town, and on a much more modest scale.

When they reached the Graves' driveway, Selina flipped down the visor mirror to check her makeup.

"Jarvis, I think your burst of speed was more effective than an hour with concealer and highlighter." Her cheeks were still rosy and her eyes bright. She added a bit of gloss to her lips and then gave him a nod.

On that cue he steeled himself to run the gauntlet with the various items on his agenda. He came around to her side and opened her door, extending a hand. She emerged with such perfect grace he assumed she'd practiced the maneuver. Or maybe it was one of those things that society women instinctively knew how to accomplish. His mind inevitably drifted to Mia, recalling paparazzi photos that documented her vehicle exits through her modeling years. Beautiful, enticing photos of long, shapely legs and that stunning smile that made anyone she looked at feel like the only relevant person on the planet.

Selina slipped her hand around his elbow, bringing him back to the moment. Her fingers clutched his arm through his suit coat, tightening with every step they took toward the house. She didn't lean too close, but she made it clear she wanted him to stick with her. He played along, stealing glances and smiling as if they shared a secret, all the while imagining Mia beside him.

Norton and Regina Graves were not waiting to greet them. The doors of the magnificent home had been thrown wide open, light spilling out over the walkway. Two men in catering uniforms stood sentry, checking identification and invitations.

"My place at the ranch has more square footage," Selina said quietly as they stepped into the foyer. "But Regina upgraded with more marble when she remodeled and brought Norton's decor into the current era."

Jarvis bent his head to her ear. "Bigger is better," he said, knowing it would make her smile.

"And younger is a plus, too," she replied, her eyes twinkling as she caressed his biceps. "Let's go raise some eyebrows, cowboy."

He recognized many of the faces as he worked the room as Selina's oversize accessory. She surprised him by making genuine introductions while they chatted with industry leaders from across the Southwest. He'd expected to be dismissed breezily if not outright ignored.

She paused between conversations, angling her body closer. Her fingertips stroked his lapel. "Here we go," she said for his ears only.

Regina glided up, a glass of champagne in her hand. She wore her hair up, but that was the only similarity to the first time he'd seen her at the courthouse. Tonight the dress and heels, along with the jewelry, made a clear statement that she was the trophy wife every man should want.

"Selina!" she gushed. "I'm so glad you've made it." She turned a bold smile on Jarvis. "Is this the nephew I've heard so much about?"

"No, no." Selina laughed easily, but he felt the bite of tension as she slid her arm around his waist. "This is Jarvis Colton, the man who has simply made the last few months a *delight*. Jarvis, this is Regina Graves, our hostess and Norton's wife."

Jarvis glided his hand down Selina's back in a gently familiar and possessive move. In the past the gesture might have felt gallant or warm. Tonight he just felt sticky. "You have a lovely home, Mrs. Graves."

"Thank you." Her gaze narrowed, her lips tilting as she assessed him.

"Where is Norton?" Selina made a show of looking around while pressing close to Jarvis's side. "We haven't had a chance to say hello to the guest of honor."

"He's out on the deck with a cigar and a few close friends," Regina said, the insult clear though she'd delivered it with a sugary smile. "Do enjoy yourselves until he returns."

With a lingering gaze for Jarvis, she walked off. He wanted a shower.

"Oh, well done," Selina said under her breath. "She's fuming."

"Happy to help," Jarvis said, moving his hand along her spine again.

He let Selina guide him to and fro through the house, until the conversations blurred together. Per Asher's request, he kept Selina sipping on champagne. Not enough to allow her to wreck her own agenda, but enough that she might feel talkative while he drove her home.

Selina couldn't be persuaded to interrupt the cigar smokers on the deck, so Jarvis had to bide his time until he could get a good look at Norton. Hopefully, hanging with his "close friends" meant he was safe. Unless Regina had tampered with the man's cigars. He wouldn't put anything past her.

Selina shooed Jarvis away once she was immersed in a conversation with several women. He seized the opportunity, selecting a sparkling water and giving himself a tour of the grand house. With luck, he might get to Norton's office or even upstairs before anyone noticed.

Everywhere he looked, he was greeted by high-end luxury. The furnishings were perfect, the colors and textures and accent pieces creating a flawlessly coordinated effect. He was sure every piece was comfortable, but nothing was comforting.

As he wandered through, he realized the decor was light on family memorabilia. Even his aunt had framed their school pictures each year. He assumed the house had been staged for the party and the personal items removed for safekeeping, until he found photos of Regina and Norton on a mantel and more candid shots of the couple framed and featured on a bookshelf. Notably absent were any photos of Mia or Silas. Hearing a slow click of high heels on the tile floor, he paused to admire the selection of books.

"Here you are," Regina purred at his shoulder.

Jarvis stepped out of her reach, barely suppressing a shudder.

"You've wandered a bit from the party." She closed the distance again, her perfume snaking around him. "Is the crowd too much?"

"I do enjoy the quiet," he replied. "I hope it's not a problem."

"No, of course not." She watched him with a shrewd gaze. "You're welcome to make yourself at home."

Ugh. She was testing him. He was torn between calling her bluff and calling her out. Embarrassing Selina would wreck his chances of gleaning any information for Asher. And Regina didn't strike him as a woman to succumb to an ultimatum from a stranger. He'd believed Mia before that Regina would strike if pressed. Now he could see it in her eyes. She was wondering how to steal him from Selina.

"Norton has quite a collection here," he said, gesturing to the bookshelf.

"How do you know the collection isn't mine?" she countered. "Maybe we share it."

The emphasis she placed on "share" made his skin crawl. He evaded her next attempt to touch him. "Classic philosophy and modern business must lead to fascinating conversations with your husband." Jarvis spotted a man Selina had introduced earlier and made his escape. "If you'll excuse me. Please, give Norton my best."

He figured Selina would give a cheer when she heard about it, but he wasn't sure one shower would be enough to erase the ick-factor. He spoke with a few more people as he made his way toward the back of the house. Being familiar with Norton's career and having a thorough understanding of industry and business ventures in the region gave him a leg up on the typical eye candy. He used it to his advantage, gathering snippets of conversations and comments to share with Mia later.

Jarvis learned Norton had been golfing twice since she'd gone into hiding. He hadn't missed any meetings and no one voiced any concerns about his health or behavior. All of that should ease Mia's concerns.

What he found more distressing was the lack of concern for Mia or her baby. She was Norton's only child and had been visible and influential as a model and as Roderick's wife. No one seemed to miss her. In fact, any sign that Mia had ever lived here or had any relationship with her father was gone. He assumed Regina was behind that, clearing out anything that diverted Norton's focus on his wife. Rounding a corner, Jarvis came up short as he found himself in front of a painting of Norton and a young Mia. They looked happy and connected, and her natural beauty was already shining.

He wondered if Regina had tried to remove it entirely or if she hadn't yet dared.

Norton walked up right then, his eyebrows lifting when he saw Jarvis.

Jarvis offered his hand and his name. "I've followed your career for some time, Mr. Graves."

Norton met his handshake with a firm grip. "A pleasure to meet you, Mr. Colton. Hope you've followed my advice, as well."

"Naturally. And I'm better off because of it," Jarvis admitted. "Is this your daughter?"

Norton faced the painting, his hands clasped behind his back and a frown pleating his gray eyebrows. "Mia, yes. I miss the girl she was back then."

"She's off with a family of her own these days?" Jarvis queried.

"Family? No." Norton's mouth firmed. "Not anymore. Her mother and I had such hopes for that girl. She squeaked through college, refusing to apply herself to her studies. Then she married an upstart tech genius from New York City." He sighed. "His business flourished, but the marriage failed, as I warned her it would. Now she's all but disappeared, taking my grandson with her."

That was far more than Jarvis had expected. He felt like Norton had siphoned all the air from the room. "I—I'm sorry, sir."

"I'd hoped, despite Mia being beyond reach, that her son would mark a fresh start for us, but she seems determined to disappoint me." He rocked back on his heels. "I really thought that would pass once she was out of her teens and twenties. Sometimes common sense skips a generation."

"I've never thought of it that way." Jarvis didn't know what else to say. He wanted to leap to Mia's defense, was in fact trying to come up with some way to clue Norton in that his daughter was in trouble. He was about to tactlessly blurt out the message from Mia when Regina appeared.

"There you are, my love." She slid up close and rubbed his shoulder. "This isn't the time for melancholy."

"Oh, I know." He gave her a tired smile. "The young man here asked about Mia."

"Jasper, is that right?" Regina said with a bored expression.

"It's Jarvis, ma'am." He corrected her politely and nearly blew it with a laugh when he saw the "ma'am" register on her face.

"Jarvis," she repeated, her tone chilly. "Mia was a lovely girl and we miss her terribly. I've tried to shield Norton from the worst of her carelessness." She caught her husband's hand between her own. "Children are forever hurting their parents. Something I'm sure she'll learn soon enough." To Norton she said, "You'll have another chance, dear. I'm sure it's only a matter of time before she comes to the door groveling for help again."

"Tried to help her launch a business," Norton grumbled.

"Of course you did. That's who you are."

"Such a disappointment." His face crumpled. "I don't understand it."

"She's selfish, Norton. And self-absorbed. On the bright side, you'll always have me, my love." She kissed her husband. Not anything brief or classy or even affectionate. No, she took the time to fuse her mouth to his in an intimate display that made Jarvis's stomach curdle. "Now, happy thoughts. I came looking for you because the mayor just walked in. You should say hello."

When he was out of earshot, her sharp gaze locked onto Jarvis. "I'll thank you not to upset my husband further this evening."

"Not my intention at all. I was merely admiring the painting." He smiled when Selina found him and hurried over. "Enjoying yourself?" He drew her close to his side.

"It's a fabulous night." She grinned up at him. The expression softened when she saw the painting over his shoulder. "I'm surprised this survived the remodeling, Regina."

"It will go to storage soon enough," the woman snapped. "Mia ran off," she said, her voice just loud enough to carry. "He just needs time to accept it. Norton is heartbroken. I always knew she was a lost cause, but the baby—" she pressed her hands over her heart "—he was crazy over that little boy."

"That's terrible." Selina didn't sound too broken up about it.

"Eventually, he'll come around," Regina continued. "After the way she left…" Regina shook her head sadly. "Some scruffy, gold-digging boyfriend had been by a few times. Only when Norton was at work, of course. Then poof, without a word, she's moved out and taken the baby. But not before stealing all the cash from my purse and clearing out a fund Norton set up for the little tyke. She hasn't spoken to either of us since. He's heartbroken," she repeated, her gaze drifting to her husband across the room. "I haven't told him I've started searching for the child. I documented everything and I'm sure we can get custody of the baby when the time comes."

Jarvis had never wanted to strike a woman until this very moment. Regina and her lies brought out the worst in him. He focused on Selina and this time he used her for support.

"Good luck with that," Selina said. "It's been a lovely party, Regina, but we should be going." She batted her lashes at Jarvis. "We both have to be up early tomorrow."

"Of course." Regina's smile didn't reach her eyes and her mouth was pinched at the corners. "We'll have to make time for lunch soon."

"Definitely. Just call." Selina extricated them from the conversation and aimed straight for the door. "Having ungrateful, greedy stepchildren is the worst. I almost feel sorry for her."

Jarvis made a sound of agreement, but his temper was about to boil over. Regina was a world-class liar and he hated that it was on him to inform Mia of how misinformed her father was. He'd leave out as much as he could and she'd be happy to hear her dad appeared healthy.

For how long?

"Do you think she meant it, about suing for custody?" he asked, driving away from the Graves home. He hadn't meant to bring it up, especially not with Selina, but it bothered him.

"Not a chance," Selina waved that off. "Regina is making the right noises to appease that old coot. She loves to flaunt her money and pretend she has all the power."

Jarvis agreed with that assessment one hundred percent.

"There was a time when I felt sorry for Mia. She and Norton were close before he met Regina."

"You don't feel sorry for her now?"

"Are you kidding? She landed on her feet. Her husband was sinfully rich and even better looking." Selina slid the bangles up and down her arm. "People don't realize how quickly things can change. I used to have more money than Regina. Back when I was Mrs. Payne Colton."

Jarvis snapped out of his Mia worries. This was exactly the opening Asher had hoped for. "From where I stand, it seems you landed on your feet, too."

"Of course it looks that way, to you. And I do have some pull, although being his ex-wife means more trade-offs." She reached over and squeezed his thigh, just above his knee. "These days Regina might have the bigger bank account, but I can be seen out and about with whomever I please. She's stuck fawning over that love-blind old man."

Jarvis stopped her wandering hand before it crept too much higher on his leg. With a giggle, Selina subsided. "I hope she's being smart about things."

"What things?"

"Well, if Norton catches on to her antics and affairs, she's doomed. And if she's been spending as wildly as she seems to be, life after divorce will be a bear. Voice of experience."

"Was the adjustment difficult?" He really didn't care, but he needed to keep her talking.

"In some ways." Selina yawned. "But I'm set for life. A beautiful home, an excellent salary and bene-

fits, plus all the help I need is just a finger-snap away."
She snapped and then stroked his knee again. "Payne
used to complain and taught his kids to resent me, but
he really should've been more discreet."

"About what?"

"Oh, everything and nothing," she said. "His secrets
and misdeeds are my gold mine."

Asher would go nuts when he heard this.

"I'll let you in on a secret, cowboy." She reached out
and petted his shoulder this time. "A smart woman is
always paying attention. Don't you ever underestimate a
pretty face." She sank back into her seat once more, and
before Jarvis could prod more out of her, she was out.

"Great."

Parking in front of her house, Jarvis roused Selina
enough to get her inside. He didn't venture any farther
than the foyer, though he'd done enough errands here
that he knew the layout well enough. Once she was
steady on her feet, he pressed the Jag keys into her hand
and urged her to lock the door behind him.

Back outside, he couldn't get away fast enough. He
rumbled across the sleeping ranch in the older pickup
and parked near his room. He wanted out of the suit
and into a shower.

Jarvis had once found Selina calculating and clingy.
Tonight he'd gone a few rounds with the new champion
of manipulation, Regina. Knowing Mia was eager for
news on her dad, he planned to text her as soon as he
was back in his room.

Walking to his door, he nearly jumped out of his skin
when the shadows moved. "Asher. You nearly gave me
a heart attack."

"You've never been jumpy," his boss replied. "Did something happen?"

It took a moment for the genuine concern to sink in. He'd only spent a few hours with high society, but he wasn't cut out for that level of sniping and veiled threats. He'd made the right choice coming to work at the Triple R. "Dodging Selina's wandering hands makes me jumpy," he admitted.

"Was she chatty?"

"A little." He unlocked his door and invited Asher in. "She let me drive the Jag."

"Lucky you."

He smiled and tugged his tie from his collar. "I'll say. That was the bright spot and it was so early on I nearly forgot it." He shrugged out of his coat and draped it over the chair.

Each room in this bunkhouse was a small apartment, furnished with a bed, dresser, small table, two chairs and a private bathroom. Each man on the crew who stayed in these quarters could add what he wanted to the setup. Jarvis hadn't added much beyond a good television. He'd put most of his belongings in storage since hiring on here.

Asher braced his hands on the other chair, impatient now. "Don't keep me in suspense."

"You were right to think blackmail. She definitely knows something damaging about Payne," Jarvis reported. "She warned me not to underestimate a pretty face, that smart women are observant."

"She didn't tell you what it was?"

"No. Said he wasn't discreet and that his secrets and misdeeds were her gold mine."

Asher swore. "She was the one who slept around. All of the financials from their marriage look clean."

"I'd say it's more than that." Jarvis held up his hands. "Gut instinct, that's all," he added. "I wanted to ask more, but she fell asleep."

Asher swore softly. "It was too much to hope for a written confession. And confirmation that she does have legitimate leverage is helpful. I know it couldn't have been an easy night." He popped Jarvis lightly on the shoulder. "Thanks for going the extra mile. Take tomorrow off."

That startled him. "You sure?"

"I am."

"Thanks," Jarvis said with feeling.

Once Asher was gone, Jarvis sent Mia a text to confirm her father was healthy, promising to explain everything tomorrow.

He waited, but she didn't reply immediately. She was probably asleep or dealing with the baby. Desperate to wash off the clinging scents of heavy perfume and cigar smoke, he went to take a shower. He'd check for a reply once he was clean.

His short shower went long and when he finally felt like his skin was his own, he turned off the tap and toweled off. With the towel wrapped around his hips, he picked up his phone. Still no reply from Mia.

With Regina's nonsense ringing in his ears, his gut clamored for him to get out there and check on her. It was nearly one in the morning and startling her at this hour was crazy. Rude.

He needed to go to bed and he sure as hell didn't need to interrupt her sleep. Even if he wasn't on the schedule tomorrow, his body was used to ranch hours and he would be up with the sun, anyway. He could check on Mia then. Maybe take her some breakfast.

He was about to toss the towel on the rack and climb into bed when his phone buzzed. The screen showed a text message from Mia.

Are you still awake?

He sent back an affirmative reply immediately.

Can we come in?

He stared down at his phone, momentarily dumbstruck. What was she doing here? If anyone saw her, she'd have to leave before word got back to Regina.

A soft knock at the door followed and he rushed across the room to invite her in. She stood there, her hair loose around her shoulders, both hands gripping the handle of the car seat. Silas was sound asleep.

The threat of disaster crashed over him and he pulled her inside, reaching around her to close and lock the door. "Mia. You shouldn't have come," he said, his voice a low growl.

"I know. I—" Her gaze dipped, then came back up to his face. "I was worried about Dad." Her eyes cruised over his mouth and lower again. "Thanks for the text…"

He would've sworn she was touching him, the way his skin tingled under her gaze, but her hands were locked onto the handle of the car seat. If she kept looking at him like that, he was going to want a lot more than kisses. He already did.

Chapter 8

Mia stared at Jarvis. He didn't even have to touch her and she was speechless. She knew coming here was a huge risk, but she'd thought the danger revolved around Regina finding her hiding place.

No. Not even close.

In this tidy room filled with Jarvis—his tempting scent, his presence, his heated gaze—she was risking much more. Personal humiliation was only the start. Jarvis stood before her, essentially naked. If she gave one small tug of the towel, she could enjoy the full view. She wasn't as ashamed as she should be that her fingers itched to do just that.

Thank goodness her hands were busy with the car seat. Car seat. Her son. A cowboy who claimed he didn't want a family. Those should be all the reasons she needed to behave herself.

"You're sure Dad's okay?" she managed.

He reached over and took the car seat out of her hands, setting it gently on the floor. Silas didn't even twitch. "Norton is fine. I heard his friends talking about recent golf outings and meetings over a few lunches or drinks and cigars after work. No one expressed any concerns about his health or well-being."

"Okay. Good." Since he'd relieved her of the car seat she didn't know what to do with her hands. Weaving her fingers together, she tried to keep her gaze away from his body. She'd known Jarvis was in shape, but to see most of his potent build on display was messing with her head.

While working as a model, her sense of modesty had died a quick death. Behind the scenes at photo shoots and fashion shows, all kinds of things happened and all types of bodies were on display, by accident or design. She'd been up close and personal with many men the world considered perfectly photogenic, including her husband.

Jarvis had just elevated the standards of perfection for her. He was sculpted from hard work and the demands of an active ranch. His muscles had purpose from those wide, ripped shoulders down to his strong forearms and calloused hands. Hands that had stirred up cravings she'd convinced herself she could live without. At least, she'd planned to forgo those physical needs until she found someone willing to stick around and be her partner through this thing called life.

Right this minute, she didn't care how temporary Jarvis might be. She wanted him.

"You really shouldn't be here," he said.

There was something akin to guilt in his eyes. Her

presence rattled him. She shouldn't take any delight in that, but she did. She glanced toward the bathroom and saw the light through the bottom of the door. Did he have company? The bed was neatly made, but maybe they hadn't gotten that far yet. "You, um. Oh, crap. I didn't mean to interrupt."

"What? No. No." He shoved a hand through his damp hair. "I'm alone. Check if you want."

She shook her head. "I trust you." Even if she didn't, it would be petty to check. They didn't have any kind of understanding. Not to mention how foolish it would be to expose herself to someone who might know Regina.

He cocked an eyebrow and as if he'd read her mind, he went over and shoved the bathroom door open. "Alone," he repeated. "The party was…" He spread his arms wide. If he didn't dress soon, her self-control would spontaneously combust.

"Pants." Her voice was as rough as sandpaper. "Please."

She focused on her sleeping son. There was the perspective she needed. When he grew up, she wouldn't want women marching into his room to ogle him.

"Right. Just a sec." A drawer opened and closed behind her, followed by the rustling of more movement. "Dressed," he said. "Sorry about that."

"I'm the one who should apologize," she began. Her thoughts vaporized. His version of dressed didn't do anything to quash her desire. He was in a soft T-shirt and loose gym shorts that were just as enticing as the towel had been.

"Mia, sit down." He pulled out a chair for her and sat in one across from her. "I was planning to come out first thing tomorrow to tell you everything."

That had been the agreement and she'd been too impatient to stick to the plan. "I expected you to be out late, but no one is up at this hour." And she'd wanted to see him.

"Asher was."

True. "I saw him walk back toward the house. He didn't see me."

Jarvis scowled, clearly unhappy with her decision. "And if Silas had cried?" He closed his eyes, pinched the bridge of his nose. "Forget it. Mia, your dad looks healthy. I wouldn't call him happy, but he doesn't look weak or sick. He's upset about your disappearance and he misses you and Silas, but there's no sign that Regina is causing him any physical harm."

To her amazement, the surge of relief still ran second to her sizzling attraction for the man sitting across from her. He was helping her because being kind was part of his nature. Whether they indulged in hot kisses or not, he didn't change his stance on being involved with her and Silas beyond this crisis.

"My mind has been reeling all night, playing through worst-case scenarios," she confessed. "I know you didn't dare send a message while you were there."

"I reached out to you as soon as I could."

"I know. I knew you would." She rubbed at her temples, wishing she'd had the courage to kiss him when he'd been standing there in that towel, fresh from the shower. This was all on her, her fears and issues. She was a hypocrite, caving to fear and worry after everything she'd said to him about loss and grief and moving on to live again. "Call me paranoid. I couldn't shake the feeling that Regina had gotten to you." It had consumed her, pushed her to be reckless. If she'd lost Jarvis to her stepmother's games, she'd truly be alone in this mess. "And then you didn't act very excited about me dropping in."

"I'm not. Under normal circumstances it would be great, but taking this kind of chance, when Regina is actively searching for you, makes me worry. You were right that she's dangerous. I saw that tonight. The woman lies as easily as she breathes."

Mia closed her eyes. Jarvis had seen through the woman who consistently fooled everyone else. "What did she say?"

"Nothing that matters." His lip curled and he squinted one eye in an expression of extreme distaste. "The worst was watching her kiss your dad." He groaned. "Like they were alone. It was…"

"Awkward?"

He nodded. "And gross. I wanted to bleach my eyes." He blinked as if he could erase the images from his mind. "She is spreading rumors about you and how you left. I'm not sure who believes her."

Only one person mattered. "Dad believes her." She could see it in Jarvis's dark eyes. "Love is blind," she muttered. "I really should be used to this by now. I've been an idiot thinking anything would change."

"Has your dad sent any more texts?" Jarvis asked.

"No. He made some crack about being disappointed in me, didn't he?"

She could tell by the furrow between his eyebrows that she was right about that, too. "You don't have to protect me. He's been disappointed with me pretty much from the moment he met Regina."

"How did she get in his head so fast?" Jarvis asked. "I saw the painting of the two of you. You were close."

"That's why it hurts. It's like he just forgot everything he knew about me, everything we'd been through. Looking back, the timing was the biggest factor, I think. I was a teenager, poised for a normal rebellion, anyway. She made the most of it. He was lonely and she was perfect for him."

"She wasn't perfect for him if she didn't like you."

Mia's heart twirled in her chest. How did he always know exactly what to say? "She really doesn't like the idea of losing money if Silas and I are around to claim any inheritance. Catching her with another man at the country house is just an excuse for the timing." A shiver caught her as she watched Silas sleep. Her son was utterly defenseless.

"So catching her might have upped her time line," he said. "Didn't they have a prenup?"

She shook her head. "Dad's will was amended to provide for her and she simpered and cooed that it was the perfect solution. Convinced him she was there for him, not the cash."

"He believed her?"

"He always does. She came to the marriage with a pretty hefty net worth. He had no reason to think she wasn't sincere." Silas shifted in his sleep and Jarvis reached over, rocking the car seat gently. "But she is greedy. She wants it all. However she gets us out of his life, she can then rework the will in her favor. And make herself a wealthy widow."

"Selina told me tonight that no man should underestimate a pretty face."

"She's not wrong." Mia grinned, thinking of Regina and Selina's long and strained friendship. "Were you everything Selina hoped for tonight? Tell me Regina was jealous."

"Yeah." He swallowed and shifted in the chair. "It worked."

"Has Selina booked you for an encore performance?" It wasn't easy to hide the jealousy creeping into her voice. If only she and Jarvis had met in a normal fashion, they might've had a chance.

"No." He stood. "Let's get you out of here before someone notices my truck is back. I'll follow you."

"You don't need to do that," she protested. "I know the way."

"I won't let you drive across the ranch alone again." He went to his dresser. "Don't argue," he said, returning to the table. He pulled on socks and running shoes. Hands braced on his knees, he looked at her. "Should I plan to stay over?"

"I, um." What a good question.

"Let's keep it simple. Yes or no, Mia."

There was nothing simple about his question or the answer she wanted to give. She watched him, wary as he moved in, resting a hand on the back of her chair, his gaze dark. He wasn't looming over her, but she felt surrounded, anyway. She breathed him in.

"Yes."

He caught her reply with a kiss, his lips tantalizing and teasing. There was none of the usual urgency this time. All that longing and need that had been ready to combust settled into a warm thrum low in her belly. The sense of incredible pleasure just waiting for the right moment rolled through her. His bed was only a few paces away, her son sound asleep.

He eased back without a word, his dark gaze unfathomable. She pressed her hands between her knees to keep from grabbing him and holding on for dear life. He made quick work of shoving clothing into a backpack and shrugging it over a shoulder. With a pair of boots in one hand, he plucked up the car seat as if it weighed mere ounces and declared himself ready to go.

She was ready, too. For far more than the drive across the ranch.

On the short drive out to the bunkhouse he'd turned into her safe haven, Mia thought of all the things she should say when they arrived. She should thank him for going with Selina tonight and checking in on her father.

He hadn't wanted to mingle with strangers tonight, but he had. For her. He was the first person in years to do something for her without expecting anything in return. Even her marriage had turned into a series of bargains and deals.

Silas stirred when they reached the refurbished bunkhouse and Jarvis volunteered to walk with him before he woke up all the way. The man looked damn perfect when he wasn't holding Silas, but when he did, white picket fences, Sunday dinners and holidays with Jarvis danced across her vision.

Technically, she didn't *need* a life partner; she wanted one. And now any future applicant for the role would have to measure up to the high standards Jarvis had set. It really was a shame she hadn't met him before marrying Roderick.

"What will you do with your day off tomorrow?" she said once Silas was out. She and Jarvis were stretched out on opposite bunks, but she was too wired to sleep.

"Dig," he said, grinning. "I'm planning to follow more of the research you came up with." His voice was a soft rumble through the dark space. "Maybe tomorrow will be the day we prove Isaiah wasn't hallucinating."

"I hope the family legend is true."

"If it is and I turn out to be the crazy rich owner of Triple R land, should I watch out for your pretty face?"

She laughed uncontrollably. The idea of her trapping him was so ridiculous. Her heart might be harboring fantasies, but she wasn't foolish enough to think they could come true. Jarvis had his own life, his own goals. She was a detour for him at best, no matter how those kisses made her feel.

As her giggles continued, he tugged her out of her bunk and over to his. "You'll wake the baby, shaking the bed that way." His breath was warm against the shell of her ear.

The contact quashed her humor instantly. She tried to hold herself away from him, but he wouldn't have it. Lying on his side, he pillowed her head on his biceps and pulled her back against his chest. With his mus-cled arm across her waist, his hips were snug against her bottom.

It was the coziest she'd been in ages. "You're better than a pregnancy pillow," she whispered.

"I don't want to know what that means," he said. "Go to sleep."

How could she possibly *sleep* when he surrounded her this way? "And if I can't?"

"Then odds are good we will definitely wake the baby." He nuzzled the back of her neck with his lips, soft, feathery touches that set her on fire.

"It'll be your fault," she teased. "You dragged me over here." She traced the bones and tendons in the hand that kept her snug against him.

"I dragged you over here to sleep." His thumb caressed the curve of her breast. "We can talk in the morning."

She wanted to talk now. Questions and wishes and what-ifs bounced around like popcorn through her mind. She knew what she wanted and knew that she was overthinking his every action, hopeful that he was changing his mind about what he wanted. From her, from life. From them.

Please, let there be a them.

Could there be anything here but wishful thinking on her side? He kept showing her this incredible tenderness and a protectiveness she could get used to. She never thought protectiveness would be a turn-on, but it ranked high on her list right now. Easy enough to explain that away because Regina threatened everything Mia held dear.

If her stepmother found out about Jarvis helping her, he would become a target. The idea made her queasy.

Shifting to talk with him, she realized his breath was deep and even and his hand was slack on her belly. He really was sleeping as soundly as the baby. The awareness delighted her. He trusted her. Resting her palm over his hand she held him close as an unprecedented contentment lulled her.

She'd always found the saying "home is where the heart is" trite. Here, in this modest bunkhouse surrounded by grassland, she was living it. Jarvis felt like home, the home she'd treasured before her mother had died. Back when the Graves family was strong and solid, and the house a haven where she was welcome to be herself.

If there was one thing she categorically resented

about Regina, it was the way she'd razed all those memories in favor of the "right" colors and "refreshing," updated style.

Mia dashed away a tear.

There had to be a way to knock the blinders from her father's eyes. Only when he saw Regina for the snake she was would Norton and Silas have a chance to know each other. Only then would their broken communication and crushed expectations have enough room to heal.

Chapter 9

Jarvis stopped digging long enough to swipe the sweat off his forehead. He was a fool for continuing this search on such a hot day. Opening another bottle of water, he considered calling it a day. Isaiah had waited years to tell him the whole story, assuming it was true. Another few months wouldn't change anything.

The day after the party, he'd eliminated one long stretch of possibilities that fitted Isaiah's story and the deed records for parcels less than a mile away from the warming hut. In the days since, he'd searched areas based on Mia's research and recommendations, hoping to find something conclusive. It was frustrating to know he could miss the box by only a few yards. Unless he brought out heavy equipment to turn over every square inch, he would have to settle for one average hole at a time.

From his back pocket, his phone chimed and he smiled when he recognized Mia's number. He slid the icon and said hello.

"Hi."

Her voice trembled on the single syllable and he froze. "What's wrong?" He tucked the phone between his chin and shoulder and started filling in the hole. He'd brought the horse this afternoon, enjoying the slower pace and the quiet solitude. Now he regretted the decision. It would take him forever to reach her if she was in trouble.

"I'm okay," she said in a rush. "There's another text from my dad a-and I'm letting it upset me. Sorry for bugging you."

"You never bug me," he said. It was more than reflex; it was the truth. He'd have to wrestle with that later. "Was it another demand to come home?"

"Yeah."

A few days after the party, Norton had reached out to Mia, surprising them both. Jarvis wanted to be encouraged, but he was guarded. When he was talking to Norton that night, it had seemed as if Mia's dad had all but given up on seeing his daughter and grandson again. They suspected Regina was behind the new text messages somehow, but they weren't sure how to respond.

No matter how he much he assured her of Spencer's discretion, Mia wasn't ready for him to share any of this with his brother. She was too fearful her dad would pay the price.

"No email, not a phone call?"

"No." She sighed. "I'm being silly and impractical to take it at face value."

"You're being a hopeful daughter," he said. In the

background he heard Silas gurgling. "How's the little man today?"

"Goofy." This time he heard a smile in her voice.

Since the night of the party, when she'd let him hold her while they slept, he was getting better and better at reading her, in person and over the phone. He spent most of his nights with her on that narrow bunk. On the rare occasions when he couldn't get out to her, he missed her and the baby more than he was ready to admit.

Sleeping beside her didn't eliminate the clawing desperation to make love with her, but it was better than not touching her at all. Although she'd made her willingness to get physical with him clear, he resisted taking that leap while her life was still in turmoil.

"How goes the search?" she asked.

"I came up empty here," he said. "It's too hot anyway, though it might be worth a closer look tomorrow. You'll be okay a while? I need to get back, stable Duke and clean up. I'll be there as soon as possible with dinner."

"I'll be fine," she replied. "Thanks, Jarvis. I really appreciate you."

Appreciation was safe. Smart. So why did he want her to say something more meaningful? He hadn't said anything of the kind to her. "Text me if something sounds good."

"Okay."

After ending the call, he stowed the shovel and climbed back into the saddle. He urged the horse into an easy canter, eager to see Mia's face. And the text message. When he reached the stable, he forced himself to take his time with Duke. Routine tasks kept him grounded. Always had. He'd been one of the weird kids who liked doing dishes and vacuuming because it gave his mind time to wander. It really shouldn't have surprised him that this straightforward life as a cowboy would fit so well.

Not easy, not simple, but straightforward.

Mia was tied to all of it. And she shouldn't be. She kept researching the questions in the Colton family tree and land records while he dug up small pockets of the Triple R. She wasn't doing anything he couldn't have done alone, but it was going a whole lot faster with her as his partner. They had a system, a friendship with the promise of heat, more than a relationship.

He reminded himself of that fact every single day. He wasn't relationship material, though this time with her and the baby eroded his confidence in that theory. Her sunny outlook and persistent hope in the face of her stepmother's manipulations made him reconsider options he'd sworn off years ago. Her philosophy challenged him and made it increasingly difficult to remember why he shouldn't follow the example his siblings set, taking chances on love and life.

The difference, he reminded himself, was crystal clear. Eventually, Mia would go back to her life and raise her son. They wouldn't need him to bring her groceries and supplies or watch their backs. Eventually, a woman like Mia would find the right man, a man who believed in love and plans, and all the possibilities of the future rather than all the pitfalls.

As nice as he felt with her, he knew himself. He enjoyed her and this interlude in part *because* it couldn't be permanent. Women from Mia's background didn't look for the long-term gig with cowboys who were raised on the lower end of middle class. She came from money, was used to luxury.

Sure he'd made a name for himself in business for a time, but he'd tossed that reputation aside for a quest to prove his Colton name was as valuable as those who sat around the Colton Oil boardroom.

As he took the older truck into town, he was grateful it was still here. Since coming to the ranch, he'd become fascinated with broken things, things that could be fixed with time and patience and elbow grease. He'd assumed an operation with Payne Colton at the helm wouldn't bother with repairs, tossing out anything that didn't function and replacing it with something new. But he'd discovered that Asher had an eye for profit that included being practical and he didn't throw money or men around without careful thought and planning.

Driving toward Lucia's Italian Café to pick up a pizza, he thought about taking Mia on a real date. Mustang Valley was a step down from parties in New York City or Paris. Still, he'd enjoy going out, just the two of them, or going somewhere with Silas. Dancing could be fun. Or maybe a baseball game, in honor of how they'd met, he mused as he parked and headed for the café.

Distracted, he didn't notice Regina walking over until she was practically on top of him.

She raked him with a hungry look that chilled his skin. "Jasper, isn't it?"

"Jarvis," he corrected again, smiling politely. He wouldn't let her feel like she had any advantage. "Nice to see you again."

"You're certainly casual this evening. How…rugged."

"Everyone needs a bit of downtime," he replied diplomatically.

She emitted a tiny, brittle laugh. "I suppose so." Something was off. She didn't appear as polished as she'd been at the party. "Is Selina meeting you? I'd love to say hello."

"Not tonight," he said. "I'll pass that on when I see her."

Regina's delicate eyebrows arched. "So the two of you aren't exclusive." She inched close enough that the skirt of her dress brushed around his jeans. "That's fascinating."

"I'm flattered you think so." He didn't add any of the warmth or charm that consistently amused Selina. "Give my best to your husband."

She blocked him when he moved toward the pickup counter. "Norton mentioned you," she said, her gaze searching him for any reaction. "After the party," she clarified. "He was sure he'd met you before."

"I have one of those faces," he said.

"No." She tilted her head, studying him. "You really don't."

"My brother is on the police force here in town," he said. "People confuse us all the time." It wasn't true, but she didn't know that. This time he managed to sidle past her to the counter.

Regina hemmed him in. "Maybe I should speak with your brother."

"About what?"

"Our missing daughter." She enunciated each word.

He swallowed the urge to correct her. Regina had no right to claim any piece of Mia. "You mentioned her at the party. Still no word?"

She clutched the pendant on her necklace. "It's tragic the way he misses her and our grandson. I'm sure she's just acting out, but with every day that passes, Norton worries that she's actually gotten herself into trouble."

The kid at the counter called his name. "I'm sure Spencer can help. Good luck," he said, using the bulky pizza box to give him some distance as he scooted around her. "No one in town wants to see Norton unhappy."

It was the only warning he dared to give her, since he was supposed to be just Selina's current fling. Dressed as he was tonight, she'd probably figured out he worked at the Triple R. How else would Selina have met him? There was no reason for her to think Mia was hiding at the ranch, but he sure didn't want Regina coming by and poking around.

Jarvis hated making Mia wait, but he refused to take a chance on Regina having him followed. He carried the pizza into his room and dropped it on the table. He wanted to call, but he sent a text so no one could possibly overhear him.

He was officially paranoid.

Got hung up. Will be there in a bit.

Her reply came back immediately.

Can't wait.

Pacing like a wildcat, he forced himself to sit down and think it through. What did he know and what could help Mia?

There was no reason for Regina to assume he had any connection to Mia. Regina had been at Lucia's without Norton, making this a prime opportunity for Mia to reach out to her father. He sent her another quick text suggesting she call her dad, explaining why.

If they could just find a way to get Norton somewhere safe long enough to trap Regina with that disgusting video, this entire mess could be over. Then Mia could explain everything to his brother and Spencer could take it from there.

He really wanted this to be done—for her.

Mia stared at the text message, her earlier worry replaced by hope. Jarvis wanted her to call her dad while Regina was too far away to interfere. What would she even say to him?

It didn't matter—she had to act. She dialed quickly, swearing when it went straight to Norton's voice mail. She didn't dare leave a message, certain her stepmother had a way to review those as well. Instead, on a hunch, she dialed her dad's office.

"Norton Graves."

Her knees went weak at the sound of his voice. "Dad. Hi."

"Mia? Where are you?"

His shock shamed her. She should have done this weeks ago. "I'm, um, away," she said. "Visiting friends in Tahoe." She didn't have any friends in Tahoe that Regina could hurt.

"Without listing the country house? Mia." She could picture him turning toward the panoramic view outside his window, his gray eyebrows pulled into a disapproving scowl. "That's disappointing."

Of course it was. "I did meet with the buyer I mentioned. No offer yet. Then I had a problem with my phone and didn't see your messages until today," she improvised, babbling. "I didn't mean to worry you."

"Messages? Honestly, Mia, you've been so flighty I didn't bother reaching out."

A chill slid over her skin. So all of those messages were more traps set by Regina.

"As Regina reminded me," Norton continued, "you should be focused on the baby. Our contract with you expires at the end of next month, anyway. I'll just relist it with someone who has the time and focus."

"Dad." Tears clogged her throat.

"Enough business. We both know things don't always work out. You'll land on your feet. Tell me about my grandson."

She shared the latest milestones, including how Silas was smiling often, enjoying time on his belly, and babbling. "You'll see it all for yourself soon," she promised.

"I want to believe—" Another voice interrupted and she heard him give her name. "Mia? Regina just brought over dinner. We'll have to finish this later."

"Sure," she managed. "We love you," she added only to see her screen flashing that the call ended.

Her nerves rattling, she berated herself for failing. That had been her chance to explain it all and she'd blown it. It was like getting tossed back in time to her teenage self. No authority, no influence with the one adult in her life who mattered.

She sat down at the computer, hoping Jarvis would be here soon. It was time for her to either give up and leave Mustang Valley or call Regina's bluff. With Silas still sleeping and no sign of Jarvis, she reviewed the notes she'd made since catching Regina at the country house.

She'd carefully documented every threat, direct or

implied, against her, her son and her father. She'd down-
loaded her call and message logs as a precaution, taking
screenshots as well. Over the past weeks, she'd spent
hours poring over Regina's social media posts, looking
for any pictures of the man she'd been cheating with,
the same man Jarvis had seen at the courthouse.

Jarvis had urged her time and again to speak at
length with his brother and let the police set up a secret
meeting with her dad. It was time to use that connection and create an advantage. With her report complete,
she uploaded it to a cloud file until she and Jarvis could
decide how to proceed.

They'd been out here, playing an odd version of
house and becoming something more than friends and
not quite lovers. Eventually, someone else from the Triple R crew would wander out this way, and then where
would she go?

She didn't want to *go* anywhere. Since leaving Roderick, she'd planned on creating a real home for her and
Silas. A home close enough to her friends and father,
right here in Mustang Valley. Free to be the mother
and professional woman she'd always envisioned. She
wanted to zip into town for business meetings or play-
dates, or even enjoy a butterfly-inducing date with a
certain sexy cowboy. Whatever simmered between
them should have a chance to grow once she was out
from under this mess with her stepmother.

She'd find a way to triumph over Regina's plans.
Silas deserved all the love, family and roots she could
give him.

At last she heard the truck. Her heart skipped ahead
and her stomach rumbled. She was hungry for dinner,
but hungrier for the man delivering it. Pausing just long

enough to be sure it was Jarvis, she dashed outside and gave him a hug.

"Did it go well?" he asked, his arms coming around her.

"No." She pressed her cheek to his solid chest, taking the comfort he offered. "He's still effectively brainwashed, but hearing his voice helped me. Thank you."

He smoothed a hand over her hair, then tipped up her chin and gave her a soft kiss. The tears she'd held back escaped now as his tenderness surrounded her. She forced herself to smile before she turned into a watering pot. "You smell like pizza."

He grinned. "Lucia's. Sorry I didn't get it to you hot."

She released him long enough to take the pizza from the car. "Smells heavenly, hot or cold. Let's eat."

"One thing," he said, following her into the bunkhouse. "Those texts weren't from your dad, were they?"

She shook her head, temper and sadness battling within her heart. "I knew it and still it's a gut punch."

"I'm sorry, sweetheart."

The apology and endearment, though he'd said it before, washed over her like a cool breeze. She tried not to read too much into it but might as well have been trying to hold back a sunrise. There were so few things in recent weeks that made her smile and gave her joy. She wouldn't ignore a single one of those gifts.

They ate their fill of pizza while she told him about the call and the file she'd compiled and uploaded.

"So the messages were definitely a setup," he said, clearing the table. He returned to his chair and reached over, covering her hands with his. "That can't be easy to digest. What if I went to your dad's office to speak with him? Or asked Spencer to deliver him a message?"

"A policeman walking into an investment-banking firm doesn't send the right message. And Regina is mean, but not stupid. If you walked in there, she'd storm the ranch just like you were worried about at first."

"Fair." He stretched his neck. "If you trust someone else, I'll go to them."

"I'll think about it," she said. Silas stirred and she opened her laptop. "Go ahead and take a look at the file. Make sure there isn't something else your brother might need."

"He's the cop, not me." He read through the file, swearing occasionally under his breath while she fed her son. "These threats need to be on an official record somewhere," he said at last. "If you're ready, why don't I take this to my brother and let him decide what comes next. I visit him often enough at the station that it's not suspicious."

"Okay."

"Okay?" Jarvis echoed. "Just like that?"

"Isn't it past time?" She sighed. "Hearing Dad's voice flipped a switch for me. As things stand right now, I lose him either way. By hiding or pushing Regina to do her worst. It's a huge risk, and it scares the hell out of me, but I'd rather lose him while trying to win, than just roll over."

Once Silas had a full tummy, he didn't want to settle down. He kept turning toward Jarvis's voice as they talked, smiling and babbling and making Mia wish for so many impossible things.

Jarvis had found her while looking for his roots. He didn't have family in mind for his future. She respected that, she did, but Silas was the next generation and that meant making plans and building up hope for the days and years ahead.

Her internal debate must have translated to Silas. Her son was happy enough but clearly had no intention of going back to sleep. "At least he isn't screaming this time," she said. "But it promises to be a long night."

"We could take him for a drive," Jarvis suggested.

She glanced over and noticed he was serious. "Where?"

He hitched a shoulder. "Around the back roads. Don't babies like that kind of thing?"

"They do." Her foolish heart fluttered. Had Jarvis been reading up on baby care, or did he remember that about Silas in particular? "He fell asleep when I drove to see you after Regina's party."

"Then let's go."

They took his truck because the car seat bracket was already installed. He drove because he knew both the truck and the area better than she did. That left her free to pop Silas's pacifier back into his mouth whenever he spit it out.

"Far cry from Selina's Jag," he said as they reached the paved road that bordered this side of the ranch. "She let me open it up on this road."

"How fun for you."

"It was. I got it to ninety-five before I brought myself back down to earth. Selina giggled like a teenager."

"I bet. Have you always wanted a sports car?"

"I used to dream of driving a Mercedes," he said. "That daydream is a rite of passage for business majors."

"One quick drag at ninety-five cured you?" She studied his handsome profile, wondering what he wasn't saying.

His lips tilted up on one side. "I wouldn't say that. The truck is comfortable. It suits me better right now."

"Well, I'm sure you look just as good driving the truck as you did driving Selina's car." She admired his capable hands on the wheel, wished she had the guts to ask him to put those hands on her.

At last Silas fell asleep and they turned back toward the bunkhouse. "Oh, look, a shooting star." She leaned forward, pointing through the windshield.

He craned his neck and then sat back in the seat, a smile on his face. "Better make a wish."

She didn't tell him she already had.

Back on Triple R land, he drove on past the bunkhouse. The tires bumped over the ground, but he kept on going until at last he stopped and cut the truck lights. Looking proud of himself, he rolled down the windows, allowing the cooler night air to flow through the truck.

"What are we doing?" she asked.

"It's a surprise." He hopped out of the car and pulled a blanket from behind his seat. "Come on." That sexy, irrepressible grin flashed. "If Silas wakes up, we'll drive some more."

He managed to lower the tailgate in near silence and she gawked while he spread out a blanket over the truck bed. Then he walked back to where she waited and extended a hand.

She placed her palm in his and his fingers curled around her as he assisted her up. Into the truck bed and his strong embrace. His arms banded around her, his fingers locked together at the base of her spine, just above the curve of her backside.

His lips touched hers softly, the urgency building with each heartbeat, each dreamy touch as her lips parted and his tongue twined with hers. A wicked, eager thrill rushed over her, from her scalp to her toes and she moaned against his mouth, wanting so much more than she had a right to ask for.

She longed for a deeper connection, more than these tantalizing kisses. Sex. Affection. Love.

He'd demonstrated such warm affection for her and she could probably persuade him to have sex with her, though she knew it wouldn't feel complete without love. Maybe that made her old-fashioned, but she had endured enough disappointment. She eased away, resting her head on his shoulder and her hand over his thudding heart.

He gave her a squeeze. "Let's watch the stars," he said.

She peeked through the window, confirming that Silas was still asleep, then she and Jarvis stretched out side by side in the pickup bed.

As stars shot through the dark velvet sky, Mia's thoughts meandered through the past and present. Her husband hadn't loved her enough to adjust and adapt when she got pregnant. And here she was with Jarvis, who demonstrated wonderful care for her and Silas, yet claimed he wasn't cut out for family life.

She watched another star fall and made another wish, this time for one more season of the type of happiness she'd known before her mother had died.

"Did you make a wish?" he asked.

"I can't seem to stop," she admitted. "You?"

"Not really. I stopped making wishes when I was a kid."

"After your parents died?" She shifted to her side

so she could see him as well as another section of the starry sky over his shoulder.

"I think it was later," he said, his wistful tone breaking her heart. "Our aunt couldn't seem to give us anything beyond the basics of food, shelter and clothing."

"I'm sorry for your loss, Jarvis."

"Life can play dirty," he said. "Then and now, I think we were all grateful to stay together. That singular factor saved us more than anything else."

They were quiet then, content to rest with only the sounds of Silas's soft snores and the occasional hoot of an owl.

"It's peaceful out here," she said softly, not wanting to shatter the spell. "It makes me feel small and gives me hope at the same time."

"Hope to go home?"

"Well, yes. You know I want my life back." They watched another streak of starlight. "I also hope to find someone to love and build a family with. I've always craved that special bond my mom and dad shared. They were so in love."

"Love?" He shifted to stare at her, incredulous. "You still believe in love after everything you've been though?"

"Yes. Every time I look at Silas," she said with confidence.

"Oh, sure. That's different."

Was he almost agreeing with her? Hope flared that he might defeat the grip of his past. "How can love be different from love?"

He immediately pulled back, from her or the conversation, far enough that the cool air moved between

them. It was mere inches, but it felt like a canyon holding them apart while she waited for his answer.

"You know what I mean."

She was so tempted to comfort him, to gloss it over.
If she did, the opportunity might never come around
again. Boldly, she said, "I'd like to."

He sighed, surprising her by pulling her close. "Aside
from my brother and sister, love has let me down every
time," he admitted. "Mom and Dad loved us and it
didn't save them."

"Everyone dies." She watched another star fall. "*Not*
loving someone won't keep you safe, either."

"I don't understand you. You elevate optimism to
an art form."

"How can I not?" Snuggling into his warmth, she
searched for the right words. "I've seen true love first-
hand. So have you. Granted, I settled for an illusion of
the real thing. Roderick loved the image of us. He didn't
love *me*. Love is adaptable. Steadfast and devoted, in
any facet or form, love sticks."

He shifted again but didn't release her. Maybe she
was getting through. If she could do nothing else for
him, she'd give him a chance to heal from his devastating losses. "Whatever you call it, loyalty or responsibility or commitment, you show love, Jarvis. It might not
be the romantic facet of love, but love is there, in your
choices and your actions."

His body tensed. "I really want to disagree with you."

She tapped her shoe to his boot. "Why argue when
we could enjoy the stars?"

Giving her shoulder a squeeze, he relaxed and they
watched the sky until her eyelids were drooping. "You

should take us back," she said, sitting up a bit. "We all need some rest."

"In a minute." He laced his fingers with hers, his face tipped up to the sky.

"Do you know your constellations?" she asked.

"That's Cowboy 101," he said.

"Really?"

"No." He bent his head and kissed her. "But these views are a big perk on night shifts."

"You love being a cowboy."

"Does that bother you?" he asked.

"No." She'd spent her life around powerful business-men and been groomed and educated so she could hold her own in any setting, social or professional. Her time around barns had included the glossy, luxury side of ranch operations, not the more functional side. She liked what Jarvis did, the obvious pride he took in his work, and the honest-work scent of sunshine and sweat that lingered on his skin after a long day outside. "Does it bother you?"

"Not a bit. I don't have any desire to go back to an office, whether or not I find evidence that this ranch belongs to my side of the family."

"So you'll work for Asher forever?"

"Not forever." He took his eyes off the sky and shot her a confident look. "I'm still learning. He's an excel-lent manager on all fronts."

"That shouldn't come as a surprise," she said. "He has a tremendous reputation."

"We didn't exactly run in the same circles, Mia. We still don't. Not yet, anyway." He pushed a hand through his hair, mussing the dark locks. "More than once I've thought, if this place is mine, I'd find a way to keep him. If it's not and I buy my own ranch, I might lure him away."

His low laugh rolled over her, as warm as melted chocolate and equally as tempting. What would that sound feel like under her hands? Her mouth watered and she yanked her wayward thoughts back into line.

"I could broker a land deal for you," she teased. Being here, feeling safe with him was such a treat. But a life in hiding couldn't last. Silas would need his regular checkups. Regina might as well stake out the pediatrician's office if she wanted to catch Mia and make good on her threats.

Mia watched the shadowy scenery on the drive back to the bunkhouse. She could make a new life elsewhere, but with Regina's threats looming over her head, worry would be a constant companion. That was no life for her son and she couldn't bear the thought of leaving her father to cope with Regina's devious nature alone. The woman was greedy and Mia had no doubt she'd continue to take whatever she wanted, whenever she chose—even Norton's life.

Tomorrow, she'd allow Jarvis to bring everything to his brother on her behalf.

Jarvis rested quietly in the bunk. Mia's sweet curves were pressed up against him and she was out. Looked like fresh air and car rides were effective sleep-enhancers for mothers, too.

Unfortunately, he couldn't stop thinking about her persistent faith in love.

After everything she'd been through, she wasn't just wishing for love; she was determined to create it, to celebrate it as though it was a reliable emotion. She wouldn't find or create love with him, obviously.

He was temporary.

That rankled more than it should, considering he wasn't in the market for a family, anyway.

He'd been telling himself this was about protecting the ranch, protecting his potential legacy and treating Mia as he would want someone to treat his sister. But he didn't feel anything brotherly toward the woman in his arms. No, he felt invested. Attached.

That attachment went beyond uncomfortable and straight into dangerous. To her. The only love he trusted, the only relationships that hadn't ended in disaster, were those with his brother and sister. And even that dynamic had changed since they were both engaged and planning weddings now. Those right and true relationships nudged Jarvis a bit more to the fringe.

He wasn't resentful, exactly. He was experiencing what might be best described as envy nipping at his heels. And bafflement. How could Spencer and Bella take the chance? What did they have that Jarvis lacked?

Oh, he could go and ask. His siblings would listen, try to help. Even if they could help him figure out the mess in his own head, he wasn't in the mood for lectures on his choices about business, ranching or women.

He breathed in the soft clove fragrance of Mia's shampoo, and pushed the envy and pointless questions aside. There would be plenty of time to sort out his issues once Mia and Silas were safe and gone.

Chapter 10

Mia read the text message from her father and pocketed her phone while she considered her reply. She'd brought Silas outside for an early morning walk while she tried not to think about Jarvis going to share the ugliest parts of her life with his brother later today. This time, she thought the sweet request for an update on the baby was probably from Norton and not one of Regina's tricks. She couldn't imagine her stepmother being kind even as a ploy.

Only last month, she'd walked with Silas through the neighborhood where she'd grown up, or through the park in town, her son in his stroller. Today she carried him in the sling, not straying too far from the remote Triple R bunkhouse, not another person in sight.

The warm sunlight painted the grassy pastures and highlighted the mountains in the distance, framed by the cloudless, blue sky. The picturesque setting made her feel like everything would eventually work out.

With a baby nearly three months old, she'd expected to be taking meetings and calls and building up a solid network for her new real-estate career by now. Instead she was still out here, hiding from her stepmother's threats.

Although she'd used her time to keep up with properties and trends in the area, she'd had far more fun helping Jarvis with his history and search. It was an easier task because she didn't have a stake in whatever he found. The deeds, acreage claims, and sales from Herman and Eugene's generation were convoluted. With luck, if Jarvis found the box, those conflicting documents might be explained.

He'd absolutely won her over with his determination to keep searching, even after she'd found documents on file that Eugene and his descendants came by the property legally, negotiating back and forth with T. Ainsley. For a man who claimed he didn't believe in family, Jarvis was going all out to prove there was merit behind his grandfather's stories. She hoped that whatever he found would be exactly what he needed for his heart and his future in ranching.

Her phone chimed again. Another text, this time a direct request for an update on the progress on the listing. Why had her father told her he wasn't going to talk business if he didn't mean it? And why had she lied about working with a buyer?

"Mommy never should've lied," she said to Silas. "Let this be a lesson—mommies and daddies always find out the truth."

Daddies. Oh, how she wanted a daddy for her son

someday. When she thought of Silas calling a man daddy, having a father figure to emulate, Jarvis's face came to mind. It was ridiculous, putting that face to her fantasy, yet she couldn't seem to remove his dark eyes, square jaw and lopsided grin from the picture.

She might've lied to her dad about the buyer, but she couldn't lie to herself about Jarvis. Her heart was firmly planted in his reluctant hands and it might as well stay there for now. As long as he didn't have any idea and she didn't blurt out that she was in love with him, her heart would be safe enough.

She rubbed her nose to Silas's and then faced her phone. What could she tell her dad that would appease him and not be a lie? She quickly let him know that the first offer was lower than his bare minimum. As in zero at the moment. She followed that with a query about why he was in such a hurry to liquidate the property.

Countless happy memories with her parents and later friends had been made at that house. After Regina's intrusive entrance into her life, the country home and the surrounding property remained the site of fond moments with her dad, hosting clients and family friends.

She couldn't imagine a reason—other than a wife who loved to shop and redecorate—why her father would need a quick influx of cash. Her hands went cold. This must be Regina's doing. She could easily picture her stepmother hovering over his shoulder and pestering him to push her. Just to flush her out of hiding.

Would the woman never be satisfied? Of course not. Regina thrived on control, from the suits and ties her father wore to the office, to the amount he spent on his weekend golf trips, all the way down to Christmas gifts.

His reply came back that his only concern was for her

and the baby. Well, that made two of them. The somewhat comforting message was trumped by the next.

You can't be in business if you aren't doing business.

She couldn't argue with that, so she didn't reply.

Come on back, Mia. We'll have lunch at the club and talk things out in person.

If only she could be sure Regina wouldn't be there, ready to poison her salad or snatch Silas. She turned off her phone and kept walking.

Her father had been an integral part of her life. Being separated from him and keeping her son away made her heart ache. Norton, who managed fortunes during the day, had helped her with homework and even coached her youth soccer teams when she was young.

Until Regina had changed everything.

"Maybe I didn't want to share," she admitted to her drowsy son. "Maybe your grandpa could've listened to my concerns or done a better job of protecting our relationship." And maybe they were both human. Her father, her hero, had put more stock in the sniping observations of his new wife than the daughter he supposedly treasured. Mia, frustrated, had only made things worse.

"I won't be perfect," she murmured, "Obviously," she added, her gaze drifting to the mountain range in the distance. A perfect mother would surely know how to get out of this mess. "I do promise to listen, to consider what's best for *you* in every decision we face." She hoped she could keep that promise.

"It takes two people to wreck a good relationship,"

she told Silas. Looking into his sweet face now, it was impossible to think of a day when they would argue, when hurtful words might fly fast and mean, undermining trust.

She wondered if the lunch invitation was worth the risk. If she went, she could talk with her dad about the house and the baby. They could walk the office space he'd recommended to her last month. They could cover everything except his wife's cheating. The temptation to accept filled her and she was doubly grateful she'd turned off the phone.

She finished her walk with Silas, passing Jarvis's truck. Inexplicably antsy, it was all she could do to settle the baby in his seat for the rest of his morning nap, rather than drive out to where she expected Jarvis to be searching today.

He hadn't seemed to mind when she'd met up a time or two before, but Mia really needed to exert some force on her future. She sat down at the table and opened her laptop. Her dad made a good point. She wouldn't have a business if she didn't *conduct* business. She did have connections with people familiar with the country house. An additional advantage was her knowledge of the people most likely to have the interest as well as the means to invest in the property.

She drafted an email with one target in mind, adding a few pictures she knew would entice. If she brokered a private sale, it would give the lies she'd told her father credence. Not only that, but the commission would be a financial cushion she could use to relocate.

Roderick had joked about buying the country house on his very first visit. More than once, while they dated, she'd been sure he stayed with her simply for the long weekends they spent out there.

Once she'd hit Send, detailing the ideal offer, she fixed herself a cup of tea. She should've done this first. If she had, she never would've found Regina with another man. Instead she'd been determined to prove she had skills, not just connections; that she was beautiful, but had a brain, too. Of course, she hadn't been eager to speak with her ex about anything. Now she was desperate.

Weary of her own problems, she turned her attention back to Jarvis's search and refused to watch the clock. With the names from the land deeds, she continued to wade through history, pleased to discover more records about when various parcels of the current ranch were purchased from the government or landowners who'd given up on taming the territory.

Jarvis worked his way through his daily assignments, not looking forward to going to Selina's house again. He knew Asher passed those calls to him, hoping the woman would open up more about the leverage she had on Payne. He wanted to help his cousin, but Jarvis couldn't bring himself to flirt with the woman anymore. One night playing the role of sexy accessory had been more than enough.

After spending time with Mia, Selina's presence felt even more cloying. According to Asher, Selina had a problem with the lighting on her patio. He hoped it was something simple as he cantered across the ranch from the stables to her house on Duke.

"Jarvis!" Selina called as he looped the reins over

the fence rail edging her patio. "You always know just how to dress. Can I get you a drink, cowboy?"

It was the opening Asher would expect him to sidle right through. He gave her his best smile and tipped his hat. "Better if we wait until I know what the trouble is," he said.

"The trouble is you won't drink with me." She winked and then gave him what he assumed was supposed to be a sexy pout. She touched him as if she had the right, her glossy, hot-pink fingernails tracking the line of his forearm. Her eyes were clear, despite the drink in her hand. Too bad. If she was drunk, it might be easier to distract her away from him.

He turned his thoughts to Mia, but that only made it worse. He'd rather be with her than anywhere else and he was stuck in the female equivalent of a tar pit.

"What do you need, Selina?" He didn't have much time before he was supposed to meet Spencer at the police station and he didn't want to be late. Mia needed him to have that meeting so she could get back to her life. "Asher mentioned something about a lighting issue?"

"Did someone put a burr under your saddle, cowboy?" She walked around him and made a humming noise as she eyed his backside. "Nothing obvious. Want me to take a closer look?"

He moved out of reach before she sank those hot-pink claws into his backside.

"You're no fun today."

"Lots of work on the schedule." He hoped to get through it all before his meeting in town so he'd still have some time to poke around a new site for Herman's box.

Selina sipped whatever was in her glass and arched a perfect eyebrow. What had Payne ever seen in her? From one moment to the next, her entire body language changed. The overblown flirt was gone and a sensible woman in her place.

"It is the lighting." She flipped the switch near the outdoor kitchen. "That section in the middle is broken or whatever." She gestured with her glass.

Why did people want to ruin a gorgeous view of a starry sky with strands of white lights? "I'll take care of it. Do you have a ladder?"

"I thought you came fully equipped," she said.

He laughed, despite himself. "Stepladder, Selina." They kept basic tools here for times just like this one.

She made a moody noise and cocked a hip. He didn't take the bait. With a shake of her head, she set her glass on the nearest table and sauntered toward the storage closet cleverly built into one of the stone pillars that framed the outdoor kitchen.

"You're seeing someone new?" she asked, opening the door and holding it for him.

The question set his teeth on edge. "I've been working too hard to see much of anyone," he replied.

"Oh, that's not what I've heard at all."

He ignored her, more than happy to use the stepladder as a shield between them.

"I heard some new cowgirl has you wrapped around her little finger." She crooked her own pinkie and wiggled it at him.

Cowgirl, no. Mia was more like a big-league hitter. He grinned, thinking of Mia and the stick she'd been all too willing to employ.

Her lips formed a surprised O. "It's true." She lifted

her glass. "Cheers and congratulations to the happy couple."

Jarvis climbed the stepladder to look over the wiring for this section of the string lights. "You don't sound all that sincere," he commented absently.

"I'd be less disappointed if you tell me it's a non-exclusive kind of thing."

It wasn't. Well, technically it wasn't anything. But if it became something, he wouldn't be sharing Mia with anyone. He just shook his head.

"Come on, Jarvis," she cajoled. "I could use a little romantic excitement, even if it is vicarious."

He tested each bulb within reach, pausing to look down at her. She was staring at his crotch. *Ew.* "Are you running low on gossip fuel?" He climbed down, moved the ladder and climbed up again.

"Knowledge is power," she said, examining her nails now. "I shared my secrets with you."

"Did you?"

"Didn't I?" She swirled the golden liquid in her glass.

So that was the reason she'd called. She was worried she'd said too much after the party. Being Selina, she would assume that he'd do what she'd done and use any secrets to her advantage. Or maybe she really was more worried about sharing juicy gossip with her friends at the next Sunday brunch.

He moved the ladder again and waited until she met his gaze. "You didn't."

What might have been relief flashed across her flawless features. "Tell me your secret, anyway." She leaned in on the other side of the ladder. "I know you can't possibly be serious about this cowboy nonsense."

He gave her an innocent smile. "A real man doesn't

joke about boots and belt buckles. Besides, being a cowboy means helpin' purdy ladies like you." He laid it on thick, hamming it up and earning her spiky laughter.

He found the problem at last. Where the nonfunctioning section connected to the previous strand, the plug had been loosened just enough to break the connection. He made the fix and verified everything worked properly again. He supposed he'd let her get away with the fake call, but it put him on edge.

"All better." He folded the ladder, keeping it between them. "Anything else, Selina?"

Color flared on her cheeks and her gaze roamed over his face. "You know how to make a woman feel special," she said. "I enjoyed our evening at Norton and Regina's party."

Just hearing Regina's name made him angry. He smothered the reaction, not willing to give Selina any reason to ask more questions. Crossing his wrists over the top of the folded stepladder, he just waited for her to spell out what she wanted. She watched his hands and licked her lips. The woman was an operator who believed he would just fall in line for the chance to land in her bed.

Asher, knowing nothing about his feeling for Mia, would want Jarvis to dive in. Although he admired his boss man, respected him and sympathized with him, he couldn't even pretend it was an option. No matter what kind of blight she was to the family, there were lines Jarvis wouldn't cross. "There is someone," he said. "Just met her last weekend."

She stroked one perfectly manicured fingertip over his banged-up knuckles. "Then it's not serious."

Jarvis chuckled at the blatant invitation. "Serious

enough." He eased just out of her reach. "Any other *maintenance* concerns?"

Her lips curved into what might be the first genuine smile he'd seen. "Not today. Thank you, Jarvis."

"You're welcome." He stowed the stepladder and headed out with a tip of his hat.

"Whoever she is, she's a lucky woman," Selina called after him. She strolled over, shading her eyes as she looked up at him sitting in the saddle.

He winked. "I'll tell her you said so." He cantered away, grateful for the wind on his face and the raw power of the horse under him.

Selina was treacherous with a hefty streak of pathetic. He supposed if he found something that negated the deed of sale, he could make Asher's day by ousting the woman. Somehow, he didn't think it was exactly the solution his boss was hoping for.

When the house was well out of sight, he slowed his horse and took the time to update the task schedule. A couple of items had been added to his list, including another pass over the fence near the warming hut where Mia had first hidden. He made a note to handle that task.

Thinking about the timing and knowing his brother, he looped Duke's reins around the nearest paddock fence while he went into his room to call Spencer.

"Catch any criminals today?" he asked when Spencer picked up.

"Better than wrangling steaks in progress," his brother replied.

Jarvis opened his laptop and then accessed the cloud file Mia had prepared. "The cattle are far more personable than your criminals."

"Probably true. You calling to bail on our meeting?"

"Sort of." Jarvis sighed. "There's a lot going on out here today. I'm sending you some information. If you want me to come in after you read it, I will."

"You're making me nervous."

"Not intentionally." He was nervous as a cat after bumping into Regina in town. "I'd rather not come to the station. Read what I'm sending and then give me a call about how you want to handle it."

"What kind of trouble are you in?"

The worst kind, he thought. He was in over his head over a woman, ready to do anything to make sure Mia and Silas came out of this on top. "Read the info. I've gotta get back to work."

Outside, he scratched Duke behind the ears and gave him a carrot before swinging up into the saddle. They headed out to the fence line on the to-do list, passing the various pastures and buildings. Other than the Colton mansion near the front gate and the necessary updates, he didn't think the ranch had changed much since Herman was burying the box that was probably long gone.

The voices of his siblings echoed in his head, scolding him for taking such a wild detour from his business career. He couldn't explain his faith in Isaiah's tales to himself; how was he supposed to explain it to them?

Besides, he expected them to accept and understand him, especially during times like this one, when he didn't fully understand himself. That was the perk of sharing a womb. Or it should've been. Had been in the past. Since losing their parents, the triplets had dealt with life as a team, supporting each other always and reflecting insights back at one another when needed.

He was probably overdue for a sounding board or

reflection session. But it would only help if he bothered to listen. They'd tried to corner him on his motives when he'd taken the Triple R job. He'd dumped his original career to become a cowboy, dealing with animals, sunburn, cuts and calluses, and Selina, just for a chance to prove their granddad was more than an aging, confused drunk.

Maybe Spencer and Bella didn't remember Isaiah the same way Jarvis did. His siblings had been aggravated when they'd been moved abruptly from Isaiah's house to Aunt Amelia's place in town. Deep down, it had been easy to keep Isaiah's secret when he knew his siblings wouldn't give any credence to the tales. Arguably, the man had done his best and come up short. Even back then, as a kid, Jarvis had understood that they needed something their grandfather couldn't give, especially not while grieving his son and daughter-in-law. Not that Amelia had managed much better, but the court had seen her as the stable option.

Admittedly, his case of hero worship for their granddad had only intensified with his work on the ranch. Not so much due to the search as the work itself. Was it weird to hit his thirties before having the epiphany that he was born to be a cowboy?

Weird or not, it was his life. Checking the app for the precise location, he found it was not far from Mia's current hideout, and it took serious willpower to veer away from the bunkhouse. He would visit later, hopefully after following up with Spencer. Just the thought of seeing her sent a surge of happiness through his veins. He really needed to get this infatuation under control.

Turning, his gaze caught on something out of place closer to the road. Most likely a trick of the light, but he knew every inch of this ranch and, from visiting Mia every day, this section specifically. He walked the horse over to where the dirt had been kicked up and rutted out around the scrubby growth between the ranch and the road.

The herds hadn't been in this area. Good news was if they'd been pushed up this way, the fence was still intact. He slid down from the saddle and walked Duke forward slowly. Even from several paces away, he could see snapped twigs and the brush pressed back, not unlike the damage he'd seen when Mia had hidden her car near the warming hut.

His blood went cold when he spotted a clear boot print in the soil. The tread was thick cut, more like a military or tactical boot than the gear worn by the crew. He held his foot near the mark and judged it of a similar size. He followed the trail of those distinct footprints where they joined the tire tracks.

It was possible someone had been drunk, driven off the road and had ambled about until they came to their senses. He'd believe it if the trail meandered or had been muddled. It didn't. One set of boot prints led toward the fence, took a brief stroll along the fence line and then turned back to the tire tracks.

He didn't like it, not this close to Mia's hiding place. Not right on top of his run-in with Regina and Mia's uncomfortable call with her father. Had someone been looking for her? He took pictures with his cell phone of the boot prints and the tire tracks and the damaged vegetation.

Questions and options raced through his mind. Call in his brother, notify his boss, ask Selina to invite Regina over for a chat so he could get his hands around that devious woman's throat.

He started with the most crucial piece and sent Mia a text message to confirm she was all right. He waited for a reply, and his heart pounded as he pulled himself back into the saddle. Duke sidestepped, sensing his distress. He took a deep breath, willing himself to calm down for the horse. For the next calls he'd have to make to Spencer and Asher.

He was about to blow up Mia's secret, force her to hide elsewhere, all because Regina was a greedy, dangerous person who would go to any lengths to keep her power, money and status.

Impatient and increasingly unsettled, he called Mia, riding toward the bunkhouse while the call went through.

"Jarvis?"

Her voice hit him like a ray of morning sunlight, and the sharpest of his worry evaporated like dew. "Yes." He forced a smile onto his face, into his voice. "I was close and wanted to check in."

"That's thoughtful. I—I'm good."

The catch in her voice sent him right back into worry mode. "You've had trouble today? Where are you?"

"No trouble," she replied. He didn't quite believe her. "We're at the bunkhouse. I've got my hands full with Silas," she said. "Did you meet with your brother?"

"I spoke with him and he's going over your information now." He didn't mention his side trip to Selina's house. "I just needed to hear your voice."

"Oh, good." She sounded delighted by that admission. "Wait. Did something happen?"

"Not really." He wanted to tell her everything and

press her for what was on her mind, too. But he didn't have facts and he wouldn't upset her without reason. "I'll be at today's dig site soon. Do you need me to bring anything along with dinner tonight?"

"That's more than enough."

Now that she sounded more relaxed, he felt better, too. Ending the call, he forwarded the pictures he'd taken to Spencer, with a request to factor them in with the information from Mia. With no damage to the fences, he wouldn't tell Asher yet.

As if on cue, his phone rang and Asher's picture filled his screen. He kept Duke at a slow walk as he answered the call.

"I saw you finished at Selina's place," the foreman said.

"It was a loose wire on those string lights on her deck," Jarvis replied. "Did she complain about me?"

"Should she?" Asher countered, laughing. "You know I'm more curious if she said anything helpful."

"No clear admission of anything. My take is that she was fishing to find out if she'd told me something important when she was so tipsy after the party."

"You couldn't use that?"

Jarvis watched the terrain for landmarks. "No. If I had guessed and been wrong, she would've known I was lying. Better to keep her off balance."

"Probably right. Where are you now?"

"I rode off into the sunset to give Selina something to ponder," Jarvis joked. Asher howled with laughter. "Have you heard about anyone interested on the northern property line? It looks like someone pulled off the road and was poking around."

"No one should be out there," Asher said. "Probably a drunk driver."

"I looked around and came to the same conclusion," Jarvis said. "The fence is fine," he added. "I took some photos, just in case, but I didn't see any damage worth reporting."

"Well, that's a plus. Keep me posted."

"Will do," Jarvis promised.

Hours later, Jarvis knocked on the door of Mia's bunkhouse. It was well past dark and his shoulders ached after another fruitless attempt to find a small metal box on the massive ranch. At least dinner would be amazing. Fried chicken, corn on the cob, green beans, biscuits and berry cobbler had been on the menu tonight for the crew. Although he hadn't expected to be on the cleanup crew, a mishap with a kitchen knife meant he had to fill in.

"Sorry I'm late," he said when she opened the door.

She treated him to that beautiful, open smile that made him feel downright heroic. "Smells delicious," she said, eyeing the bag in his hands. "You're forgiven. Get in here."

"Grab a plate." She did while he unpacked the bag, opening the various containers for her. "How was Silas today?"

"He had a great day. Fresh air and sunshine, a full tummy, playtime and good naps."

"Living his best life," Jarvis observed.

"He is." She ate while he amused the baby.

The little guy was taking in everything with those big brown eyes. Although Jarvis knew Mia's ex was part of the baby's DNA, whenever he looked at the baby he only saw Mia's features. If the genetics held, the little boy would be breaking hearts by preschool.

He and the baby smiled and played. He tried not to dwell on how natural it felt to chatter along with the baby while he waited for Mia to open up about what was bugging her. It was something to do with her son, if he read her correctly.

"Thanks for feeding me." She blotted her lush lips with a napkin. "Did you see Regina in town?" That she'd felt the need to ask was a huge clue to the issue on her mind.

"No. But I've been away from civilization most of the day. I had to handle the meeting with Spencer over the phone."

"Oh."

"Regina might be manipulating your father's phone and emails, but she can't possibly have access to the MVPD."

"True. I'm just…"

He picked up the baby and moved to the table. "Just?"

"Tired and paranoid. And sad. Dad texted me this morning, but it probably wasn't him. So I was careful."

"I don't think it will take Spencer long to get back to us."

A faint smile touched her lips. "Were you able to search at all?"

"I found another place the box is not," he said.

"Good." She took a bite of the cobbler and closed her eyes. "This is epic." She handed him a fork. "There's enough to share."

One more boundary he plowed right through for Mia. They polished off the sweet dessert and she reached for her laptop. "I think I have a better idea. Come over here."

As he sat down, he caught her minimizing a map of residential Las Vegas and a tab with home listings in Denver. "Are you thinking of moving?"

"Yes. Call it plan B. Or G, or whatever letter I'm up to by now. We can talk about it after you see what I found for you today."

His stomach cramped. His search seemed less important lately. He had all his life to find that box. Mia's situation was more urgent. She couldn't stay out here indefinitely and was clearly making plans to move on.

Without him.

Why the hell did that hurt?

Yes. She was thinking of moving. Said it as if that was the most obvious solution. It was. She couldn't live in secret out here forever. He looked down into Silas's face, his ears ringing and his heart hammering that his time with this little guy was limited.

"Jarvis. You're not listening."

"Sorry." He focused on the map of the ranch filling her screen and the point where her finger hovered. "Your son is a terrible distraction."

Her expression softened. "I know."

An unsettling feeling of rightness sifted over him. This woman, with that warm, uninhibited love shining in her eyes and her child in his arms, was right. For him. He could almost hear the click as everything snapped into place. He hadn't counted on this at all.

Was her love worth the effort and risk theory rubbing off on him? He'd initially blamed her philosophy about life and living on motherhood and a daughter's tender heart and devotion. He had no idea how to explain the reaction rocketing through him.

He felt Silas getting sleepy and he stood up, swaying gently with the baby. "Why add this spot to the search?" he asked, the unfamiliar emotions making his voice rough.

"I made a few calls this afternoon. Many of the public records have been scanned in and I was able to access them online. I'd rather be there in person, but..." Her voice trailed off and she stroked a curl of hair over Silas's ear.

"Anyway," she cleared her throat. "I took a closer look at which acreage was acquired when." She zoomed in. "We're here," she pointed. "And this sector northwest of us is a prime spot to look." She tipped her face up, smile blooming. "I think it's *the* spot."

In his arms, Silas gurgled. "He seems to agree," Jarvis joked. "Tell me more."

"Either Herman or Eugene Colton picked up this strip of land just a few years before the date on that deed of sale that shows Herman sold the property to Ainsley."

She clicked and opened a new window on her screen and a spreadsheet opened. "This is hardly proof of anything, but this is the list of when which parcels changed hands. Between Herman and Eugene and the Ainsley family, the acreage that melded into the Triple R was in flux for a long time."

"But we're not sure that first deed of sale between Herman and Ainsley was legit." He said it out of habit as much as belief. He still had faith in his grandfather's story, but that properly filed deed of sale would be hard to overcome. "It doesn't make sense that Herman would sell the land *and* keep searching for the card cheat while telling anyone who'd listen that the property was rightfully his."

"I know." She looked at him, sadness filling her lovely eyes. "You may never know exactly what happened."

Well, he had no chance of separating fact from legend without the box. "So that's the spot?"

Her teeth nipped her lower lip and her mouth quirked to one side. "All it needs is an *X*," she said with confidence.

"Can I take a look?"

She scooted over and he handed her the baby, before taking the seat she'd been using. He scrolled in and out on the image as he read through the documentation of this particular acreage. "This is even farther out than I expected."

"We know the land and landmarks can change over time."

He nodded. "Weather, usage, roads and development. Earthquakes."

She rested a hand on his shoulder. "You won't offend me if you disagree."

He gave in and leaned into her comforting touch. "It's worth a look." He smiled, pulled out his cell phone and noted the position. He added a star to it, his reminder that the location was her suggestion. It was strange having help in this endeavor, a quest he'd relegated to white-whale status.

"I guess I have my marching orders," he said. Sitting back in the chair, he moved the cursor over the Las Vegas tab, but he didn't open it. "So tell me why you're thinking of moving away."

"An email came through earlier. It was an update on

the college fund my dad and I set up for Silas. Someone closed the account. The money is gone."

He knew Mia was thinking about her stepmother's previous theft. "Who has access?" he asked.

"Only my father and me," she said. "It has to be Regina. Either she convinced him to move the money or she managed to fake the signatures. Again."

It was exactly what he'd been thinking. "Convincing your dad to move the money seems like a hard sell. Even if he's upset with you, he wants what's best for your son."

She gave a low growl of frustration. The sound was far from intimate, but it slid under his skin, anyway. Made him wonder what kind of pleasured sounds he could draw out of her.

"Did you try to call?"

"As soon as I saw the email," she said. "My calls went straight to voice mail. I sent text messages, but he hasn't answered. Regina hasn't answered for him, either."

He knew she was thinking the worst, that Regina had finally attacked her father to draw her out. "Wouldn't closing or moving an account like that have to be done in person?"

"It can be done online," she said. "I don't care about the money. That account was entirely a gift for Silas from Dad."

The baby had dozed off in her arms and he hoped her distress wouldn't wake him. One thing that struck him time and again was how down-to-earth Mia remained. Practical, kind and genuine.

"Online or in person, there has to be a record, whether it's security cameras or electronic documentation. This is something Spencer can dig into. Let me loop him in," Jarvis urged. "Your dad handles accounts for many high-profile people and businesses. If he's being coerced, people need to know."

"That's true. Do it."

He sent the information on to Spencer, then studied her profile. While talking about his search, she'd been animated and confident. Now she looked more defeated. "What's also true is that moving away won't guarantee your dad's safety. Regina is greedy and conniving. That won't change no matter what you do."

He ignored the small voice in his head that whispered he was being selfish by urging her to stay. She needed a life, a full and vibrant life, and once Regina was under control, she could have it right here in Mustang Valley, where he could still see her around town. It wasn't like they were destined for wedded bliss. He wasn't the man who could keep her and Silas happy and content in the long term.

Carefully, so he wouldn't wake the baby, he pushed back from the table. He stretched his arms overhead, then arched his back, easing the aches that affirmed an honest day's work on the ranch.

"You really do love being a cowboy." Her soft smile lit up her face and ignited something deep in his chest.

"You're right." Could she love him as a cowboy? He swallowed the question before it embarrassed them both. "I don't see it changing."

An operation this size always needed something, and each day was a slight variation on the last. Yet it was the constancy amid all of it that appealed. And like a fool, he kept wondering if she could be happy with an average cowboy rather than a slick, wealthy businessman. Even if his old career miraculously put him in the same financial league as Mia, he couldn't go back to that life, not even for her.

"Will you stay again tonight?" She peered up at him through her lashes.

"Sure." Of course he'd stay. It wasn't just about keeping watch. He was too attached to her and her son. The smart move would be creating some distance before he spouted promises he couldn't keep. "And with a little luck, tomorrow night I'll be here with dinner and Herman's box in hand," he said lightly.

With Silas down for the night, they talked of other things, lighter topics until they were ready for bed, as well. Mia was a woman who deserved promises and a man who would keep them. Jarvis came from a long line of men who drank heavily and died early, leaving the people who dared to love them behind. He wasn't an alcoholic, but that wasn't enough to convince him he'd be different in the long run.

His siblings, the only two constants in his life, had found the courage to fall in love. That was great and fine for them. Jarvis couldn't muster up the same faith in a happy ending for himself.

"Jarvis?" She twisted around to face him in the bunk. "Will you be here for coffee?"

"I'll probably need to get out of here early." His mouth touched hers almost against his will. He needed that sweet taste of her to carry him through the night. She was warm, her lush lips tempting. His self-control fraying, he pulled her close, his fingertips caressing her generous curves.

"I want you," she whispered. The invitation fluttered against his throat. Butterfly wings carrying world-altering cargo. "I don't want to wait anymore."

The idea of spending the night with her body tangled with his hit him like a kick in the chest. With another woman, child or not, he might jump at the chance. He'd been the rebound guy before and been fine with it.

An easy, compatible one-night stand wouldn't be enough. Instinctively, he knew Mia wouldn't be out of his system with just one night. That was why he'd been avoiding anything more than hot kisses and sizzling caresses. He feared she was an addiction as detrimental to him as alcohol and bitterness had been to his grandfathers.

"We shouldn't," he said. "I want to," he insisted as her disappointment sagged against him.

"Because of the baby?" Her fingertips dragged down his chest and lower until he trapped her hand under his.

"Because of everything." An owl called and Jarvis listened. There was no reason to think Mia was in danger, and yet he remained alert.

"I understand." Her words brushed against his throat.

He was glad one of them did. "Get some rest." He brushed a kiss to her lips and heard himself make her a promise. "When this is over, if you still want me, I'm all yours."

"I'll hold you to that."

He was already hers. And he was increasingly convinced that nothing would alter that fact.

Chapter 11

Mia wondered how Jarvis was doing. She'd hoped to say good morning, share that magical first cup of coffee with him this morning, but he'd been gone before Silas had woken her.

As the day wore on with no contact from him, she started doubting herself for being direct last night. But she did want him, had wanted him from that very first kiss. One way or another, her time here would end. It was selfish and possibly arrogant to think making love with Jarvis would somehow bind him to her when she and Silas came out of hiding.

Needs and temptation aside, it wasn't fair to push him when she didn't know where she would end up. But it would've been amazing. Would *be* amazing, she reminded herself. She just had to be patient because

Jarvis would keep his word about being all hers when this was over.

Mia looked at the calendar displayed on her computer screen and wondered exactly when "over" would get here.

Regina was still out there, still pushing and working the rumor mill to undermine Mia's credibility and her relationship with her dad. Nearly a month had passed and nothing outside of this bunkhouse felt safe.

It was an illusion. Temporary. Just because she didn't know what would crop up next, didn't mean she could keep leaning on Jarvis's kindness and kisses. When she'd divorced, she expected it would take years to find a man worthy of her affection and her son's trust. Finding them, Jarvis had changed everything from her relationship time line to uncovering a well of desire she'd never known before.

She shook off the wayward thoughts. There were far more important things to think about than the day she would finally get intimate with Jarvis.

Aggravated and restless, Mia opened the front door of the bunkhouse, making sure the sunlight wouldn't disrupt Silas's nap. The fresh air and open country should feel full of promise. This rugged land was beautiful, but it was time to make a move. She had a son to raise, a career to launch. It was impractical to think she could move out of town and stay safe. At some point, someone would recognize her and Regina would start her threats all over again.

Jarvis had asked her to give Spencer time. And why not? It wasn't like she had anywhere to be. Maybe once he verified the information in the file, he'd have a suggestion about how she should proceed.

Her phone vibrated in her pocket and she checked the alert on her screen. It was a text from her father. At least from his number, she thought grimly.

Mia, I need to see you.

What's wrong, Dad?

I'm afraid Regina has done something unforgivable.

Mia's heart soared with hope, even as logic insisted it was most likely another one of Regina's traps.

Are you in town?

She hesitated, wishing she could be sure it was really her father sending these messages.

Yes. Call me.

I can't. I'm so sick my throat's raw. I think Regina put something in my breakfast.

What? Her heart slammed against her rib cage. Another text came through before she could ask any questions or suggest he call an ambulance.

Honey, have you been hiding from my wife?

Could her dad have finally figured out he'd married a crocodile in designer clothing?

Please meet me at the house. Regina will be away for another hour. Bring the baby and let's talk this out. If you have evidence against Regina bring that, too.

That last line gave her a moment's pause. But if Spencer had reached out about the college fund, it made sense. This was an opportunity to gain an advantage.

Dad, where did we spend my eighth birthday?

In Disneyland. You went nuts for the princess parade. Hurry, honey. I need you.

OMW

Mia closed her laptop, her latest search unfinished. She shoved supplies into the diaper bag and called Jarvis. He didn't answer. She'd try again from the car and apologize when she got back. She couldn't *not* go to her father.

Moving as quickly as possible, she buckled Silas in to the car seat. Looping the diaper bag and her purse over her arm, she headed for the truck. Mia drove toward the house as fast as she dared, eyeing the clock. He hadn't given her much time. She'd known Regina was bad news from day one and finally—finally—her father's eyes had been opened to his wife's true nature. Using the hands-free option, she called Jarvis again and left a message this time.

"We'll take Grandpa to the hospital," she told Silas. She would insist on a full blood workup, an analysis of what had made him sick and a plan to flush it out of his system. The police could meet them there and take his statement. Jarvis's brother could smooth the way for that solution.

Oh, the idea of reclaiming her stable, loving relationship with her dad put a smile on her face as she parked the truck in the driveway. With Silas in his car seat, her purse and diaper bag over her shoulder, she rushed to the front door. Her father had left it unlocked; she didn't even need to use her code. That shouldn't have been such a high point, but it was. She and her father had been at odds for so long.

"Regina," she said, stopping short in the foyer. "How nice to see you."

"Is it?" She sneered. The woman who'd been a thorn in Mia's side for too many years, who'd effectively wedged her out of her father's life, aimed a gun at her. "Welcome home."

Dread flared along her spine, turned her palms damp with nervous sweat. "What are you doing?" She tucked the carrier behind her back to shelter Silas. "Where's Dad?"

"Upstairs, asleep. He's not as young as he used to be."

"He called me," she began. Her voice faltered when Regina laughed. "No, my dear, he sent you a text message." Keeping the gun steady in one hand, she held up a device and wagged it side to side. "Look familiar?"

Mia's stomach cramped. Both the phone and the gun her father kept in a lockbox in the bedroom were familiar. She'd known better and made a serious miscalculation, anyway. "What have you done?"

"Only what's necessary to protect my husband and his interests."

"*Your* interests, more like."

She shrugged one shoulder. "Your father and I are more frequently on the same page when it comes to you." She leaned a bit to the side. "And your brat."

"How did you answer the Disney question so well?" She had to keep Regina talking. She had to buy time for Jarvis to see that she'd called or for the housekeeper to come home or another miracle. Any miracle that would prevent Regina from killing her and Silas.

"Since you had the baby, your father will not shut up about your childhood. He pores over those scrapbooks every night." Her heart pounded in her chest. She absolutely believed Regina would pull that trigger. And she'd get away with it because Mia had walked right into the trap with her son. So many violent, furious thoughts ran through her head that she was tongue-tied.

"You were invited here for one purpose, Mia." Regina stared at her over the barrel of the gun. "Give me that damned video and anything else you think you've got on me."

"I don't have the video."

Regina rolled her eyes. "Cooperation is your only play," Regina snapped. "You've lost. You'll hand over your phone and give me all the links to where you've stashed copies. Do it now and I'll spare your son."

"No. I don't believe you." It wouldn't be that easy. "You've threatened him too often already."

Regina's eyes went wide and she gave a little scream but the gun remained on Mia. "All the more reason to cooperate. You have no power here. Give me all of your supposed evidence and your father won't die today."

Mia forced herself to speak her worst fear. "You've killed him already."

"Oh, Mia. You've thought the worst of me from the start. I *love* him. I'd never hurt him."

"Save it," Mia snapped. "You're an evil, manipulative excuse for a human being."

Regina lowered the gun slightly, her mouth agape. "I can't decide if you're too stupid or too brave. If I'm so terrible, you should damn well cooperate with me."

"Never." Mia held her ground. "You've done enough damage to this family."

"You selfish *tramp*!" Regina screamed. Her lips twisted into a grotesque snarl. "After everything I've put up with since marrying Norton. You have *no* power here. No room to negotiate."

She stalked across the room, the gun a very real threat between them. "You always do everything Daddy says. I know you brought that video with you. Along with anything else you think will turn him against me."

Mia took brief comfort in Regina's use of present tense when speaking about Norton. Maybe he was still alive.

Her comfort shifted to alarm as Regina stalked closer and, using the threat of the gun, forced her out of the foyer toward the front room, shoving her to the floor. The car seat landed with a thump and Mia sheltered Silas as best she could.

Grabbing Mia's purse, Regina stepped back, dumping out the contents. "Why do people hail mothers as saints?" she muttered. "This is a mess." She snatched Mia's phone and then glared into Mia's face. "*You* are a mess. What is the code?"

Mia gave it to her. She'd used a new phone, one strictly for business when she'd caught Regina with another man at the country house. And, just as Regina assumed, she'd stored the incriminating video on the cloud. Two separate servers, in fact, with one copy in the hands of the police. She was tempted to tell Regina all of that, but she'd made enough mistakes today.

Regina swore when she didn't find the video. "Where is it?"

"You have the wrong phone," Mia said calmly.

Regina's face contorted with rage. "I've always hated you. You're nothing but a leech."

Mia ignored the familiar rant, her mind on how to escape without jeopardizing Silas. "Give me that video and I'll make sure Norton doesn't mix up his medications again."

"I don't believe you," Mia said. "I'm not handing anything over to you until I see my father."

Regina cursed a blue streak. "Fine. I'll indulge you one more time." She gestured with the barrel of the gun. "The last time," she added. "Go on upstairs and see him for yourself."

Mia moved as slowly as she dared, not wanting to aggravate Regina any more than necessary, yet buying as much time as possible.

Surely, Jarvis had seen her text by now or picked up her message. Yes, he'd be furious that she'd fallen for Regina's trap, but when she didn't call, he'd follow up. He'd find her.

She had to believe in him. That faith was the only thing keeping her heart beating in her chest. Fear for Silas was a beast, clawing at her gut. She had to find a way to prove she wasn't merely a spoiled brat and that Regina was the monster.

* * *

Jarvis's shovel sliced into the earth and metal clanged hard against metal. The vibration ringing up his arms froze him in place. His breath stalled, trapped in his chest, until it exploded on an exhale.

"I'll be damned." Mia was right.

Of course she was. She'd thrown herself into his search, pulling strings and piecing together leads that he hadn't considered. Maybe she should give up real estate for treasure hunting.

Dropping the shovel, he fell to his knees and scraped dirt away from the top of an old metal box. He eased the box from its resting place and stared at it as shock and potential rippled through his system. Pulling a bandanna from his back pocket, he poured water on the fabric and rubbed the top of the box clean. His heart pounded as the *H.C.* scratched into the surface was revealed. "Just like Isaiah said."

His grandfather's story flitted through his mind. "You weren't crazy, Granddad." And by default, Jarvis wasn't, either.

Herman Colton had dug into this earth generations ago, and buried this box for his sons and their sons. Could there really be evidence inside that this massive, thriving enterprise belonged to Jarvis and his siblings now?

A chill ran through him and Jarvis sat down hard, suddenly afraid to open it. This could change everything. Or nothing. His sister and brother weren't into the Triple R. Jarvis was currently the only cowboy in the immediate family.

He tried to imagine Asher's face, hearing that Jarvis was the new owner. Jarvis didn't want to be the boss.

He couldn't work this place any better than Asher. Hell, he wasn't ready to take sole responsibility of an operation this size. He scrubbed at his face as hope and fear zinged through him in equal measure.

The contents, assuming they confirmed Isaiah's story, would put the long-ignored Colton triplets on the map. A complete reversal of fortune. Their parents would have flipped out.

It was dumb to sit here wondering after investing so much time in the search. The answers were at his fingertips now. His hands shook as he reached for the lock and he pulled back. Mia should see this. She'd suggested this place, and finding the box was as much her victory as his.

If there were documents inside, it was probably better to open this in the presence of a lawyer. And somewhere other than outside under the bright sunshine, where the breeze might carry off something important.

Carefully setting aside the box, he picked up the shovel and filled in the hole. With the location marked on the app, just in case someone challenged his claim, he secured the box behind his saddle and rode for the bunkhouse.

"Mia!" he called as he pulled Duke to a stop. He tempered his excitement and lowered his voice, worried about waking Silas from a nap. It was such a "honey, I'm home" kind of moment, but he didn't care. Didn't even feel awkward about it.

"Mia, you were right," he said softly as he opened the door. He stopped and stared around the space. She wasn't here. The baby wasn't here. The blanket where he napped was near the bed. Her computer was on the table, closed.

His blood ran cold. Had Regina found her? He tore around to the back. The truck was gone. That didn't necessarily mean she'd left on her own. Maybe she'd gone for a drive so Silas would sleep. She might even be scoping out another likely search site.

That worried him. He saw a missed call from her number, but no voice mail. Sometimes those alerts were slow out here. He sent her a text that he'd found the box. With luck, that would bring her back sooner rather than later.

Unable to stand it any longer, he broke the lock and opened the box. There were letters and some old, grainy photographs and a Bible. The writing had faded with time, but most of it was still legible. His hands trembled when he realized he held the original deed for a chunk of Triple R land.

He read a letter from Herman and could almost smell the liquor on his ancestor's breath. It rambled on and on, not bothering to be tactful at all or hide his contempt for Eugene's poor character. Herman alleged that not only had Eugene reneged on the plan to reclaim property lost in the card game, he had also forged Herman's signature on a second sale of land to T. Ainsley. It was a slice of his family history, possibly true, but not likely to hold up in court against the documentation Mia had found on file.

The surge of relief startled him.

Jarvis carefully opened the old Bible, mindful of the cracked leather cover. He squinted at the births and deaths listed on the fragile front pages. Tucked inside was a piece of paper. Unfolding it, he smiled at a Colton family tree.

Herman and Eugene weren't brothers at all. The men

had been cousins, he noted, tracking the names and marriages, the children that followed. The revelations in the collection of letters, the names and important dates of people he'd never known left ripples across his soul, changing his mind about the kind of family he came from.

He tucked everything back into the box. He wasn't comfortable leaving it out here unattended. Where were Mia and Silas? She hadn't replied to his text and he was getting restless. Had the baby gotten sick?

He tried to call her and got a service error. Better to stow the box in his room until he figured out what had happened to Mia. He and Duke weren't far from the main stable when his phone chirped from his shirt pocket. A voice-mail alert showed up from Mia's number. He scrambled to listen to the message.

"Hi. Dad thinks Regina poisoned him. Had to go. I'll call when I know more."

Jarvis swore, urging Duke into a gallop, his heart thundering with the worst-case scenarios. Regina was behind this. Had to be. Every minute gave that witch an advantage, but he couldn't ride hard and talk on the phone at the same time.

Reaching the stable, he handed off Duke to Jimmy with his apologies. Box under his arm, he called Spencer as he ran for the old ranch truck. "I think Mia's in trouble," he said without preamble. "Can you meet me at Norton Graves's place?"

"What kind of trouble?" his brother queried.

"You've been through the file I sent? You saw the threats her stepmom made?"

"Yes. In fact, I called Regina this morning and asked her to come in and talk."

Jarvis swore. That was the catalyst. "Supposedly, Mia's dad asked her to come over with the baby. I don't have evidence yet of a crime in progress, but it smells like a setup." Would that be enough for Spencer?

"On my way."

"Thanks."

At his truck, Jarvis placed Herman's box under the dash on the passenger side and tossed a towel over it. Then he drove as fast as the old engine would go to Norton's house, using his speakerphone option to call Mia. She didn't pick up, so he called again. And again. As dread pooled in his gut, he kept trying her phone, praying the next time she'd answer.

Every minute felt like an hour. Though he tried to put his churning emotions into context, he knew he wouldn't calm down until he saw Mia and Silas healthy and whole.

"See. I told you he was fine," Regina said.

Mia watched her father's chest rise and fall. "What did you give him?"

"Nothing fatal." Regina's smile could curdle milk. "This time."

"How do you expect to get away with this?" Mia demanded. If she could keep her talking she could find an opening. Where was Jarvis?

"You've been gone, out of sight, no contact for weeks. Your poor father has nearly worried himself to death." She cackled. "He'll be so disappointed to hear you relocated and refused to visit. Don't worry, I'll be here to soothe him through your heartless betrayal."

So the woman planned to impersonate her as she'd impersonated Norton. If Regina had her way, Mia wouldn't leave this house alive. She had to *do* something or Regina would get away with murder. Hers, her father's and, probably, her son's.

Staring into Regina's pitiless eyes, Mia felt her blood ignite. No way would she let this woman walk off as the sole beneficiary of the Graves estate, playing the part of a grieving widow.

"Go." Regina waved the gun, motioning Mia out of the bedroom.

She backed up, deliberately bumping her shoulder and then the baby carrier into the door frame. Silas started to fuss. Setting the carrier down, she made an issue of rubbing her shoulder while soothing her son.

"You're as clumsy as a cow," Regina snapped. "Worse than before you were pregnant. Trust me, a bullet will hurt more than a door frame. Pick up the brat and *move*."

Mia braced for the worst as she twisted around, but instead of picking up Silas, she grabbed a stone bust from the pedestal in the hallway. Only Regina would consider this cheap knockoff an artistic statement.

Swiveling around, she threw the bust at Regina. The woman screamed, squeezing the trigger as Mia wheeled back and tried to duck. The bullet hit the ceiling and dust rained down on them as Mia launched herself at Regina. But something caught her at the waist and hauled her back out into the hallway. Did Regina have help?

With a scream, she clawed at the thick forearm, desperate to escape with her baby.

Someone else shoved past her, shouting at Regina.

"Easy, Mia. Mia! It's me."

"Jarvis?" She slumped to her knees and he followed her to the floor. "What are you doing here?"

"Keeping Silas's mother out of jail."

Indignant, she looked around. "Where is he?"

"Spencer put him in the bathroom."

Despite the sounds of an ongoing fight in her father's bedroom, Mia jumped up and darted through the closed bathroom door across the hall. Jarvis's voice followed her, warning her to wait, but she couldn't possibly. Silas was awake and gurgling happily, flapping his arms. The car seat, safely in the center of the bathtub, rocked with his motions.

"Oh, my baby." She couldn't help herself—she had to hold him. Lifting him from the seat, she cradled his head to her shoulder, kissing his chubby cheek. "It's all over now, my sweetheart."

"He's okay?"

"Perfect." She twisted to find Jarvis staring at her. "It's over, right?"

He nodded.

"Thank you." She realized what a fool she'd been rushing out here alone. As her errors stuttered through her mind, she realized how she'd played right into Regina's plans. If Jarvis hadn't shown up, with police backup, there was no telling how badly this might have ended.

"Jarvis—"

He cut her off with a sharp look. "Why would you do this? You could've been killed." His face was pale and she knew she had to find a way to reassure him. "I—I was only thinking of my dad. He asked for my help."

Jarvis folded his arms. "You called but didn't wait. You didn't give me much chance to help you."

"And yet you showed up in time. Thank you," she said again.

But timing wasn't the point. She saw the pain in his eyes and realized how her lapse in judgment, how putting herself and the baby at risk, hurt him. This man had gone above and beyond for her and she'd returned his kindnesses by being cruel, forcing him to worry that another person he cared for would be injured. Or worse.

"I'm sorry, Jarvis." He turned away, as if he couldn't bear to look at her. "You would've told me it was a trap."

"It *was*!" He hitched a shoulder, shuffling his feet. His brother called for him and he stepped into the hallway. A moment later he returned. "Regina's in cuffs," he told her, his voice flat. "I've called an ambulance."

Of course he had.

"They should be here any minute. Wait in the bedroom with your dad. All three of you are safe now." He held her gaze for a long moment, then his eyes shifted to her son, lingered there. "I'll see you around, Mia. Be well."

She stood there, feelings and words a logjam in her throat. He couldn't be walking away. Yet, this wasn't the time or place to demand he uphold his promise.

As she rushed into her father's bedroom, gratitude and relief soared through her. He wasn't awake, but he was alive. A chair and table had been upended, items and pictures from the top of his dresser scattered and broken. A framed picture of Silas and Mia was distorted by shattered glass.

Still, her father slept on, oblivious to the chaos Regina had staged. Jarvis had been right. There was no telling what might have happened if he and his brother hadn't shown up in time. Guilt blotted out the relief and tears threatened. She'd ruined everything, damaged something beautiful between her and Jarvis.

When the paramedics arrived, she stepped aside, watched with a new fear as they gathered the pill bottles from the nightstand and transferred her father from the bed to the stretcher, wheeling him away.

Chapter 12

Jarvis listened to the updates on Spencer's police scanner as Regina fumed in the back seat. She tossed out threats even after Spencer read her her rights.

The ambulance was transporting Norton Graves to Mustang Valley General Hospital. He was sure Mia was with them. At the very least, she was following. Maybe he'd see her again when she returned the truck. A pulse of heat zipped through his veins at the idea. He was a fool.

Seeing her again wouldn't change the facts. She was more than a beautiful woman he'd fallen for. She and Silas were a ready-made family he wasn't convinced he could have.

"How do you do it?" he asked Spencer when Regina had been hauled deeper into the police station for processing.

"Do what?"

"Love. Your relationship with Katrina." He shoved his hands into his pockets. "You put your life on the line in this job."

"Not too often," Spencer said. "Is there a question in there?"

"*Everyone* left us," Jarvis said. "Everyone has let us down. What made you take that kind of chance?"

"Mom and Dad didn't exactly choose that car wreck," Spencer said. "Aunt Amelia did her best by us, considering she wound up with three kids when she didn't want any."

Jarvis slumped into a chair near his brother's desk, one normally reserved for criminals in processing. He should be happy Mia and Silas were out of danger, but he kept thinking about that expectant look on her face. Thinking about the promise he'd made that he had to break. Anything else would be emotional suicide.

"I've let her down," he muttered.

"Mia?"

Jarvis nodded. To be fair, she'd let him down, too, when she rushed into danger. "I can't be what she needs."

"Why the hell not?" Spencer demanded.

"Come on." He stood up, restless. "She has a kid. Me and fatherhood? That's a joke."

Spencer leaned back in his chair, fingers drumming on the armrests. "Is it? Do you love her?"

"How would I know?"

Spencer glared at him. "Only you can answer that." From the back, they heard Regina shouting. "Get out of here," he said. "I'll keep you posted." He clapped Jarvis on the shoulder as he walked by. "You do the same."

Twitchy as the adrenaline faded, Jarvis didn't know what to do with himself. He wasn't ready to go back to the ranch and talk with Asher. Spencer didn't need him here and neither did Mia. She was set now that her stepmother was in custody and she had her father back.

Family sucked, he thought. Always had. He walked out of the police station, guilt digging into the back of the neck. Mia and Silas were a family and they didn't suck at all.

No, Mia and Silas were a sweet temptation he'd never expected to crave.

Jarvis slid into the driver's seat of the old pickup and tried to imagine how he'd fill his time without them. The idea left him hollow. He'd found evidence that his family, several messy generations ago, had tried their best with various degrees of success. All the way down to his parents.

Lost in his wandering thoughts, Jarvis drove through town, a little surprised to find himself at his aunt's old house. They'd sold it right after she died. He wouldn't find absolution here. He drove on to the cemetery where his parents, Amelia and his granddad were buried.

Herman's box had slipped out from under the towel, like some ghostly challenge. Jarvis owed it to Isaiah to let someone know the old man had been right about the family legend, even if those folks weren't around anymore.

With the box under his arm, he walked out toward their graves, staring down at the headstones. "I found it," he said to the hushed cemetery. "The old family legend is true. Isaiah wasn't just drunk or confused." He sat down, resting the box on his crossed legs. "I found the box Herman buried."

He looked to Amelia's headstone. "I was helping a friend with a baby the other day," he said. "I had to look up what to do on Google." He thought he had a better perspective now, being furious with Mia and still desperate to hold her and tell her it would all work out. "I'm sorry we were so mad at you. A friend made me realize we were all grieving. Thanks for being a safe person to be mad at."

The admission lifted a weight from his shoulders, relieving a pressure he'd lived with for too long.

"Thank you. All of you." He toyed with the broken latch on the box. "I should've said that a long time ago and a lot more often."

With a sigh, he flipped open the lid and pulled out the old Bible. "I figured we could go through this together. I'll fill in Spencer and Bella later. Turns out Herman Colton and Eugene Colton were cousins, not brothers. Payne can't deny we're all related, but we're not as close as Isaiah thought."

Jarvis gingerly leafed through the fragile documents in the box. "The original deed is here, in Herman's name. He was spitting mad about Eugene being a thief, but it wasn't true. All of that land around the Triple R changed hands as fortunes changed. I'll show this to Asher, but it's only a matter of curiosity. Nothing in here disputes Payne's ownership. Which is fine. I couldn't take on all that by myself."

He was talking to gravestones and yet it felt right. A normal, peaceful interlude underscored by an intense sense of connection. "After Mom and Dad died, I felt cut off from everything but Spencer and Bella. This helps." His ancestors were far from perfect, but they'd cared and they'd done their best for those who came after them. "Maybe my generation can overcome some of Payne's nonsense." He'd never wanted the family ties just to make a claim on Payne's precious fortune. He'd simply been looking for roots. Now he'd found them. With questions answered, by this box and the records Mia had uncovered, the bitterness faded.

Contrary to his siblings' concerns, he'd never felt like he'd given up anything by leaving the office for the ranch. He'd simply changed his direction to make something better happen. Something he'd hoped would change the conversation around his siblings.

The search itself, along with what he'd found in this box, had unlocked something inside him. Something fresh and hopeful that wanted to flourish.

"Thanks," he said again to the gravestones. "I'll come back again soon." And next time he hoped to have his family with him. It would take a bit of planning, but it would be worth it.

Mia's eyes were gritty from fighting bursts of tears for hours. She'd love to blame it all on hormones, but she had to accept responsibility. She was crying out all the stress of the past month. Weeks of wondering how to protect her son and her father had taken a toll. Without Jarvis… She started tearing up again.

She'd lost him and she hadn't been prepared for that price. Here they were, both safe. Her son snoozed in her arms while her father rested under the capable observation of nurses as the heavy sedatives Regina had dosed him with wore off.

Two of the three most important men in her life, she thought wryly, swaying side to side gently to keep

Silas asleep. His car seat was handy, but she wasn't ready to let go.

She rapidly blinked away another wave of emotion. Why did she keep falling in love with men who wanted nothing to do with fatherhood? The pain cut deeply and a night without Jarvis hadn't eased the sting of reality. If time healed all wounds, getting over him would take years.

It might be better, just her and Silas. If she'd learned anything from her time with Jarvis, it was that giving her son a solid foundation of love and being valued was essential for his future.

She could do that. Clearly, she had to do that.

"Mia? Is that you?"

She turned at the rasping sound of her father's voice and hurried to his bedside. "Yes, Dad." She gripped his hand. "I'm here. We're here," she added.

"Oh, honey." He squeezed his eyes closed. "Honey, I'm so sorry I didn't believe you about Regina."

"Love does that," she said. "And you loved her." She loved Jarvis and a piece of her always would, whether or not they ever managed to reconcile. It was the most challenging thing to accept. The heart was stubborn.

"I love you, too. Loved you first." He coughed. "Love blinded me to her faults." Another cough interrupted him.

"Rest now," she soothed. "Don't stress about it. We're all fine now."

"I'll make it up to you," he said. He shifted, fiddling with the bed controls so he was sitting up. He patted her hand and beamed at Silas. "Can I hold my grandson?"

"Of course." She could see the regrets swirling in his gaze. "He's overdue for grandpa time."

"Because I'm an old fool," he crooned to the baby. "No more. Your momma is a smart woman. The sooner you learn that, the happier you'll be." He lifted his face to meet her gaze. "You come first, Mia. Take the country house, for as long as you need it."

As much as she appreciated the gesture, she couldn't erase the image of her stepmother's infidelity. Her dad still didn't know about that. "What if we sell it and donate the proceeds to charity?" she suggested. Single mothers, victims of crimes, an orphanage were just a few options that came to mind. There were countless places that money could make a difference and then she'd never have to step foot on the property again.

He lifted an eyebrow. "You loved that place."

"It's time for a change," she hedged.

"A fresh start is a good idea for both of us." He smiled down at the baby. "All of us. But where does that leave us? I can't bear the idea of going back to the house where she…where she abused both of us."

"Well, it's technically a crime scene at the moment," she said. "I know of a property between the Rattlesnake Ridge Ranch and town. It's not as grand as the house in the neighborhood or even the country house. But it's closer to your office and it could work for the three of us while we sort things out."

A week ago, in a dreamy, love-induced haze, she'd put in an offer, hoping to tempt Jarvis to build a life there with her. Close enough to the Triple R to keep him in the job he loved, close enough to town to make her real-estate career viable. Though Jarvis might never call it home, it was still perfect for her and Silas and her dad for as long as he wanted to stay.

A nurse walked in, all smiles. "Now, this is what

I like to see." She took Norton's vital signs while he bragged on his tiny grandson. "You have a lovely family, Mr. Graves. The doctor will be around soon."

She'd barely stepped out before a volunteer knocked on the open door. "Is there a Silas Graves here?"

Mia bristled, moving between her father's bed and the doorway. "Silas is my son. He isn't a patient."

The volunteer looked down at a card he held. "We actually have deliveries for Silas Graves, Norton Graves and Mia Graves."

Wary, Mia planted her hands on her hips. "Deliveries from whom?"

"This card doesn't say."

"Then we can't…" Her voice trailed off as Jarvis filled the doorway.

"Can't what?" he asked.

She stared, utterly dumbstruck. She hadn't expected to face him this soon. Wasn't she allowed some time to pull the ragged pieces of her heart together? There should be rules about this kind of thing. She should definitely be allowed a shower and fresh clothes before facing him.

"I'll take it from here," he said to the volunteer. "Can you please bring in the cart?"

With a nod, the volunteer stepped aside and pushed a cart into the room behind Jarvis.

"How are you feeling, sir?" he asked Norton, striding right past her to the bed.

"Grateful to be alive," her father replied. "Thanks to you and your brother."

"Your daughter had it under control," Jarvis said. "We just batted cleanup."

He caught her eye across the bed and she felt the heat

in her cheeks, remembering their first meeting when she'd been nearly knocked his head off with that stick.

"She's my pride and joy," Norton said. "Even when I'm a fool. And she has excellent intuition."

Mia blinked. It was the first time she'd heard that kind of compliment out of her father since before he'd married Regina.

"I agree." Jarvis grinned. "I brought a few things, just to brighten the room until they kick you out."

She noticed several items on the cart. Flowers, a few wrapped boxes and a portable crib on the bottom shelf. What did this mean? Hope bloomed, bright as the lilies in the floral arrangement. Tears stung her nose and she sniffed them away. Whatever he was about, she would survive this and cry about it later, when she didn't have an audience.

"Mr. Graves, these are for you." He set the vase of colorful flowers on the counter where Norton could see them easily.

Her father's brow furrowed. "Thanks."

"You're welcome." Jarvis turned back to the cart. "This is for the precious guy in your arms."

"We won't need the crib," she snapped ungraciously. "I think they'll discharge him today."

But it wasn't the crib he'd pulled from the cart, but a deep square box. "Go ahead and open it," he said, putting the box in her arms.

Her knees were jelly and she sank into the chair before they failed her. She heard the voices, but not the words as Jarvis and her father chatted.

She opened the box and stared at the contents. A small baseball cap and the smallest baseball mitt she'd ever seen were nested in with a soft, squishy ball stitched like a baseball.

"Jarvis?"

"Just thinking ahead. If he inherits your batting stance, you should get him started early."

It should've been funny, a flashback to their first meeting. Maybe she'd find the humor and kindness behind the gesture later. But he'd said *you*, not *we*. Why was he crushing her heart this way?

"This one is for you." He set the box of tiny baseball gear aside and rested a longer box across her knees.

"A bat? You're definitely ahead of yourself." Would she even share these things with her son? Silas was too young to remember this month, so full of upheaval, and she wasn't sure she'd ever be strong enough to share even the happier stories with him.

"Just open it."

She didn't know what to make of the quirk of his lips. Avoiding his gaze, she slid the ribbon off and raised the lid. She frowned at the contents. It wasn't the baseball bat she'd expected. It was a length of hickory, polished to a gleam and cushioned in a bed of midnight blue velvet. There was a sheer ribbon tied around one end of the stick. A sparkle in the center of the bow caught her eye. It couldn't be…but it sure looked like a diamond engagement ring.

"What's that?" Her father leaned over Silas for a peek.

"Nothing. It's a long story," she answered, scrambling to put the lid back on the box. She couldn't make sense of what was happening.

"Let's put the right ending on that story." Jarvis dropped to one knee in front of her. "I love you, Mia.

You and Silas. You've changed me, shown me what lasting love looks like. Will you marry me and be my family? Will you let me love you both for the rest of our days?"

"Say yes!" her father encouraged.

"What happened to trusting my judgment and intuition?" she asked, shooting her dad a look. To Jarvis she said, "I'm more of a package deal now than I was before. You said—"

"I've said a lot of stupid things. It was all fear talking."

"Fear?"

He nodded. "All my life I've lost the people I love most. Love felt more like a curse or a burden, until you."

She remembered how he'd resisted her attempts to give him some perspective.

"I was out there searching for my past and when I stumbled onto you and Silas I found my future. Marry me, Mia. Let's build the family we both deserve."

"Oh, Jarvis, yes." Her heart swelled with joy. "I love you, too. I was afraid to admit it and run you off."

The smile that creased his face melted away every cold spot inside her. Hope and love gleamed in his brown eyes. He glided his thumb over her cheek, wiping away a tear. It seemed she was crying in front of everyone after all.

At least this time, for the first time since Silas was born, she was weeping tears of joy.

Jarvis could hardly believe his proposal had worked out. Soon he would have a wife, and with a little paperwork, Silas would legally be his, too. It had all come together and he was the happiest man on the planet.

Every time Silas fussed or cried, he jumped in, eager to provide whatever his little guy needed. He'd have to curb that tendency in time, but at this stage there was no such thing as too much love. He'd never thought he had so much love inside him, ready to pour out over the people who mattered.

This evening, after another long day of work, he'd hustled back home—his *new* home—to pick up his fiancée. Norton had moved with them to the property Mia had found and was babysitting so Jarvis and Mia could go over to the Triple R for dinner with his siblings and Colton cousins.

As he pulled through the main gate and followed the drive toward Ainsley's wing of the Colton mansion, it felt remarkably normal to be here as family rather than just as an employee. Not family like Mia and Silas, but family with shared history. Roots he would be sure to nurture for the next generation.

"Are you okay with this?" she asked.

"Perfect," he replied honestly. "Since finding Herman's box, I'm more at peace with all of it than ever before. You gave me that, Mia. Thank you." He held her hand as they walked up to a sprawling deck where Ainsley was setting out a charcuterie board on a long table.

"Welcome, welcome." She invited them up to join her on the expansive deck. "You're the first to arrive. It's a gorgeous evening," she said, grinning. "The two of you look so happy."

The two of them. It was a heady sensation going from solo to a family. He had a fiancée and a son to raise and, hopefully, more children in the years ahead. He and Mia were creating something that would stand the test of time, no matter what life threw at them.

He turned as another car pulled up, and grinned as Spencer got out. Mia gave his hand a squeeze. It was a wonderful reminder that he had love beyond his brother and sister now. Now. Forever.

"Katrina's on her way," Spencer said as he joined them. "I couldn't wait to tell you the good news. Regina pleaded guilty to everything."

Mia relaxed against Jarvis and he slipped an arm around her waist. "Everything?"

His brother nodded. "Threats, extortion, drugging Norton, all of it. She even gave us the name of the man she'd been with in the video. Same guy knifed Mia's tire at the courthouse and came poking around the ranch, too."

Mia gaped at Jarvis. "He what?"

"I spotted tracks at the warming hut and didn't see the sense in alarming you." He bore up under the hard glare, lifting her hand to his lips. "It's the last secret I'll keep from you."

She and Ainsley traded a skeptical glance. "This calls for champagne," Ainsley said brightly. "Four glasses?"

"I'll have to take a rain check," Spencer replied. "I can't stay."

"That's a shame," Ainsley said. "Join us for the toast at least. Have you heard anything more about Ace's situation?"

Jarvis had heard bits and pieces of the accusations that the former Colton Oil CEO had been switched at birth with another baby at Mustang Valley General. Spencer hadn't discussed every detail of the investigation with him, but his cousins had started opening up since he'd shared the contents of Herman's box with Asher.

"I have a working theory," Spencer said. "It's taking time to come together."

The four of them settled around a heavy ironwork table and Ainsley filled three champagne glasses and poured water for Spencer. They toasted to newfound family.

"I'm tracking down verification," Spencer continued. "Everything in my gut says Micheline Anderson *is* Luella Smith, the other mother at the hospital the night Ace was born. I'm sure she switched the babies."

Ainsley studied the bubbles in her glass. "If you're right, where is the real Ace Colton?"

"That's the question, isn't it?" Spencer shook his head. "Micheline's Affirmation Alliance Group feels like a cult to me. She swears it isn't and I can't prove it, yet, but the woman might not be as benign as we thought."

"How will you be sure one way or another?" Mia asked.

"Time," he said again. "I'll keep asking questions and we'll follow every thread until we have the facts."

"You're not the only one with a gut instinct," Ainsley said. "I have a terrible feeling that Micheline is our Ace's biological mother." She sipped her champagne. "This is such a complicated mess."

"It is," Spencer agreed. "If you'll excuse me, I have to get back to the station."

"Don't worry." Jarvis lifted his chin toward the car as his brother drove away. "With Spencer on the case and all of us invested in finding the truth, he'll figure it out."

"Maybe," Ainsley said, thoughtfully.

Jarvis knew Ainsley by reputation more than personal experience, but he couldn't help worrying that she might do something rash in an effort to find something to help her family.

His family, too.

Fortunately Katrina, Bella and Holden, Bella's fiancé, arrived, followed by Asher and Willow. It was a fabulous evening of good food and laughter, and the relaxed kind of family dinner he'd never expected to enjoy quite so much.

On the way home, he voiced his concerns about Ainsley to Mia. It was amazing to have someone to talk with about anything and everything. She listened attentively, assuring Jarvis that his rapidly expanding family would find a way to work together to get to the bottom of the Ace Colton mystery and all the other recent troubles.

After kissing Silas goodnight, they retired to their bedroom and, in the luxury of their king-size bed, Jarvis made up for all those nights when he hadn't done anything more than kiss her. When they were both sated, he pulled her close, as he'd done night after night on that narrow bunk, and reveled in the bliss of having a family of his own.

* * * * *

**WE HOPE YOU ENJOYED
THIS BOOK FROM**

**HARLEQUIN
ROMANTIC
SUSPENSE**

Danger. Passion. Drama.

These heart-racing page-turners will keep you guessing
to the very end. Experience the thrill of unexpected
plot twists and irresistible chemistry.

4 NEW BOOKS AVAILABLE EVERY MONTH!

HRSHALO2020

COMING NEXT MONTH FROM

H HARLEQUIN

ROMANTIC SUSPENSE

Available May 5, 2020

#2087 COLTON'S UNDERCOVER REUNION
The Coltons of Mustang Valley • by Lara Lacombe
Ainsley Colton hasn't seen Santiago Morales since he broke
her heart years ago, but he's the best defense attorney
she knows. To get him to agree to defend her twin brother,
though, she has to pretend to be Santiago's wife while he
goes undercover to save his sister—and they reignite their
passion in the process!

#2088 DEADLY COLTON SEARCH
The Coltons of Mustang Valley • by Addison Fox
Young and pregnant, Nova Ellis hires PI Nikolas Slater to find
her missing father, who could make her a Colton. They work
together, uncovering danger and mutual attraction—and a
threat that's after them both.

#2089 OPERATION SECOND CHANCE
Cutter's Code • by Justine Davis
The only one who blames Adam Kirk more than
Amanda Bonner for her father's death is Adam himself. And
yet the tragedy brings them together to uncover one last
secret. Can the truth of what happened that night bring
forgiveness to them both?

#2090 INFILTRATION RESCUE
by Susan Cliff
FBI agent Nick Diaz enlists Avery Samuels, a former cult
member turned psychologist, to help him take down the
cult—undercover. She's just trying to save her sister, but the
unexpected attraction to Nick is proving to be more than a
mere distraction!

———

**YOU CAN FIND MORE INFORMATION ON UPCOMING HARLEQUIN TITLES,
FREE EXCERPTS AND MORE AT HARLEQUIN.COM.**

HRSCNM0420

SPECIAL EXCERPT FROM

(H)HARLEQUIN
ROMANTIC SUSPENSE

*The only one who blames Adam Kirk more than
Amanda Bonner for her father's death is Adam himself.
And yet the tragedy brings them together to uncover one
last secret. Can the truth of what happened that night
bring forgiveness to them both?*

*Read on for a sneak preview of the next book
in Justine Davis's Cutter's Code miniseries,*
Operation Second Chance.

She ended up on his lap. And the first thing he saw when
he caught his breath was Cutter, standing right there and
looking immensely pleased with himself.

"He bumped me," Amanda said, a little breathlessly. "I
didn't mean to…fall on you, but he came up right behind
me and—"

"Pushed?" Adam suggested.

She looked at him quizzically. "Yes. How—"

"I've been told he…herds people where he wants
them to go."

She laughed. He was afraid to say any more, to explain
any further, because he thought she would get up. And he
didn't want her to. Holding her like this, on his lap, felt
better than anything had in…at least five years.

"I'd buy that," she said, as if she didn't even realize
where she was sitting. Or on what, he added silently as

he finally had to admit to his body's fierce and instant response to her position. "I've seen him do it. But why…"

Her voice died away, and he had the feeling that only when she had wondered why Cutter would want her on his lap did she realize that's where she was.

"I…" she began, but it trailed off as she stared down at him.

He could feel himself breathing hard, felt his lips dry as his breath rushed over them. But he couldn't stop staring back at her. And because of that he saw the moment when something changed, shifted, when her eyes widened as if in surprise, then, impossibly, warmed.

She kissed him.

In all his imaginings, and he couldn't deny he'd had them, he'd never imagined this. Oh, not her kissing him, because sometimes on sleepless nights long ago he'd imagined exactly that. He'd just never known how it would feel.

Because he'd never in his life felt anything like it.

Don't miss
Operation Second Chance *by Justine Davis,*
available May 2020 wherever
Harlequin Romantic Suspense
books and ebooks are sold.

Harlequin.com

Copyright © 2020 by Janice Davis Smith

HRSEXP0420

Get 4 FREE REWARDS!

We'll send you 2 FREE Books plus 2 FREE Mystery Gifts.

Harlequin Romantic Suspense books are heart-racing page-turners with unexpected plot twists and irresistible chemistry that will keep you guessing to the very end.

FREE Value Over **$20**

YES! Please send me 2 FREE Harlequin Romantic Suspense novels and my 2 FREE gifts (gifts are worth about $10 retail). After receiving them, if I don't wish to receive any more books, I can return the shipping statement marked "cancel." If I don't cancel, I will receive 4 brand-new novels every month and be billed just $4.99 per book in the U.S. or $5.74 per book in Canada. That's a savings of at least 13% off the cover price! It's quite a bargain! Shipping and handling is just 50¢ per book in the U.S. and $1.25 per book in Canada.* I understand that accepting the 2 free books and gifts places me under no obligation to buy anything. I can always return a shipment and cancel at any time. The free books and gifts are mine to keep no matter what I decide.

240/340 HDN GNMZ

Name (please print)

Address   Apt. #

City   State/Province   Zip/Postal Code

Mail to the **Reader Service:**
IN U.S.A.: P.O. Box 1341, Buffalo, NY 14240-8531
IN CANADA: P.O. Box 603, Fort Erie, Ontario L2A 5X3

Want to try 2 free books from another series? Call 1-800-873-8635 or visit www.ReaderService.com.

---

*Terms and prices subject to change without notice. Prices do not include sales taxes, which will be charged (if applicable) based on your state or country of residence. Canadian residents will be charged applicable taxes. Offer not valid in Quebec. This offer is limited to one order per household. Books received may not be as shown. Not valid for current subscribers to Harlequin Romantic Suspense books. All orders subject to approval. Credit or debit balances in a customer's account(s) may be offset by any other outstanding balance owed by or to the customer. Please allow 4 to 6 weeks for delivery. Offer available while quantities last.

Your Privacy—The Reader Service is committed to protecting your privacy. Our Privacy Policy is available online at www.ReaderService.com or upon request from the Reader Service. We make a portion of our mailing list available to reputable third parties that offer products we believe may interest you. If you prefer that we not exchange your name with third parties, or if you wish to clarify or modify your communication preferences, please visit us at www.ReaderService.com/consumerschoice or write to us at Reader Service Preference Service, P.O. Box 9062, Buffalo, NY 14240-9062. Include your complete name and address.

HRS20R

**IF YOU ENJOYED THIS BOOK
WE THINK YOU WILL ALSO LOVE**

HARLEQUIN

INTRIGUE

Seek thrills. Solve crimes. Justice served.

Dive into action-packed stories that will keep you
on the edge of your seat. Solve the crime
and deliver justice at all costs.

6 NEW BOOKS AVAILABLE EVERY MONTH!

HIXSERIES2020

Dear Reader,

As an author, it's always a delight to be part of a Colton family adventure.

Generations ago, the Colton family in Mustang Valley was fractured by a card game gone wrong. After years of listening to his grandfather's stories, Jarvis Colton is determined to sort out where he fits on that family tree.

While Jarvis is searching for his roots, he comes across Mia Graves and her newborn son. The pair is hiding from unspeakable danger in a remote, abandoned cabin. Though Mia wants him to forget them, Jarvis can't walk away. Soon he has his hands full dealing with his tasks at the ranch, his personal search, and wrangling his growing affection for a single mom with a target on her back.

I hope you'll enjoy reading their story as much as I enjoyed writing it.

Live the adventure!

Regan Black

"We shouldn't," Jarvis amended. **"Seriously."** He looked around, his gaze as hot and bewildered as Mia felt. That was a small consolation that she wasn't in this alone, but it steadied her.

"The baby," he said desperately.

"Is asleep," she pointed out. She reached up and smoothed a hand over his cheek, loving the feel of his whiskers against her palm. She loved every nuance and discovery Jarvis allowed. He had so many textures and layers beneath that rough-and-ready exterior.

She clamped her lips shut and didn't protest when he stepped back. Pride would not allow her to beg for the connection or passion he wasn't ready to give.

"Mia." He pushed a hand through his hair, his chest expanding on a deep inhale. "I want you, but I don't think it's smart. For you."

"Uh-huh." She crossed her arms, reflexively preventing her heart from leaping into his hands. "Do you always lie to yourself?"

* * *

Book Eight of The Coltons of Mustang Valley

* * *

If you're on Twitter, tell us what you think of Harlequin Romantic Suspense! #harlequinromsuspense